THE CLOVER GIRLS' NETWORK

CLAIRE ANDERS

A CIP catalogue record for this book is available from the British Library.

Published by TLC Publications Ltd

Cover Design by MiblArt

ISBN 978-1-7395389-2-7

ISBN ebook 978-1-7395389-3-4

For Betty

THE CLOVER GIRLS' NETWORK
A WWII HISTORICAL FICTION NOVEL

In the shadow of World War II, a young woman's life is forever changed.

Krista Schulz, a 17-year-old German girl living in Poland, faces a harrowing loss as the Nazi occupation shatters her peaceful life. After witnessing the brutal murder of her beloved grandparents, the Nazis are now hunting her. Krista flees her village, carrying the weight of unanswered questions and a heart heavy with grief.

Determined to survive and find purpose in the chaos, Krista makes her way to Warsaw. As she grows from a frightened young girl into a resolute young woman, Krista discovers the strength within herself to navigate the dangers of war and aid those in need. But it's not long before the past catches up with her in the most unexpected of ways.

The Clover Girls' Network is a poignant coming-of-age story that captures the quiet strength of a young woman swept up in the turmoil of history. It's a tale of loss, love, and the unbreakable bonds of friendship that can illuminate even the darkest of times.

1

The furious roar of the motorcycle approaching the sleepy village of Zawica could only mean one thing – the Germans were coming. Krista's heart pounded as she looked around at her friends and neighbours, terror etched on their faces. Mothers clutched their children with white-knuckled grips. Others were already running away, not waiting for their worst fears to be confirmed. Krista felt like an imposter among them. She had spent the last seven years of her life in Poland, barely remembering her childhood in Berlin. But her documents declared her a German citizen. Surely she had nothing to fear. But that didn't stop her stomach twisting into knots as Marcin Bukowski roared into the square on his motorcycle, heading towards the council building overlooking the heart of their village. The crowd parted for him, and he stopped his bike and shut off the engine. A tense silence fell over the group as they awaited his news.

Marcin removed his helmet and scanned the faces of the gathered crowd, his dark coffee-coloured eyes finding Krista's as if she had activated a beacon that only he could see. His eyes were narrowed, and his brow furrowed with worry lines. The usual spark of life and mischief in his expression seemed to have dimmed. It had been five long days since German and Soviet forces had claimed full control over Poland. The bombs had stopped raining down on her bruised and battered community, but the nightly air raid sirens still wailed as the Luftwaffe flew overhead as a reminder that two decades of independence were on the verge of being over. The villages had been expecting the arrival of the Germans any day now, and it seemed today was that day.

'They're coming,' said Marcin.

The crowd gave a collective gasp, their worst fears confirmed.

'What did you see?' someone asked.

'At least five trucks and a few cars,' said Marcin, his voice loud so everyone could hear, but his eyes never leaving Krista. 'And a line of soldiers that I couldn't see the end of.'

'Any tanks?' someone else asked.

'Not that I saw,' said Marcin. 'But I heard motorcycles. More than one or two.'

Someone brushed up against Krista and she turned to see Olesia, her friend and Marcin's sister. Krista felt her cheeks colour and she wondered if Olesia had noticed the recent shift in Krista's feelings towards Marcin. Krista was almost certain that Marcin felt the same way, but they had been dancing around each other for weeks now, neither willing to say anything out loud.

Olesia was accompanied by Anna, their Guide Captain. 'So this is it,' said Anna.

Poor Anna had attempted to dye her sleek black hair blonde. The peroxide had caused her hair to become so dry that it had snapped off in chunks. Her newly short hair now had a prominent black stripe down the middle of her head as her natural hair colour grew back in.

Krista observed her surroundings. The once-thriving community was in ruins, barely functioning. Wooden benches scattered around the square for people to sit and enjoy the peaceful surroundings were scorched and unstable. The school was closed. The library, where the Guides were meant to meet today, had lost half of its books in an air raid. Yet amidst the rubble, there were still remnants of beauty. Pots of colourful flowers lined the pathways and villagers still had a smile and a kind word or two for each other. But there was nothing here for the Germans. They had to be passing through. Perhaps they'd stay a day or two and then continue marching towards the bigger towns and cities.

'I'm part German, you know,' said Olesia, in the same bright and breezy tone that she said everything. It was as if she hadn't heard her brother announce that the Germans were on their way.

'Really?' asked Anna. 'You don't look very German.' She took a step back to peruse Olesia's appearance. Olesia had the same dark hair and dark eyes as Marcin.

Olesia reached forward and twirled her finger around one of Krista's delicate chestnut brown curls. 'Not all Germans have blonde hair and blue eyes.'

'You've never mentioned this before,' said Krista.

'I didn't know before. My grandmother was born in Germany. She died when I was only three, so I don't remember her. Her family moved to Poland when she was a baby so even my mother doesn't think of her as truly German.'

Krista clasped Olesia's hand, grateful for the unwavering acceptance she'd received from her Guide unit. None of the other girls in their unit had ever treated Krista differently because she was German, not even at the outbreak of war.

A single gunshot reverberated through the air like a sudden crackle of thunder. Krista flinched, looking around frantically for the source of the shot, but saw nothing out of the ordinary. Olesia gripped Krista's hand tighter.

Anna placed her hand on top of theirs, creating a bond between the three girls. 'Let's remember,' she said, her voice cracking with emotion, 'the Germans can occupy Poland and stop Guides from meeting, but they cannot stop us from living the values that define our characters. We're good people and we will get through this.'

The sound of anxious whispers and stifled sobs filled the air. Krista tried to maintain her composure, but even Olesia, who usually radiated positivity, struggled to muster a smile. Fear and uncertainty lingered between them as they clung to each other's trembling hands.

'Let's go home,' said Krista.

The others agreed. Anna headed off and Olesia hurried towards her brother who was still surrounded by a crowd of people once again throwing questions at him. Krista pushed her way to the other side of the crowd in the direction of her grandparents' farm. The Germans were coming. Everything was about to change in ways she could barely imagine. Her grandfather had told her to prepare for the worst. The Nazis would tear through the village, he'd said, leaving nothing but destruction in their wake as they overrun the country like rats in an abandoned warehouse.

As she reached the edge of the square, Krista picked up

the faint rumble of slow-moving vehicles. She pressed herself against the wall of the cafe on the corner and waited. She had to see them for herself. She had to know if they were as sinister as her mind had conjured them to be.

A procession of German military cars, motorcycles, and trucks arrived first, their dark grey forms devouring the lush green surroundings of Zawica as they advanced towards the heart of the village. Behind them marched soldiers in crisp uniforms with shining black boots. Their boots thudded on the same ground Krista walked on every day. She touched her hand to the sinking feeling in her chest. One day she lived in a free nation and the next an occupied territory under German control. It wasn't that simple, but that was how it felt.

As the first soldier rounded the bend, Krista locked eyes with him. The others marched behind him in precise rows of four, their steely glares focused ahead as they made their way to the village square. By now, most of the villagers had retreated to the edges of the square to witness the spectacle. The soldier staring at her flicked his gaze to the ground before returning it to her. It struck her how young he looked. He couldn't have been much more than her seventeen years. He didn't look like the brutal men she had envisaged while waiting for this day to come. Did he even know why he was here? Did he believe in Hitler's cause? He was so close she could reach out and touch him. His eyes were the same shade as his uniform, not quite grey, but not quite green either. She thought she glimpsed regret in them.

Despite the still-warm October air, Krista shivered as the Germans marched past. She'd expected them to be bloodied. Exhausted. Dirty from the battlefields. But they were clean. And smart. And they had walked into the heart of her village unimpeded, having already killed or arrested those Polish warriors who had fought so hard to keep them away.

The soldiers in front came to an abrupt halt. The ones on motorcycles revved their engines and sped past their comrades until they reached the front of the procession. They switched off their engines and everything fell silent except for the thud of boots on concrete as Germans on foot continued to flood in.

The upper two windows of the village council office were opened. With what appeared to be practised synchronicity, streaks of red appeared at the windows and Nazi flags unfurled and cascaded down the front of the building. The giant swastikas were a clear symbol to the villagers that the Nazis were now in charge. Krista's stomach felt like a raging cauldron, bubbling with unbearably hot liquid.

Finally, the last of the soldiers arrived. Her chest tightened and her ragged breaths felt as though they were bouncing off the walls around her. Krista had seen the square crowded many times before. But this was different. It was like market day, except everyone wore identical uniforms and stood in perfectly straight rows. It was unnatural, and unnerving.

The silence was broken by hundreds of voices chanting in unison. 'Heil Hitler!'

Krista jumped with fright. She dabbed at a tear in the corner of her eye and turned her back on the men with their arms in the air saluting evil himself.

2

THE SKY HAD TURNED DARK BY THE TIME KRISTA ARRIVED BACK at the farm. Their home was surrounded by acres of agricultural land, a fortunate placement that had spared it from the intense bombing that had devastated many of the other houses in Zawica. Despite there being no military targets nearby, the Luftwaffe attack had been vicious and unrelenting.

Their quaint two-storey house was nestled in a dip in the countryside, providing an idyllic place to grow up. Or it would have been if she had moved to Poland under different circumstances. Her hand instinctively reached for the scar running the length of her thigh, the physical reminder of the car crash that had claimed the lives of her parents and had spared her.

Her grandfather, Kristian, was waiting for her, perched on the remains of the old tree between their house and barn. A storm last winter had snapped it in half before bringing it down, a stroke of good fortune that had saved their home and barn from its potentially destructive fall.

Kristian took a final drag of his cigarette before tossing it on the ground and working it into the soil with his boot. He stood up and gripped the rifle he'd had resting across his lap. 'Did you see them?' he asked.

Krista nodded. 'I did,' she said, knowing immediately he was referring to the Germans. It took her a few seconds to realise he'd spoken to her in Polish. He only ever spoke German at their home. Polish was reserved for trips into the village or the rare occasion when visitors were in the house.

'That's that then,' he said, still in Polish.

Kristian turned and shuffled back to the house. Each step seemed to take a great effort. His broad shoulders, usually held tall, sagged under the weight of his worries. It was as if confirmation of the Germans arrival had instantly aged him. He had never spoken of war, not to Krista at least. She was sad he was having to see another war in his life-time, but grateful he was too old to go off and fight. Many men from the village had gone to defend the country and hadn't been heard from again. Rumour was that those who hadn't been killed had been imprisoned and she hated to think what that might mean for them.

As soon as Krista appeared in the doorway, her grand-mother, Ilse, let out a sigh of relief. 'Krista, thank goodness you're back safely,' she said, the words tumbling out of her in rapid succession. Ilse ushered Krista into the house and bolted the door, securing them all inside. She double-checked the lock. 'It's almost time for dinner.'

Krista hung her coat by the front door. She looked between her grandparents, waiting for a barrage of ques-tions about the Germans, but her grandfather headed into the sitting room without another word.

Ilse ran her hands down Krista's hair, smoothing it out. 'Did you have time for your meeting?'

Krista shook her head, unable to speak through the

lump that formed in her throat. The eerie calm of her grandparents' reaction sent shivers down her spine, a stark contrast to the almost frenzied chaos of the villagers and the endless questions they threw at Marcin. But it wasn't the absence of questions that unnerved Krista, it was the lack of reassurance that everything would be alright despite the arrival of the Germans. Dread crept through Krista's veins like a venomous snake.

Ilse smiled, but it was one that failed to reach her eyes. 'You don't need meetings to organise yourselves,' she said.

Her grandmother was right about that, at least. Krista knew Anna would find a way for them to continue meeting in secret, but it wouldn't be the same. They'd be defying the Germans, sneaking around, and not everyone would be prepared to do that. Their numbers had already dwindled since the beginning of Hitler's onslaught on the Polish people. Only seven of them had turned up to their last meeting. But that didn't matter. Now was the time when Poland needed its Guides more than ever. Guides knew how to make themselves useful. Even the Guides too frightened to come to the meeting had spent the weeks since war was declared serving meals to soldiers, helping nurses to treat the wounded, and clearing rubble. Guides had even been digging trenches and building air raid shelters. Krista picked at the dirt under her fingernails. No amount of scrubbing had dislodged the grit under there.

'Do you want to help me finish dinner?' asked Ilse.

'I have something I need to do first,' said Krista.

Her grandmother nodded and disappeared into the kitchen while Krista hurried upstairs.

She pulled her Guide uniform out of her wardrobe and carefully folded it into a neat square, running her hand along the smooth fabric. Hitler's army was so paranoid and fearful that even children were not allowed to organise themselves into groups. Girl Guides, like the Boy Scouts, were banned. Some of the other girls' parents had made them get rid of their uniforms entirely. Her grandparents would never do that. They knew how much being a Guide meant to Krista. She had been ten years old when her parents died, and her grandparents whisked her away from everything she had ever known and taken her to live in the tiny Polish village of Zawica. Krista had barely understood the language. They had signed her up for the Girl Guides as a way to make friends and it was there, with Olesia and Anna and many other girls, that the Polish side of her had blossomed over the last seven years.

Krista's fingers trembled as she unpinned the metal shiny trefoil badge from her uniform and gently placed it on top of her chest of drawers. She retrieved a sheet of brown paper from her top drawer and meticulously wrapped her uniform, securing the edges with precise folds. She reached into another drawer and pulled out a sturdy metal pen, which she wiggled between a gap in her floorboards until one of the boards popped loose. As she placed her packaged uniform into the gap underneath her bedroom floor, she felt a twinge of sadness, as though she were somehow burying a part of her identity.

'Krista?' Her grandmother's voice called from downstairs. 'Dinner is ready.'

With a quiet click, Krista slid the floorboard back into place and ran her hand over it to make sure it was flush with the others. She stood up, picked up her trefoil pin, and made her way downstairs. She flipped over the collar of her coat hanging by the door and secured the pin to the underside of it, making sure it was hidden from plain view.

Dinner was already waiting for her. Roast pork, mashed

potatoes, and sauerkraut from Ilse's plentiful supply in the pantry.

'Have a seat,' said Ilse in Polish, as she placed a jug of water on the dining table.

'Why are you both speaking Polish?' Krista asked, taking her seat.

'To blend in,' said Ilse. 'We don't want to give the Germans a reason to come poking around.'

Before Krista got a chance to point out that there were no Germans in their home, her grandfather dragged his chair back from the table and sat down.

'What happened in the village?' he asked.

Finally, Krista thought. She sliced into her pork and loaded her fork with meat and a generous scoop of potatoes. 'There were a few cars and five trucks, but most of them arrived on foot. They marched right into the square as if on some military parade.' Her skin prickled at the memory.

'Huh,' said Kristian.

Her grandparents exchanged a glance that Krista couldn't decipher. 'They just look like us,' she added.

Kristian slammed his fist onto the tabletop. 'They're not, though. Don't you forget that. Many of them will do unspeakable things under the command of the Nazis.'

Krista's shoulders tightened. Her grandfather's certainty was frightening. He had never talked much about the Great War, as it had become known, but Krista knew from little comments her grandmother had made here and there that the experience had changed him. He'd seen the best of humanity, and he'd seen the worst. All she could do now was hope that humanity had learned its lesson and would not repeat the horrors of the past.

Ilse placed her hand across her husbands and his fist

unclenched. 'Did any of them talk to you? Did they take your details?' her grandfather asked.

Krista shook her head. 'I didn't stay long, but from what I saw, they didn't seem to be talking to anyone at all.'

'That will change,' said Kristian.

'They hung swastikas from the council office windows,' said Krista.

Kristian looked at Ilse again. 'This is how it starts.'

'We'll be safe, though, right?' Krista asked, fearing what the answer might be. When the reassurance she'd hoped to get wasn't forthcoming, she stuffed another forkful of food in her mouth and chewed. She'd lost her appetite, but the food supply was already becoming precarious. By the time Krista had reached the front of the queue at the bakery only yesterday the bread had just sold out for the day. Ilse's pickled cabbage was about the only thing not in short supply. She couldn't very well squander one of her grandmother's delicious dinners not knowing how much longer she'd be able to enjoy them.

Kristian stood up, stalked across the room, and turned the radio on. 'Let's listen to the radio while we're still able to.'

'Why won't we be able to?' Krista asked.

'Because soon enough the Germans will control everything we see and hear.'

Krista felt her meal turning over in her stomach. She thought of the book her grandfather kept on his nightstand, with its flawless spine and crisp pages. She had once asked him why he hadn't read it. *"I don't want to read it,"* he had said. *"But I value the right to read it if I choose to."* Before bed, she'd sneak that book away and hide it beside her Guide uniform. If the Germans knocked on their front door, she didn't want them to find anything incriminating inside.

As they finished their meal, the radio on the other side of the room buzzed picking up only snippets of static-filled conversation.

Frustrated, Kristian stood up again and turned the radio off with a flick of his wrist. He looked at Krista. 'After dinner, I have a story to tell you. About our family and why we are here.'

His words ignited the spark of curiosity within Krista. She had always known there more to her family's history than met the eye. She'd grown up hearing bits and pieces of hushed conversations, catching fragments of memories that never quite fit together. She looked between her grandparents, but they both avoided her gaze. The room felt heavy with unspoken truths, secrets waiting to be told. Krista was about to get the answers to the questions that had plagued her for so many years, but now she wasn't so sure that was a good thing.

3

_____

WITH THE DISHES WASHED AND PUT AWAY, KRISTA DROPPED
onto the worn armchair opposite her grandfather. Despite
the hours that had past and a good meal in her belly, she
still hadn't shaken off the anxiety she'd felt seeing the
Germans arrive and her grandparents' odd reaction. She
wondered what the Germans were doing. They'd all heard
the horror stories of what had happened in other cities and
towns across Poland. People had been slaughtered, there
was no other way to describe it. And it hadn't just been
soldiers. Men, women, and children had been brutalised by
the Germans. Or so they'd heard. Krista closed her eyes for
a moment and wished that the rumours were nowhere close
to the truth. The Germans had won. For now, Poland was
theirs. There was no need for further violence.

She sensed her grandfather's watchful gaze on her, but
when she met his eyes, he quickly looked away.

'You had a story for me,' said Krista.

Her grandfather leaned forward and straightened up a
newspaper on the table between them. He was dithering.
The man was a born storyteller. It was he who soothed

Krista after her many nightmares about the car accident that had taken her parents from her. He told tales full of adventure, a little mischief, and always a happy ending. But whatever story he had to tell now, was real life. It was the truth of their shared past, and it was a story he didn't seem keen to tell.

'Why did we leave Germany?' Krista asked. It was a question she'd asked before and her grandparents had always said "for a fresh start".

Her grandfather looked at her again. She could see him struggling for the right words. He let out a deep sigh. 'If we'd stayed in Germany, you would have been forced to join the League of German Girls so they could indoctrinate you with Nazi ideology,' he said.

Krista's eyes widened. She'd seen images of rows upon rows of young people, carrying Nazi flags, and parading like they were in the military. And she'd seen the real thing only hours before.

Ilse joined them in the sitting room. 'The Germans are not like us,' she said. She cradled a delicate vase in her hands, filled with vibrant purple flowers. 'Not anymore.'

'But you're German,' said Krista.

Her grandfather let out a heavy sigh and wiped a hand across his wrinkled forehead. 'I'm the wrong kind of German,' he said, with a sad shake of his head. His piercing blue eyes, just like Krista's, locked onto her. 'You are German too. Don't forget that. Speak Polish, blend in, but if the Nazis ask, show them your German documents with pride.'

Krista shook her head. She'd been born in Berlin and had spent the first ten years of her life there, but she didn't feel German. 'I feel more Polish now,' she said. 'Poland is my home.'

'No, it's not,' her grandfather said with a force in his

voice Krista had rarely heard. 'Until this war ends, you are German. You were forced to come here after your parents died, that's all.'

Krista looked at her grandmother who was nodding along, her expression serious. 'It's the best way for you to be safe,' said Ilse.

Safe? During the nightly bombings, Krista had been constantly afraid and uncertain. But now that they were over, she'd thought she was safe. But that seemed like a foolish notion now. How could she have ever believed safety was attainable while war raged on?

Ilse's hand trembled as she placed the vase of flowers on the low table between them. She sat down and stroked a purple petal. 'The most beautiful flowers bloom in the coolest weather.'

Krista gazed at the delicate blooms, trying to decipher whether her grandmother's words were meant to be taken literally or if there was a deeper meaning she couldn't yet grasp. The frailty of the petals seemed to mirror her grandmother's own fragile state, amplifying it even more in Krista's eyes.

'Kristian?' Ilse prompted.

Kristian sat forward on his chair and reached for Krista's hand. 'Everyone is vulnerable to the whims of this irrational enemy. But our family has more reason than most to keep out of their way. We must stay low, avoid drawing attention to ourselves. There's more I need to tell you.'

The steady rumble of tyres on the gravel outside their home dragged their attention away from each other. The noise grew louder and closer with each passing second.

Ilse's hand shot to her mouth. 'Have we left it too late?' she asked.

Kristian shook his head. 'Not already. It must be something else.'

Her grandparents stared at each other; an immediate tension thick in the air. Ilse got up and hurried to the window, her fingers nervously tugging at the blackout curtain as she peered outside.

'I can't see anything for headlights,' she said.

Kristian sprung to his feet and looked out; his face etched with deep lines of worry. 'Four vehicles at least. This isn't just a patrol.'

Krista caught the exchange of glances between her grandparents and knew that they had somehow already discussed whatever was happening now. Ilse hurried from the room. She returned moments later, clutching her old satchel tightly in her hand.

'Krista,' her grandfather said, taking the bag from Ilse. 'Take this and run. Go out the back door, up through the trees, and onto the track that runs alongside the cornfield.'

'What? Why?' asked Krista. 'What's going on?'

'There's no time to explain. Just take it.' He forced the strap of the bag over her head and her grandmother held out Krista's coat for her. She shoved her arms through the sleeves. A glimmer of light shone through the gap in the curtains and a car stopped outside. 'Go to Mr Gertz and tell him what's happened. He will look after you.'

'I don't know what's happened,' said Krista, with a crack in her voice. Her legs were heavy, and she didn't want to go anywhere, not without her grandparents. She turned to her grandmother. 'Come with me. Please.'

Ilse shook her head and nudged Krista towards the back door. 'No, my love. My place is here now. You'll be safer on your own.'

Tears welled in Krista's eyes and her heart thudded

inside her chest. It was as if her grandparents knew exactly what was going to happen next. 'It's the Germans, isn't it? Why are they here? Are you being arrested?'

'Go to Mr Gertz. He will explain everything. You must go now.' Her grandmother nudged her towards the door again, more forcefully this time. She cupped Krista's face, tears visible in her green eyes. 'You must go now. And remember that we love you.'

There was no more time. Car doors slammed. Her grandparents both pushed her, with more force now, towards the back door.

'We love you,' her grandfather repeated. 'Hide. Stay out of the spotlight and you'll stay safe.'

Krista slipped outside into the early evening shade and ran. Once sheltered in the cover of the trees, she stood still, listening and waiting for her eyes to adjust to the fading light. She looked back but the house blocked her view of whatever was happening in front of the building. More car doors slammed, and German voices grunted and barked orders. Whatever was going on, they weren't concerned with keeping it quiet.

As instructed, Krista sprinted through the woods and emerged onto the track. Going left would take her into the village, and she could go straight to Mr Gertz's house. He was a lawyer. His office would already be locked up for the evening, but Zawica was tiny, and she knew where he lived. Turning right would take her back to the farmhouse.

She turned right.

Slipping into the field of corn, she crouched and made her way through the narrow paths between the stalks, grateful the corn hadn't yet been harvested. Eventually, she reached a point where she could look down into the dip that sheltered her home without being noticed. The air was still, with no breeze to disguise any suspicious noise from the rustling plants. She peered down at the house. Light streamed out from the wide-open door to the farmhouse. In the headlights of a German vehicle, her grandparents faced the barn, their hands alongside their heads. Two soldiers aimed weapons at them. The vehicle's lights bounced off the metal. Three soldiers appeared to be having a conversation between themselves, but Krista was too far away to hear more than mumbling. Her gaze flicked back to her grandparents. She had no parents, and no brothers or sisters. Her father had been their only child. Those two people who hadn't hesitated to take her in when she needed it most were the only family she had in this world. If the Germans were taking them somewhere, Krista would go too. She straightened up and stepped forward. As she did, her grandfather moved his arm and clasped his wife's hand in his.

The stillness of the air around them was shattered as gunfire exploded, the noise reverberating around the sparse landscape and destroying Krista's world. She watched helplessly as her grandparents fell to the ground, their lifeless bodies staining the earth with their precious blood as it pooled around them.

'No!' Krista screamed. She clasped her hand over her mouth and retreated into the cover of the tall plants, her body shaking from the panic and fear consuming her. Beams of light from the Germans' torches shone her way, skimming the landscape, hunting her – a witness to their brutal actions. Krista stumbled backwards a few more paces, before turning and running as fast as her feet could carry her.

4

KRISTA'S BREATH HEAVED IN HER CHEST AS SHE LEFT THE country roads behind her and arrived back in Zawica. The streets were eerily quiet when Krista arrived. The windows of every house were shuttered and locked. People returned home before dark these days and stayed there until it was light enough to queue up for what little food arrived each day.

Mr Gertz lived a few streets before the centre and Krista was grateful she didn't have to enter the square itself. As far as she knew, the Germans were still there. Some of them anyway. Other Germans were up on her family's farm; perhaps standing over the bodies of her grandparents or rifling through her home. They only had to step inside her grandparents' house and they would find photographs of her and a girl's bedroom. It would be easy for them to guess that she was the one who had seen what they'd done.

An image of her grandparents falling to the ground flashed in her mind. She wiped the sleeve of her coat across her sweaty forehead, squeezed her eyes shut, and shook her head. Now was not the time to stop and replay what she had seen. If she did that, she'd never make it to Mr Gertz's house.

When the farm had become too big for her grandparents to manage on their own, Mr Gertz had helped them to break it up and sell off everything except two fields of corn and an apple orchard. As far as Krista was aware, her grandparents' relationship with their lawyer had been strictly professional. Now she was supposed to go and see this man and expect him to look after her. That's what her grandfather had said. *He will look after you.*

She circled Mr Gertz's street once, scanning the dark road and side streets as she did. They were empty. She knocked on Mr Gertz's door and pressed her ear against the sturdy wood, hoping to hear movement inside. When there was no response, she grasped the polished metal door knocker that glimmered even in the dark. A single tap echoed through the quiet street. Holding her breath, Krista resisted a glance behind her for any onlookers who may have now been alerted to her arrival. The door creaked open, and Mr Gertz appeared, his mouth agape and his eyes wide as he took in the unexpected visitor standing before him.

Krista looked down at her herself. These early autumn weeks had been dry so far and the fields were parched, yet she'd managed to find what must have been the only patches of damp ground to run across. Her shoes were covered in thick clumps of mud, with bits of grass and dirt clinging to their edges. Her coat was damp. The fabric felt sticky against her body thanks to the layer of sweat covering her skin.

'You can't be here,' Mr Gertz said, his words rushed and breathless. He leaned out of his door and peered up and down the street behind her. 'You have to go home.'

'But I need help,' said Krista. 'My grandparents, they've been...' She couldn't even bring herself to say it out loud. 'They told me to come to you. That you would help me.'

Mr Gertz shook his head and seemed to shrink back slightly. 'Not tonight. Come to my office in the morning. You can't be seen here.'

He slammed the heavy door shut, leaving Krista alone in front of his house, her eyes fixed on the glossy black paintwork, her feet rooted to the spot. She struggled to catch her breath and finally turned away. Unsteady steps carried her back up the street as she fought to push away the waves of confusion and heartbreak crashing over her. She had no idea where to go or what to do next.

'Krista?' a voice called behind her.

Krista's tense shoulders dropped with relief at the sound of her friend's voice.

Olesia skipped towards her, her parents trailing behind. She reached her arms forward to hug Krista, but froze, her gaze roaming across Krista's filthy appearance. 'My goodness. What happened to you?'

Olesia's parents caught up with them. Their eyes widened at the sight of Krista. Before Krista had a chance to explain her bedraggled appearance, the sound of a car racing along the cobbles of a nearby street filled the air. All four of them froze, awaiting its arrival. None of the locals used their cars anymore. Everyone walked. Those who still had fuel were saving every precious drop for essential, longer journeys. The bright glow of the headlights came into view briefly before fading away as the vehicle sped off in the opposite direction.

'I told you we should have left earlier,' Mrs Bukowski said to her husband. She put a hand on both girls' shoulders. 'Come on, let's get off the streets. Krista, Mr Bukowski will walk you home.'

Krista shook her head. 'I can't go home.'

'Of course you can, dear, it's not that far,' said Mrs Bukowski.

Krista's shoulders shook and tears rolled down her cheeks. She put a trembling hand to her chest, fighting to contain the sobs that ached inside of her.

'Oh, Krista, it's going to be OK,' said Mrs Bukowski. She wrapped an arm around Krista's shoulders and squeezed her tight, not seeming to mind about the dirt and grime. 'Let's get you home.'

'I can't go home,' Krista said again.

A military vehicle turned on the corner ahead of them, its heavy wheels trundling over the narrow pavement. Krista peeled away from Mrs Bukowski and covered her face with trembling hands, not daring to even glance towards the truck for fear of making eye contact with whoever may be inside. She felt Olesia's arm touch her own as her friend moved beside her and was grateful that she wasn't alone.

The truck stopped at the side of the road and Krista peered around the side of Mrs Bukowski. A German soldier leaned out from his open window. His stern gaze swept over the group, suspicion in his eyes.

'What are you doing on the streets?' he barked.

Mr Bukowski stepped forward, his back straight despite the tension crackling around them. 'I'm just seeing my daughters safely home after checking on an elderly neighbour,' he said.

The German soldier narrowed his eyes, assessing them for a moment that seemed to stretch too long. The weight of his scrutiny pressed down on Krista, making her limbs feel heavy. *Was he looking for her?*

Finally, the soldier's expression shifted from suspicion to irritation. 'Go straight home,' he ordered. 'You should not be out here at this hour.'

The soldier withdrew back into the truck, and it set off, the low growl of its engine echoing in Krista's ears as it passed by, its destination and purpose unknown.

'Has something happened?' Mrs Bukowski asked.

Krista grabbed her stomach and screwed her eyes shut, trying to will away the nausea that threatened to overwhelm her. Her whole body trembled.

The Bukowskis exchanged a few hushed words before Mrs Bukowski again wrapped an arm around Krista's shoulders. 'Come with us. You can stay with us tonight. If the telephones are working, I'll call your grandmother and let her know you're safe.'

Krista tried to speak, to explain that her grandmother wouldn't answer the phone. But the words choked in her throat as the memories of what she had witnessed on the farm flooded in. Her sweaty hands clutched tightly at her chest as if to stop her heart from breaking. She couldn't move. It was too painful. Her breath came in jagged gasps as someone grabbed her shoulders, pushing her forward. With all her energy, she focused on her legs, willing them to move, as she allowed herself to be ushered off the streets.

5

————

KRISTA WOKE IN DARKNESS AND SNUGGLED DEEPER INTO THE warm blanket covering her body. She rolled over in bed and tried to push away thoughts of the terrible dream she'd had.

'Good morning,' came Olesia's cheery voice. 'How did you sleep?'

Krista jolted upright in bed. Her heart sank, and tears stung her eyes as she realised that it hadn't been a nightmare at all. Her grandparents really were dead. Murdered in front of their own home.

'Morning?' Krista asked, now confused by the darkness.

Olesia's silhouette shuffled around in the dark. The soft click of the door opening was followed by light spilling in from the hallway outside. Krista squinted at the sudden brightness.

They were in Olesia's bedroom, and Krista was in Olesia's bed.

'You were really out of it last night. What happened?'

Mrs Bukowski appeared in the doorframe holding Krista's clothes. Krista glanced down. She was wearing a nightdress that she presumed belonged to Olesia. She couldn't remember anything beyond meeting the Bukowskis in the street after Mr Gertz had turned her away.

Olesia's mother dropped the bundle of clothing onto the bed beside Krista. 'Washed and dried for you. Come downstairs for breakfast when you're ready.'

'Thank you,' Krista mumbled still trying to figure out how it was that she had arrived at Olesia's house, undressed, and climbed into Olesia's bed without remembering any of it.

Her friend eyed her curiously. 'You look confused,' she said. 'My father said you were in shock. He's seen it before.'

Krista nodded. That was the first thing to make sense since she'd opened her eyes. It was only natural that she'd be in shock. She ran her hand along her clean clothes.

'I'll leave you to get dressed,' said Olesia, fumbling in her wardrobe and pulling out a dress and a chunky woollen cardigan. 'The bathroom is right next door. I'll go first, if you don't mind. Come to the kitchen whenever you're ready.'

In the corner of Olesia's bedroom, the bag Krista's grandmother had given her was propped up on a chair. Pangs of guilt crept over Krista as she spotted a pile of blankets crumpled on the floor where Olesia must have slept.

Krista slid out of the warm bed, picked up her bag, and brought it back to the bed with her. She opened it, instantly overwhelmed by memories of her home: the floral scent of her grandmother's perfume and the smell of her grandfather's tobacco. She could almost see the bag hanging on a hook by the door in her mind, and she could hear her grandmother urging her to run.

Krista rifled through the contents of the bag. There was a change of clothes, her identity documents, an envelope with some cash, her Girl Guide's first aid kit and whittling knife, and half a dozen of her grandmother's oat biscuits wrapped in paper. She took out one of the biscuits. With a gentle twist, she snapped it in half, popped the piece into her mouth and savoured the sweetness. She closed her eyes and imagined her grandmother in her trusty apron, hands covered in flour, with her infectious grin lighting up her face. She wondered how long the bag had been packed and how many times her grandmother had replaced the parcel of biscuits to keep them this fresh.

Krista dressed in her freshly washed clothes and joined Olesia and her mother downstairs just as Mr Bukowski flung open the back door, bringing a rush of cool morning air inside with him. He stormed into the kitchen and slammed the door behind him, the hinges squeaking in protest. His face was pale.

'It's an outrage,' he said with ragged breath. 'Everyone has been arrested. Anyone with any political or religious affiliation has been rounded up. The mayor and his entire staff. The priest. The rabbi was shot dead in front of his own synagogue. The poor man's blood is still pooled on the street. Even Mr Gorecki, the headmaster, has been arrested. His only crime seems to be intellect.'

Olesia's hand flew towards her gaping mouth. Krista didn't flinch. She wondered if she would have been just as shocked as Olesia if she hadn't witnessed the Germans' brutality for herself only hours before.

'Krista,' said Mr Bukowski, turning to her. 'I'm sorry to have to be the one to tell you, but I believe your grandparents are dead.'

'I know,' Krista replied.

'Oh, Krista. No!' said Olesia, tears bubbling over and spilling down her cheeks.

'Oh no!' said Mrs Bukowski. 'What on earth happened? They're farmers. They're not political or religious. Did the

Germans want the house? Or the farm?' she asked, directing her questions to her husband.

'Perhaps, but they can do that without killing the current occupants. I think it's more likely that they believed the Schulzs were involved in something.' Krista felt Mr Bukowski's eyes on her, as if waiting for a reaction. Getting none, he turned to his wife. 'They might be looking for her.'

They *were* looking for her. Krista knew that for certain. She suddenly felt anxious just being in Olesia's house in case she brought the Germans to her friend's front door.

'What do we do?' asked Mrs Bukowski with a slight quiver in her voice that shook her words.

They all looked at each other, as if seeking guidance, but no one was quite sure what the answer was. Mrs Bukowski turned and left the room. Krista heard her footsteps on the stairs and braced herself for Mrs Bukowski's return. She expected her to be carrying Krista's bag and, quite politely, to ask Krista to leave. Krista couldn't blame her. She didn't want to put her friend at risk either. She had to see Mr Gertz and pray he wouldn't turn her away once more.

Olesia reached out and gently squeezed Krista's trembling hand. There was a flicker of understanding in her eyes, sympathy mixed with fear for what lay ahead.

Mrs Bukowski returned, but instead of carrying her bag as Krista anticipated, she held a dark, glass bottle in her hand and a look of purpose on her face. 'Krista,' she said. 'I think we should change your hair colour.'

Krista's eyes widened in surprise, her breath catching in her throat. Olesia smiled and Mr Bukowski nodded at his wife's suggestion. Krista had steeled herself for rejection, but instead, she found unexpected allies in the Bukowskis.

Krista ran her fingers through her long, chestnut brown hair. It held a gentle wave that she'd shared with her mother. She had precious few memories of her parents, but she could vividly recall her mother gently running her fingers through Krista's hair, warning her not to brush it too often or she would lose the natural waves that made it so beautiful.

'This will lighten it,' said Mrs Bukowski, snapping Krista's attention back. 'If the Germans are looking for you, they're looking for a brunette.'

Krista's skin prickled. She exchanged looks with Olesia, knowing her friend was also thinking of Anna and her rather unfortunate luck trying to lighten her hair. Anna hadn't known what she was doing. It seemed the wrong thing to be worried about right now, but, still, Krista did not want to find out if Olesia's mother was any more adept with a bottle of peroxide.

'Thank you, but I don't want to be blonde,' said Krista.

'Nonsense,' said Mr Bukowski. 'It's only hair and it could save your life.'

Krista's felt her cheeks flush.

'Hair matters,' said Mrs Bukowski. 'How about a cut instead?'

Krista nodded. Losing the wave in her hair hardly compared to all the other things she had lost in her lifetime.

Olesia's mother turned out to be an accomplished hairdresser and provided a stylish cut. She swept up the inches of hair that she'd snipped off and left Krista to examine her new look in the bathroom mirror. Her waves were gone, replaced by poker-straight hair that skimmed the tops of her shoulders. It hadn't been that short in years.

Krista shook her head over the bathtub and rinsed away all remaining evidence of her haircut.

She emerged from the bathroom to find Olesia's brother Marcin leaning against the wall in the hallway. His hands fidgeted with his shirt sleeves and a small smile played on his lips. Krista leaned against the wall beside him, and he turned to face her.

His hand reached out, brushing against her hair as he twirled a lock around his finger. 'It suits you.'

Krista felt goosebumps rise on her arms as a shiver ran down her spine. She resisted the urge to reach out and touch him, her hand hovering in the air before quickly pulling back. She shouldn't get distracted. It was so wrong. Now was not the time to indulge in her childhood crush. Her mind should be focused on figuring out why her grandparents were suddenly gone.

Marcin released her hair, and it brushed her cheek like a feather floating to the ground. 'I'm so very sorry about your grandparents.'

His coffee-coloured eyes, usually brimming with mischief and youthful energy, now held a deeper level of concern. Krista felt a lump form in her throat, a rush of emotions threatening to spill over. Tears blurred her vision, and she blinked them away, swallowing hard as she mustered a grateful smile for Marcin's words.

'Thank you,' she managed to say softly, her voice trembling with the weight of grief.

They stood there in the dimly lit hallway, a world of unspoken thoughts passing between them. Marcin took a step closer to her, his presence a comforting shield against the storm of emotions threatening to break her. He reached out and gently wiped away a tear that escaped down her cheek, his touch warm against her skin. Krista felt a surge of connection that she had never experienced before.

'I wish I could take your pain away, Krista,' Marcin whispered. 'I wish I could shield you from all the darkness that has touched your life.'

His words pierced through Krista's defences, unravelling the barriers she had constructed since fleeing her home. Tears welled up in her eyes once more, but this time she didn't try to stop them. She allowed them to flow down her cheeks, soaking into Marcin's shirt as he pulled her towards him and held her tight.

6

When Krista's quiet sobs subsided, Marcin took a step back to look at her. He kept his hands firmly planted on her shoulders. 'You will get through this,' he said.

Krista gave him a small smile and followed him to join Olesia and her parents in the living room. Marcin dropped into the seat beside his father while Krista hovered in the doorway.

Olesia bounced up from the sofa to touch the ends of Krista's newly shorn hair. 'It's magnificent. And with this new side parting, you hardly look like the old Krista at all.'

'That's the point, darling,' said Mrs Bukowski, who was busy dusting the bookcases with a yellow rag.

'Oh, right. Yes,' said Olesia. 'Should we come up with a new name for you? How exciting! It's like something from a mystery novel.'

'Except it's real life,' barked Olesia's father. 'The girl has to use the name on her identity documents and hope she can talk her way out of any problems if she's caught.'

'What do you mean caught?' asked Olesia, her brow

furrowing as she turned to her father. 'Krista hasn't done anything wrong.'

Olesia's father took a slow drag from his pipe and exhaled a thick plume of smoke that curled through the air like a dark omen. 'The Nazis don't just haul people out of their homes and shoot them for no reason.'

It seemed to Krista as though that was exactly what the Nazis had done. She felt a shiver run down her spine. Mr Bukowski sounded as if he was implying that this had somehow been her grandparents' fault.

'Whatever her grandparents were involved in, Krista needs to deny all knowledge of it,' he continued, his voice a low growl.

Krista's fingernails dug into her palms as she balled her fists at her sides. 'My grandparents were farmers, that's all. They weren't *involved* in anything.'

Mr Bukowski leaned forward, his eyes narrowing. His gaze was hard and unyielding. 'The Germans think differently. They have a reason for everything, however spurious that reason might be. If they find you, you must convince them you knew nothing of it.'

'There's nothing to know!' snapped Krista. Her pulse quickened and she could feel the heat of anger flushing her cheeks.

Olesia winced, her eyes darting between her friend and her father. Krista caught the concern in Olesia's eyes as she anxiously awaited her father's reaction to Krista's outburst.

'I'm sorry,' said Krista, her voice softer now. She looked down, fighting to steady her breathing. Too many emotions swirled inside her, threatening to overwhelm her. But getting angry wouldn't help her right now. 'I don't know why the Nazis came to my grandparents farm, but I am certain that they were honest people who did not deserve bullets in the back of their heads.'

Mr Bukowski lowered his gaze and inspected the pipe he held. 'No,' he murmured. 'They did not deserve that. Whatever they've done.'

Krista took a deep breath, her frustration once again threatening to boil over again at Mr Bukowski's certainty that her grandparents had done something. Just one hour ago, he had informed them of the sudden mass-arrests without placing any blame on the victims. She couldn't understand his mindset. He had been through the outbreak of this war firsthand, returning to Zawica just days ago. He must have considered the possibility of being arrested by the Nazis for simply defending his country. Would he willingly submit himself if they came knocking at his door, believing he deserved it?

Krista's eyes locked with Marcin's, and she saw understanding and empathy in his gaze. Unlike his father, he did not seem convinced that her grandparents were at fault. It was a small comfort, but his quiet support meant everything to Krista.

'The Nazis don't need a reason to be cruel and ruthless,' said Marcin. 'They just are. All we can do now is find a way to get Krista to safety.'

'Yes, right,' said Mrs Bukowski, swiping the rag along another dusty shelf. She looked at Krista over her shoulder. 'Do you have any other family you can stay with? Long term, I mean. You can stay here for as long as you need to.'

'I'm meeting someone this morning,' said Krista. 'He has agreed to help me.' She hoped that was still the case. Had grandparents had seemed certain that Mr Gertz would help her, but he hadn't seemed keen to help last night.

'I'll take you there,' said Marcin, his voice calm and steady.

'No!' snapped Mr Bukowski. He set his pipe down on the table with a clink. 'The Nazis are suspicious of all men. You'll only draw more attention her way.'

Mr Bukowski's weathered face was stern, lines etched deep with concern for his son's safety.

'We can't send her out there alone,' said Marcin, scowling in his father's direction. He turned to Krista. 'Who are you meeting? I can go for you.'

Krista could see the worry now etched on Marcin's face and felt the unspoken tension between him and his father. 'It's alright, Marcin,' she said softly. 'Your father is right.'

'Besides,' added Mrs Bukowski. 'It will look even more suspicious if you're not at the meeting.'

Marcin crossed his arms. 'I'm not going to their meeting.'

Mrs Bukowski picked up a photo frame and swiped her cloth across the glass. Her gaze lingered on the smiling faces of her children. 'Of course you're going. I won't have you disappearing into the forest with those men. That's no life for a boy.'

Marcin stood up, towering over his mother. She turned to look at him. He gently took the frame from her hands and replaced it on the shelf. 'I'm not a boy.'

Mr Bukowski retrieved his pipe. He struck a match on the side of his chair, relighting the tobacco with ease. He held the pipe between his lips and extinguished the match with his fingertips. Taking another long drag, he turned to his son and blew out another thick cloud of smoke. 'Marcin, you'll stay here and take care of your mother and sister. That's the honourable thing to do. And you will attend that meeting.'

Marcin's hands curled into tight fists, his knuckles turning white. Krista could see the struggle raging within him, torn between obeying his father's orders and asserting his own independence. But even he had to admit that Krista would be safer alone. Marcin would catch the attention of the Germans far quicker than Krista. At least, that's what she hoped.

'What meeting?' asked Krista, hoping to calm the atmosphere a little.

'The entire village has been instructed to attend a meeting with the Germans this morning at nine o'clock,' said Olesia, a quiver of concern in her voice. 'Did you not hear them announcing it when they arrived yesterday?'

Krista felt a knot form in her stomach at the mere thought of encountering the Germans again. 'I didn't stick around to hear what they had to say,' she said. 'But I can't attend the meeting, and I can't stay here in Zawica either.' She knew she couldn't stay, but leaving meant leaving behind everything and everyone she knew. She glanced at Olesia and then Marcin. It was a decision that tore her apart from the inside out.

Olesia wrung her hands together. 'Where will you go?'

A metallic taste filled Krista's mouth as she thought of her options. She wiped her clammy hands on her clothes. 'I don't know.'

'A life on the run isn't easy,' said Mr Bukowski.

Olesia's eyebrows shot up. 'On the *run*?'

'My advice is to find somewhere to settle and do what you can to blend in,' he added.

Krista wondered if that explained why Mr Bukowski was sitting in his house, surrounded by his family, and smoking his pipe. Perhaps he had considered that the Nazis would arrest him, but the alternative was to run from them. What would that look like for a man of fighting age? She regretted her earlier anger at the man. Despite the fears he must have had for his own safety, he had still opened his home to her in her time of need. Besides, she couldn't be too put out by his persistence that her grandparents had been involved in something. They had clearly planned for a situation where Krista would have to flee through the back door alone. They had a secret from her, and she hoped that Mr Gertz could provide some answers.

7

Mr Gertz's office on the village square was still locked up when Krista arrived. Rather than stand and wait, she began a lap around the square, relieved to see no Germans patrolling the area.

Two soldiers stood guard in front of the bank, a clear indication to the locals that the Germans were now in charge. And if that wasn't enough symbolism, the Germans had made sure to leave their mark almost everywhere else that Krista looked. Polish flags had been replaced by swastikas waving proudly in the morning breeze. The patriotic posters that she and her fellow Guides had papered Zawica with during the early days of the war had been torn down and replaced with Nazi propaganda messages.

There was a long queue outside of the grocery store. A normal sight since the invasion. But what wasn't normal was friends and neighbours hurrying past each other with their heads down, avoiding eye contact. No one stopped to talk to each, to compare stories of the first night of German occupation in their village. There was an atmosphere of mistrust, and it seemed that no one wanted to do anything that might bring attention their way.

Krista walked by the cafe where her grandmother gathered with her knitting club every Sunday. It was bustling. A quick glance inside the windows revealed why there were no other Germans out on the street – they were all inside eating and drinking. The tables in the front showcased an abundance of food, a stark contrast to the food shortages that had plagued the rest of the village since the bombing began. A new sign had been added to the glass door: GERMANS ONLY.

The change in Zawica overnight was unfathomable. And overseeing it all, was a large picture of Hitler raised high above the village council office, dominating the building's stone facade.

After a slow walk around the square, Mr Gertz still hadn't arrived. Krista thought about standing in line at the butchers to at least look as though she had a purpose. The queue wasn't moving fast, and she'd have a good view of Mr Gertz's office. However, she dismissed that idea for fear of someone in the queue noticing her and spearing her with questions she couldn't answer. News had obviously spread about her grandparents given Olesia's father had heard about it.

Instead, she wandered into the only shop without a line of people waiting outside – Mrs Krol's knitting supplies shop. Browsing an array of coloured wool had to be less conspicuous than hanging about in the street.

As soon as Krista entered, Mrs Krol waved a hand in her direction. 'Anna,' she said, 'I have the wool your mother requested.'

Anna was a popular name. She knew of half a dozen people, at least, named Anna, including Krista's Guide

Captain who was a regular in the knitting shop, but Mrs Krol surely hadn't mistaken Krista for any of the others. Her new haircut was not so different as to make her unrecognisable to those who already knew her. Krista opened her mouth to speak, but Mrs Krol glared at her before grabbing a paper bag from behind the counter and dropping two balls of navy blue wool and a starter set of knitting needles into it.

'Here you go, Anna, dear,' said Mrs Krol, thrusting the bag at Krista with shaky hands. 'Run along and take that straight home to your mother.'

It was clear that Mrs Krol knew exactly who Krista was and she didn't want her in her shop. Krista reached out for the bag still being offered. 'Thank you,' she said, her fingers scrunching up the paper bag. She turned to leave the shop and only then did she see the reason behind Mrs Krol's fluster.

Two German soldiers emerged from behind a shelving unit carrying a pair of knitted gloves each. They nodded to Krista and continued past her to Mrs Krol. Krista didn't dare look back to see if they had given her a second glance. She left the shop, forcing herself to walk when her legs twitched with the desire to run.

Her departure from the shop was just in time to see Mr Gertz arriving at his office. Even from twenty feet away, she could feel his frenzied energy vibrating towards her. His gaze darted around, and he glanced over his shoulder several times. It was like witnessing a masterclass on how to draw attention to oneself.

Krista waited for him to unlock the door then dashed across the road and followed him into the building.

His eyebrows shot up when he registered who she was.

'Krista!' He shoved her out of the way and stared out into the street behind her. 'What are you doing here?'

'You told me to come. Last night, remember?' There were gaps in her memory from the evening before, but she remembered clearly going to Mr Gertz's house and his instruction to come to his office in the morning.

His eyes were heavy and his face somehow more lined than it had been the night before. He seemed as though he'd aged ten years overnight, a situation Krista felt she could relate to.

'Oh, right. Yes,' he said.

'My grandparents told me you would help me.'

Mr Gertz dumped his bag on a narrow table and shut his office door, bolting it from the inside. 'You'd better come up.'

She followed him up the stairs and into a room at the front of the building. His office, Krista concluded. It was as dishevelled as the man himself. Piles of paperwork dominated the large wooden desk. It didn't appear to be in any kind of order. A stack of unopened mail had spilt from the top left corner of the desk onto the floor. She took a seat in front of his desk and tucked the bag of wool that Mrs Krol had given her inside her bag.

Mr Gertz hovered by the window peering down into the square below. 'Are you certain you weren't followed?' he asked.

'I'm sure.' As sure as she could be given the events of the last twenty-four hours. She had known war would change things, but she couldn't ever have imagined just how much or how fast things would change.

He hadn't been happy about her unexpected visit to his home the previous night, but he had been composed enough apart from checking for any potential observers. However, now, as he paced back and forth in front of the window, his hands trembled and sweat beaded on his fore-head. He moved away from the window and slumped into the leather chair behind his desk. He dragged a hand through his hair, ruffling the already messy strands.

'Where are your grandparents?' he asked.

'They're dead.' It was the first time she'd said it out loud and she surprised herself by stating it without breaking down. There hadn't even been a crack in her voice. She willed herself to stay strong. Mr Gertz was panicking enough for the both of them.

Mr Gertz loosened his tie and tugged at the collar of his shirt. 'Both of them? How?'

'The Germans showed up at the farm and shot them. I don't know why.' 'How do you know this?'

'I saw it happen.'

He clasped his hands together and leaned forward on his desk. 'You saw a German soldier shoot your grandparents?' he asked, unable to mask the doubt in his voice.

'Two German soldiers.' Her voice remained steady as she recounted the horrifying events. The memories were fresh, and painful. She closed her eyes for a moment. The sound of gunshots and her own scream still rang in her ears. 'They made my grandparents face the barn then each soldier fired their rifle, and my family were dead.'

Colour drained from Mr Gertz face, and he wiped the back of his hand across his brow. 'How did you get away?'

'My grandparents told me to run as soon as we heard the Germans driving up to the farm. They told me to come here for help. You will help me, won't you?' As she pleaded for his assistance, doubts began to creep into her mind. If he wouldn't help her, she had nowhere else to turn.

'Well, yes, of course,' said Mr Gertz. He sat up straighter in his chair and took a breath, composed at last. 'If I can. I'm afraid this all happened more suddenly than I had expected.'

'What do you mean?' asked Krista, leaning forward in her chair, her desperation now tangled with suspicion. 'What did you expect was going to happen?'

Mr Gertz glanced down at his desk, running a finger along a dent in the wooden top. 'Your grandfather had spoken to me some time back and asked me to help you and Ilse if his life was ever in danger.'

'Why would his life be in danger?' It seemed such a silly question to ask given her grandfather was now dead. Of course his life had been in danger, but how could he have possibly known that? He wasn't in the Polish army, he was too old for that, and he wasn't a threat to the Nazis. He was a farmer, not some kind of politician or high-profile figure. He wasn't religious in any way. He wasn't at all like the others who had been arrested by the Germans.

'Krista, your grandfather was Jewish.'

8

KRISTA SAT IN MR GERTZ'S OFFICE SHAKING HER HEAD. 'MY grandfather is not Jewish. He's German.'

'Plenty of people are German and Jewish,' said Mr Gertz.

She shook her head again. 'I know, but he's not Jewish. We're not Jewish.' There was a small Jewish community in Zawica, a synagogue, and a shop selling kosher meat. Her grandparents hadn't ever set foot in the synagogue as far as she knew. Their last meal together had been roast pork. Her eyes drifted to the ceiling as she replayed their dinner the evening before. Had her grandfather eaten the meat? He must have, surely, although she couldn't now recall seeing a forkful of pork enter his mouth.

'How do you know this?' Krista asked.

'Your grandfather said he heard the way Jews were being talked about in Germany. He said he believed that this hateful rhetoric was going to end badly for Jews, and he wanted no part in it.'

'Why would he tell you this?'

'When he moved to Poland, I think he chose to leave his Jewishness behind. But he didn't believe the Nazis would respect the nonaggression pact with Poland. He asked me to help you and Ilse if the Nazis ever came looking for him.' Mr Gertz ran his hand across his jaw. 'Why would they just execute them like that?'

The word *execute* hit Krista like a blow to the back of the head. The room closed in around her, the air growing thin and suffocating. Mr Gertz's voice continued in the distance, his words muffled and distorted. She heard him speaking, but his voice was a blur of indistinct syllables, lost in the chaos that consumed her thoughts.

She grasped the edge of the wooden desk in front of her and took a desperate gasp for air. A warm hand landed on her back, rubbing in circles between her shoulder blades. She closed her eyes, focusing on matching her breaths to the rhythmic movement. Gradually, her breathing steadied and she opened her eyes.

'Are you alright?' asked Mr Gertz, standing over her, his hand still on her back.

She gave a slight nod, and he handed her a handkerchief from his pocket before walking over to open the small cupboard behind his desk.

A safe was tucked behind the door. He knelt and unlocked it, while Krista wiped her clammy face with his handkerchief. There were three shelves inside and each one was more ordered than his desk, although that wouldn't have been difficult to achieve. He flicked through a stash of envelopes on the middle shelf and plucked one out. He relocked the safe, closed the cupboard door, and sat down again, passing her the envelope. 'Your grandfather left this for you.'

It was sealed and her initials had been typed on the front. 'What is it?' she asked, holding the envelope between the palm of her hands.

'Money. You'll have to leave town. That will help you. There's a transport leaving before sunrise tomorrow morning. It will take you and some others to safety.'

'Which others? Jews?'

'Mostly.'

Krista narrowed her eyes, suspicion flaring in her gut. 'And where are we going?'

Mr Gertz glanced towards his window, his expression tightening. 'I can't reveal that information. I'm sure you understand.'

'No, I don't understand.' She leaned forward, the wood of the desk creaking slightly under her weight, and extended the handkerchief towards him. Her fingers brushed the cool surface of the desk, but he waved her away.

'Keep it, please. The truck will leave from the old footbridge. The driver won't wait for any latecomers so be there in plenty of time before sunrise. Hide somewhere until then. All residents have been ordered to attend a meeting in the village hall shortly.' His voice dropped, and he leaned in closer, his breath shallow. 'The Germans will be crawling the streets looking for anyone who has defied their orders. Stay out of sight.'

Krista swallowed hard, the weight of his words pressing down on her.

A thud came from behind and she whipped her head around to the office door. 'What was that?'

Mr Gertz sprung up from his chair. His brief period of composure was over and the anxious man she'd seen on the street had returned. 'My secretary trying to get in. Do you have any other family who can take you in?'

'No.'

Someone thumped on the front door. Mr Gertz came out

from behind his desk, took her hand, and closed his fingertips around the envelope. 'Then be at the bridge tomorrow. You have no other choice.' He opened the door to his office and ushered her out. 'Go down the stairs and out of the back door.'

She sprinted ahead of him and down the stairs. Another thump on the door.

'I'm coming, I'm coming,' he yelled.

Krista turned at the bottom of the stairs.

'Wait,' said Mr Gertz. He reached into the bag he'd left on the table and pulled out a metal flask. 'Take this.' He pressed it into her hand.

She wasted no time and ran towards the back door, flinging it open, and disappearing into the alleyway behind the office buildings.

She leaned against the cool brick wall, trying to catch her breath and calm her racing heart. How could the Nazis arrive in their village and, within hours, learn her grandfather was Jewish, something she had never known?

Krista sank to her knees and unscrewed the lid off the flask that Mr Gertz had given her. The strong scent of coffee filled her nostrils. She wasn't a coffee drinker, but in the absence of anything else to drink, she was grateful for his last-minute gesture.

After a time, Krista left the shade of the alleyway and surveyed the square. It had been a typical Polish village, everyone going about their business as best they could given the knowledge that their country was now officially under German occupation. Now, only a day later, Zawica had been transformed into what she imagined one outside of Berlin to look like. There were more soldiers now on the square. With their bellies fuller than anyone else's, they had left the cafe to do whatever it was a group of Germans were supposed to do in a country that wasn't their own. Her gaze settled on the guards in front of the bank. She stashed the envelope Mr Gertz had given her deep inside the pocket of her coat, grateful for her grandfather's extraordinary foresight.

People streamed towards the village hall for the compulsory meeting. Given what Mr Bukowski had said about the arrests yesterday, who would dare defy the Germans and not attend? Krista considered melting into one of the crowds, walking up the steps, and into the venue. She hadn't cared what they had to say when they had first marched into the village, but her entire worldview had shifted within the space of a day. Now she wanted to know what the occupiers had to say, but she never would.

She stepped into the shadows of the lane behind the bakery and, using only the side streets, made her way to the synagogue.

The synagogue stood tall, its beautiful white facade adorned with towering columns and intricate carvings. Multi-coloured light flooded through the stained-glass windows, creating a kaleidoscope of patterns on the ground below.

The wooden doors to the synagogue were closed and there were no signs of life. But the signs of death were impossible to ignore.

Bullet holes had pierced into the white flesh of the building, and one of the windows had been shattered, jagged blue glass littering the ground. Each stone step from the entrance looked like polished marble, worn smooth from years of use. But at the bottom lay a dark pool of thick, sticky blood. Her Guide first aid training had taught her how crucial it was to stem bleeding as soon as possible; too much blood loss could be fatal. This was too much blood.

The thought that the rabbi may have died right there made her heart ache. And yet, in a twisted way, it made her feel less alone knowing that her family wasn't the only one targeted by this tragedy.

Krista stepped away from the synagogue, shards of broken glass crunched under her shoes and echoed through the empty streets. The envelope in her pocket was proof that her grandfather had known the Nazis would come for him one day, but why? Mr Gertz had seemed so certain that it was because her grandfather was Jewish, but still, she wasn't sure she believed it. No one had ever mentioned Jewish heritage. *Stay out of the spotlight and you'll stay safe.* Was that why they had moved to Poland? So her Jewish grandfather could stay out of the spotlight?

She needed to find a place to hide until the transport departed in the morning. Going back to Olesia's house wasn't an option. Her family had helped Krista the night before because she was their daughter's friend. Krista hadn't even considered that there might be a risk to them for helping her. But now, she knew there would be a risk. The Nazis would consider it harbouring a Jew. That risked their lives, and she would not put the Bukowskis in that position. Suddenly, a gunshot shattered the silence and Krista jumped. Without looking back, she quickened her pace, afraid of who might be chasing after her.

9

KRISTA CROUCHED BEHIND THE GNARLED ROOTS OF A
towering oak tree. She'd spent the night sheltering in an old
barn that bordered the very edges of her grandparents'
farm, sneaking away in the early hours to make her way to
the old footbridge. She pulled her hands up into the sleeves
of her coat to warm them.

The darkness was thick, but she could just make out the
shapes of people gathering near the bridge. They whispered
to each other; their words too quiet for her to decipher. She
stood up, ready to join the group of people who, like her,
were fleeing from the Nazis. Her coat snagged on something
sharp. Squinting down at what had caught her, her skin
prickled at the long line of barbed wire stretched up the side
of the road leading to the bridge. The dull hum of a vehicle
grew louder, and Krista retreated into the shadows of the
tree.

A beam of light swept past her as the vehicle turned. She
waited for the headlights to illuminate the murky figures on
the bridge, but the driver cut the lights and crawled to a
stop. It was a car. There must have been a dozen or so

people on the bridge. This couldn't be the transport Mr Gertz had told her was coming.

With a loud click, the car's doors opened and slammed shut. Heavy boots crunched on gravel. Krista didn't need light to know they were Nazis. A chill shot down her spine and she shivered as frantic voices echoed through the air around her.

Harsh, guttural voices barked orders in German. The people were being instructed to form a line. Suddenly, a deafening shot rang out and was met with pained wails that quickly turned to fearful silence.

'Anyone else tries to run and this girl is dead,' threatened a voice in heavily accented Polish.

Krista felt helpless. Somewhere beyond the shadows was a girl with a gun to her head and there was nothing Krista could do about it. The Nazis turning up here and now was not a coincidence. She didn't know who told the others to be here, but she knew who had told her.

Mr Gertz.

She considered for a moment that Mr Gertz himself had told the Nazis, but quickly dismissed that theory. She thought of the pile of envelopes she had seen him flick through in his safe. He could be shot for helping Jews evade the clutches of the Nazis. Just holding Jewish money could cause him problems and, from what she recalled, he was holding money for a lot of people.

Further instructions were issued. The group were being moved on foot. Krista shuddered. The only thing between the bridge and the neighbouring village were a few kilometres of woodland. The clatter of feet scuffing the ground faded into the darkness until Krista heard only her own breathing. She dared not follow in case she was spotted, or the crunch of leaves underfoot gave her away.

As the darkness faded away and the once pitch-black sky showed hints of deep blue, Krista edged her way closer to the road, making sure to avoid the barbed wire. A soft glow caught her attention, along with the distinct whiff of tobacco. A figure was hunched over a pile of luggage. Krista slowly lowered herself to the ground again. He rifled through each bag, pocketing items here and there before tossing them into the back of his vehicle with a thud. She heard paper being ripped and another bag being thrown inside the car.

Slowly, she backed away from the scene, keeping her eyes fixed on the soldier and trying to match her movements to the thumps of the luggage being loaded.

She'd only made it a few paces when the crackle of gunfire rang out. She dropped to the ground. Another shot. Then another. She counted seven shots before she clasped her hands across her ears in a hopeless attempt to drown out the harrowing sounds.

The gunfire eventually ceased, leaving only her racing heartbeat pounding in her ears.

Rustling nearby was followed by the sound of someone retching.

'That bad, huh?' a voice said in German.

More vomiting and rustling of the trees. The Germans coming back to the vehicle she suspected, but she kept her eyes down, not daring to look in their direction. The putrid odour drifted through the air, making her want to gag. She clamped her hand across her nose and breathed through her mouth.

'Next time I'll take bag duty,' another voice said.

'If you can't handle it, next time you can stay back at the camp with the other cowardly rats,' a third voice sneered. 'Grab the shovels. Your work isn't done.'

The car doors slammed shut and the rustling of leaves faded as the Germans made their way back into the woods. Her legs trembling, Krista struggled to her feet and stumbled away, with two words hammering in her mind like a relentless drumbeat. *Next time.*

10

KRISTA APPROACHED MR GERTZ'S HOUSE JUST AS THE FIRST rays of sunlight peeked over the horizon. She knew he would be home. It was too early for his office to be open. She reached his front door and hesitated. Her grandfather had trusted Mr Gertz. She should, too. What choice did she have? She slammed the metal door knocker against the wood, not caring who heard her this time. The sooner she was off the streets, the better.

The door creaked open, revealing a dazed Mr Gertz in a wrinkled dressing gown, tied haphazardly around his waist. Once again, her unexpected arrival seemed a shock to him. His eyebrows shot up and his mouth fell open at the sight of her. Without a word, he grabbed her wrist and dragged her inside. He quickly wrapped his dressing gown around his body and tied it at the waist.

'What are you doing here?' he asked with a hint of panic in his voice. 'I told you to be at the footbridge before sunrise.' He turned and hurried up the dimly lit hallway. 'I fear you're too late. Oh dear.'

Krista followed him into his living room. The heavy

curtains were still drawn, blocking out any daylight, but a soft glow from a lamp in the corner illuminated the space. On a small table between two comfortable armchairs sat two mugs of steaming coffee. After hours in the cold outdoors, her body felt icy cold. She picked up one of the coffee mugs. She couldn't resist wrapping her hands around it and letting its warmth spread through her fingers.

'I went,' she said. 'It was a trap.'

'What do you mean? What... what happened?' There was a stammer in his words and a slight tremor in his tone.

Krista described in haunting detail the arrival of the Germans and the innocent people herded into the dark woods. And then, the deafening sound of gunfire that ripped through the air, drowning out any cries for help. She left him in no doubt about what had happened to those people.

Colour drained from the lawyer's face, and he collapsed into one of the armchairs. 'I didn't know,' he whispered. His expression contorted as if he was grappling with his own complicity.

Krista's body tensed. 'What *did* you know?'

He shifted in his seat, his eyes darting around the room, unable to meet Krista's intense stare. 'The Germans were looking for a list of Jews. They said that they were being sent to new settlements. It would have happened eventually. My assistance simply made it happen quicker so they would leave town, and we could all return to normal.'

'*They*?' Krista asked, anger seething inside of her. 'The people who have lived in Zawica for many years and whose business dealings and personal affairs have provided you with the means to support your family.'

Mr Gertz put his head in his hands, his shoulders slumped.

'Did you put my grandfather's name on that list?'

He lifted his gaze to meet hers, and his hands fell onto his lap. The wrinkles on his forehead deepened with each passing moment. She had her answer. Krista sank onto his sofa. She couldn't comprehend that the person who so many had trusted with securing their family's future had ultimately betrayed them in the worst way possible.

'I didn't know anyone would die,' he said.

She set the coffee mug back down on the table and balled her hands into fists by her sides. She despised him. Her grandparents had no idea who they were trusting. 'Now that you know, what do you plan to do about it?' she asked.

Mr Gertz swallowed and rolled his shoulders back. 'What can I do?' His voice was louder, steadier. 'It's not just Jews they want. If I don't keep supplying them with names, it'll be my family next.'

'Tell them they've done it,' said Krista, matching the volume of his voice. 'Tell them they've rounded everyone up and they can move on.'

'They won't believe it. Even if I don't give them names, someone else will.'

'But at some point they will have rounded everyone up. Why can't that point be now? You tell them that whoever they are looking for fled before they arrived and the only ones who hung around are now gone.'

Mr Gertz mulled over her suggestion with a doubtful expression, as if he saw her as a naive girl who couldn't comprehend the gravity of grown-up matters. But she understood all too well – he was the one who had been naive, failing to even consider that the Nazis intended to kill those people. Not only did he neglect to warn them or make any attempt to help, he actually sent them straight into the hands of their enemies. Her grandfather had not been so gullible. He predicted the danger when the Nazis arrived and took steps to protect his family. His only mistake was trusting Gertz. Yet here she was, still alive, and she would fight every day to stay that way – for herself and for her grandparents' memory in this war.

'Let me make this right,' said Mr Gertz, springing to his feet. 'I'll arrange another transport. Just give me a day to sort something out.'

'No, thank you.' Krista stood up. 'Clearly, I'm safer without your help.'

Gertz nodded. He could hardly disagree after what had happened.

'I'm sorry,' he muttered.

'Just not sorry enough to stop handing over lists.'

There was nothing more to say between them.

Krista turned and made her exit, locking eyes with Mrs Gertz who was sitting on the stairs, her face streaked with tears. If the woman hadn't already known about her husband's actions, she certainly knew now. What she chose to do with that knowledge was up to her.

Krista stormed out of the house, slamming the door behind her.

11

———————

KRISTA LEFT GERTZ'S ROAD AND WANDERED THE SIDE STREETS of her village contemplating her options. She had money to purchase a train ticket and leave town. But if the Nazis were hunting her, she couldn't risk being seen at the train station. Besides, she had no idea where she would go even if she did leave. She needed help coming up with an alternative plan and turned to one of the few people she could truly trust, her Guide Captain Anna.

She made her way to Anna's house using side streets and the narrow pathways separating back gardens between neighbouring houses. Her stomach gave a loud groan in protest at the lack of food she'd sent its way since breakfast with Olesia the day before. She had eaten three of her grandmother's biscuits and was determined to save the last three for when she felt safe. Gertz's flask still held a dribble of coffee, but she couldn't bring herself to drink it. Stopping at a store to buy food was out of the question, but she did know which of the houses in Zawica had apple trees in their gardens.

It didn't take her long to spot the branches of an apple

tree hanging over a nearby wall. Finding a foothold in between bricks, she pulled herself up and scanned the windows of the house. Their blackout blinds were still drawn. The tree's branches had already been picked clean and Krista imagined barrel upon barrel of apples sitting in the family's cellar. Her stomach grumbled loudly again. She climbed back down and continued along the path until she came across another tree. This time the owner had not been quite so diligent at picking their apples and the branches were heavy with fruit. Making sure no one was watching, Krista reached up and plucked half a dozen apples from the tree, stuffing them into her bag. She picked one more and released the branch, watching it spring up, lighter now. Krista took a big bite out of a juicy red apple, savouring the satisfying crunch and the burst of sweetness in her mouth. She had successfully fed herself and quenched her thirst – a small victory that she desperately needed.

When she arrived at Anna's house, Anna was walking towards the front door, struggling with a heavy bag of groceries in her arms. Krista cleared her throat and Anna turned.

'Oh, thank goodness,' said Anna on seeing Krista. 'Olesia has been frantic wondering what happened to you.'

Anna quickly unlocked her door and the two of them slipped inside.

'Are you alright?' Anna asked as soon as the door was locked. 'The Germans are looking for you. They called your name out at the village meeting.'

Krista slumped against Anna's wall, her heart racing. She had made the right decision in avoiding the train station, but now she was faced with the daunting task of coming up with another way out of Zawica. Fear gnawed at her insides, but she pushed it aside. For now, she was safe under Anna's roof, although she couldn't shake the feeling that time was running out for her.

'Come through,' said Anna, leading Krista to the kitchen at the back of the house. Anna placed her shopping bag on the counter and pulled out a loaf of fresh bread. She handed the bread to Krista and brought a knife and a small parcel of cured meat to the table.

'Eat whatever you want,' said Anna, as if sensing Krista's hunger.

Krista sat down at the table and tore a chunk off the bread. 'Thank you. I'm starved.' She wanted to ask Anna more about the Germans calling out her name, but at the same time, she was physically drained and couldn't bear to think about it.

Anna peeled her hat and coat off and hung them on a hook near her back door. Her bleached blonde hair was flat to her head. She ran her fingers through it then busied herself bringing butter, jam, and a random jar of pickled carrots to the table. Krista ate while filling Anna in on everything else that had happened.

'And Mr Gertz knew what was going to happen to those people?' Anna asked.

Krista hadn't felt the need to keep Gertz's secret. She did, however, keep quiet about Gertz's assertion that her grandfather was Jewish for fear that that knowledge would somehow land Anna in trouble.

'I don't believe he knew those people were going to die. But he did tell the Germans where to find them.'

Anna let out a heavy breath. 'And I thought my hair snapping off was going to be the worst thing that happened this year.'

Krista giggled followed by a sharp intake of breath as she clamped her hand across her mouth.

'You're allowed to laugh,' said Anna, gently tugging Krista's hand away from her face.

Krista allowed her hand to fall into her lap. 'How can I laugh after what has happened? To find humour amid all this darkness, it's shameful.'

'If you don't find some joy, the darkness will swallow you whole. Is that what your grandparents would have wanted?'

Krista shook her head.

'Exactly. We hold on to these moments of light because they are what we are fighting for.'

'They called out my name,' said Krista, slowly accepting the harsh reality of being hunted by the Germans.

'The meeting was horrific.' Anna was serious once more. 'They read out a list of names, ordering those on the list to identify themselves. Your name was on that list. Everyone thought they were just going to confiscate our valuables and tell us we what we could and couldn't do. They did that, too, of course. When no one on the list came forward, they organised us into groups. They separated us by nationality and made anyone who was also Jewish stand in the centre of the hall. All our documents were checked, and the Germans made lists of everything. The Jews were told to go home and pack. They had to return to the village hall that night for *relocation*. That was all they were told. Nothing about where they were going or how long they'd be gone for. They were just supposed to pack away their entire lives into one suitcase.'

Krista winced. She knew what was likely to have happened to those suitcases. She dared not think about what had become of the people.

'I've already heard of three families being forced out of their own homes to make way for the soldiers. But there are so many soldiers. Everyone is scared to answer a knock on the door in case it's the Germans. And they're too scared to fight back in case they end up like–'

Like her grandparents, Krista thought.

Anna reached out and squeezed Krista's trembling hands. The walls that held back her tears crumbled and a river of grief flooded out. She allowed herself once more to feel the weight of her loss. Her grandparents, her only family, had been taken from her in a senseless act of violence. At seventeen years old, she was completely alone in the world. And now the Nazis were looking for her. As Anna pulled her chair closer and enveloped her in a warm embrace, Krista sobbed uncontrollably into her shoulder.

When her tears had stopped, Krista lifted her head.

'Maybe you don't need to leave town,' said Anna. 'I can hide you here until the Nazis move on. They won't want to stay in our tiny village for too long.'

Krista wiped her face with the back of her hand and shook her head. 'No. I won't put you in danger like that. They might never stop looking for me and, if they find me here–' There was no need for her to finish the sentence. They both knew the potential consequences. 'I need to go somewhere where I won't have to hide. My grandparents tried hiding, and it didn't work for them.'

Anna's brow furrowed, and she pressed her lips pressed together in a tight line. 'But it *has* worked for you. The corn-field. The bridge. There's no shame in keeping yourself alive.'

Krista's gaze wandered around the room, finally settling on the ornate ceiling. She swallowed back another surge of tears. Her grandparents' sacrifice weighed heavily on her heart, urging her to do whatever it took to survive.

She turned to Anna, conflicting emotions churning within her. 'The only thing I know for certain is that I can't stay in Zawica. I need to get away from here.'

Anna stood up and placed a comforting hand on Krista's shoulder. 'I can help you with that.'

12

———

By early evening, Anna had used her network of Guides to arrange both transport and accommodation for Krista. She handed Krista a bag made of a sturdy brown fabric, its seams straining from the weight of its contents. It was filled to the brim with neatly folded clothes and a few personal necessities.

Krista had been right to seek out Anna. Her Guide Captain was organised and efficient and calm in a crisis. She felt enormous gratitude for Anna's quick work. Tonight, Krista would lay her head down someplace safe. Although that feeling wasn't as welcome as Krista had hoped. She had a nagging feeling that leaving Zawica would only amplify the grief she had been trying so hard to suppress. She feared that once she was alone, she would finally unravel and have no one to help her piece herself back together.

She pushed those thoughts aside and accepted the bag. 'Thank you so much,' she said. 'I don't know how to repay you.'

'It's what we do,' said Anna with a smile. 'We take care of each other, especially in times like these. Now, is there anything else you need? Armin will be here soon, and I expect he'll be keen to get on the road again before dark.'

Krista grabbed her coat and checked that her trefoil pin was still tucked under her collar. 'I have everything I need.'

'One more thing.' Anna held out a book. 'I've written out names, addresses, and contact numbers for people who might be prepared to help you. There are Guide Captains, some friends, and my cousin, Nelka, in Warsaw.'

Krista reached for the book. Its hardback cover was a rich, dark green leather, and the pages were divided by A-to-Z index tabs. She opened it up, revealing an intricate design of clover leaves in varying shades of green on the inside cover. She ran her fingers over the smooth, fabric-like paper, admiring its beauty. There were pages of names. She flicked through them, each person neatly listed with their contact details under the corresponding letter of their surname.

Anna laid her hand on Krista's back. 'I thought an address book was less conspicuous than a sheet of paper with a list of names.'

'Thank you,' said Krista, her voice a whisper and tears stinging her eyes. She had been alone and helpless, but now, thanks to Anna, she had a network of people who might be willing to help her. With trembling hands, she tucked the book with its precious contents into the bag her grandmother had given her.

Armin arrived only minutes later. He stood at least a few inches taller than Krista, his figure slightly looming over her. The brim of his peaked hat cast a shadow over his features.

'Are you ready to go?' he asked, wasting no time on polite greetings. His voice was deep and authoritative.

Krista nodded and they left the relative safety of Anna's house.

The street was deserted, the silence broken only by the faint sound of insects chirping in the distance. For a moment Krista was transported back to the farm at dusk. She wanted to close her eyes and escape into that memory, but it wouldn't change anything. Instead, Krista reached out and embraced Anna tightly. 'Thank you.'

'Good luck,' said Anna, squeezing her tight. 'Next time I see you, my hair will have grown back.'

Krista smiled. She pulled back and flicked a strand of Anna's wiry blonde hair. 'I do hope so. Will you please tell Olesia that I'm OK, and that I said thank you to her, too?'

'Of course.'

'And tell Marcin, too. Tell him I'm OK.'

Anna lifted one eyebrow in a wordless inquiry, but she didn't pry. 'I'll tell him.'

It seemed a cowardly way to say goodbye to friends who had helped her so much, but it was the safest option for all of them. Krista piled into the passenger seat of Armin's car, tucking her own bag and the one Anna had given her in the space at her feet.

Armin climbed into the driver's seat. 'You can put that in the back, if you'd like.'

Krista fidgeted with the bag's strap, twirling it around her fingers. 'Thanks, but I'll hold on to it.'

Armin inserted the key into the ignition and Krista breathed a sigh of relief as the car's engine purred to life. Anna closed the passenger side door, and they pressed their hands against the window, their fingers meeting through the glass for a moment before letting go. Armin pulled away from the curb. Krista looked back to see Anna standing in the middle of the road, her figure gradually shrinking until she disappeared as Armin turned a corner.

Krista turned back around, facing the road ahead.

'Thank you for picking me up. I'm grateful I don't have to make this journey alone.'

Armin glided the steering wheel through his hands as they navigated the twists and turns of Zawica's narrow streets. 'It's not easy out there. The Germans are arriving in one direction and the Poles are fleeing in the other. For now, settle in. We only live an hour away, but the main roads are impossible. Too many German checkpoints. We'll make our way through the countryside, so we'll be in this car for a while. That's the plan, anyway. The trickiest part is up ahead. We'll have to pass the Germans' camp. It's not ideal, but it's the best way out of the village to avoid the first of the checkpoints.'

As they drove, the green of the field ahead transformed into a sea of khaki tents, dotted with occasional pops of red from Nazi flags. The smell of smoke from makeshift fires seeped into the car. Soldiers in crisp uniforms were huddled together, chatting and smoking cigarettes.

Armin cleared his throat. 'We're turning just before the field up ahead.'

Just a few months ago, Krista and her Guide unit had camped in that same field. Life had seemed so much simpler back then. They had heard rumours of war, Hitler had been accusing Poland of inciting conflict for months, but Krista didn't pay much attention to it at the time. Now she felt guilty for not taking it more seriously. While she had been living in blissful ignorance, her grandparents had been preparing for the danger that knocked at their door.

'What are they doing there?' Krista asked.

Armin braked as they approached the junction, and the car slowed. 'They're living there for now. I expect some of them will requisition houses in the village and others will move elsewhere.'

The car edged towards the junction and Armin leaned forward to check the road was clear. It was and he pulled out driving parallel to the field with a high hedge between the car and the campsite. Krista rolled the window down as they drove past. Above the hum of the engine, music drifted towards her from the field. Someone was playing the violin. But it wasn't the sombre song she usually associated with the instrument. It was upbeat. A cheery melody accompanied by raucous singing. She thought of the soldiers who, earlier that day, had murdered a group of innocent people in the woods. Were they there? Were they celebrating their depravity, or were they doing what they could to block out the memories of what they had done?

'We're clear,' said Armin.

Krista exhaled a deep breath and checked the side mirror. The village she had called home for seven years faded into the distance. The future she had once imagined now lay in ruins, crushed by the brutal invasion of the Nazis who had ruthlessly killed her beloved grandparents. She had been torn once again from everything and everyone she held dear. But she refused to allow herself to be swept away by the trauma. She forced herself to look away from the mirror; there was nothing left for her in the past. It was time to face the uncertain future ahead.

She reached into her bag, pulling out the last of her grandmother's biscuits. 'Would you like one?' she asked. 'My grandmother made them.'

Armin took his eyes off the road for a second to glance down at the unwrapped biscuits. He smiled. 'They look delicious, but no thank you. I think you should enjoy those ones on your own.'

Krista bit into the first biscuit. The crunch was gone now, but the sweetness lingered on her tongue. Closing her eyes, she allowed herself to be transported back to cherished moments watching her grandmother baking. She could almost see her grandmother, with a mischievous twinkle in her eyes, liberally sprinkling extra sugar on top of the biscuits before popping them in the oven to bake. Then they would laugh at her grandfather's uncanny ability to join them in the kitchen, his coffee mug in hand, only seconds before the timer announced the biscuits were ready. A gentle smile formed on Krista's lips and a tear rolled down her cheek.

13

Krista stirred the watery porridge simmering on the stove. For the past month, she'd been living with Armin and his wife, Irena. They had warmly welcomed her into their home and told her she could stay for as long as she needed to, but Krista was already itching to move. She rarely left the house. Armin went to work every day and Irena shopped for food and volunteered for an hour each morning at the local donation centre. All Krista did was clean the house and cook. She was staying out of the spotlight as her grandparents had instructed her to do, but she didn't feel safe, she felt like a prisoner.

Irena appeared in the doorway with a half-empty shopping bag. The morning sun poured in the kitchen window, illuminating Irena's long brown hair and framing her pale face in a glowing halo. 'Something smells delicious in here,' she said.

Krista smiled and removed the pies she had baking in

the oven, their golden crusts glistening with a tantalising sheen. She resisted the temptation to take a bite. 'It's not breakfast, I'm afraid. I was getting a head start on dinner.'

Irena had sourced some butter the day before and Krista had used it to make enough pastry for three small pies. Encasing potatoes, onions, and cabbage in pastry felt like more of a substantial meal rather than just eating them separately.

'No bread today, unfortunately.' Irena placed the bag on the worktop and unpacked it. 'The shelves were practically empty and all the butcher had left was small bags of offal. We'll have to make some kind of stew with it, I suppose.'

Krista took two bowls from the cupboard and placed them on the worktop.

Irena hung her shopping bag on a hook beside the door then pulled a scrap of paper from her coat pocket. She scrunched it up and tossed it on the worktop. 'I don't know why I bother writing a shopping list. They never have anything on it.'

Krista picked up the ball of paper and smoothed it out, smiling at Irena's swirly handwriting. Her own handwriting was little more than a scrawl. She tucked the list under a jar on the worktop. 'Then we may as well keep this list for tomorrow to save you from writing it again.'

She gave the porridge another stir while Irena hung her coat up. Car doors slammed outside. Krista winced and dropped her spoon, the metal clattering against the rim of the pot. She turned the heat off.

Irena's face drained of colour. 'It's the Germans.'

Krista nodded, instantly on edge. These days, anyone arriving by car was always German. An impatient knock on the front door shook the bones of the building. Irena hurried to open the door and, not bothering to wait for an invitation, two German soldiers burst in, their polished black boots clunking against the wooden floorboards.

'Is there a problem?' asked Irena.

'Not for us,' one of the soldiers said with a sly grin on his face. He stood at least a foot taller than Krista with a slim, angular build. His uniform was oversized and hung awkwardly on his narrow frame.

The other soldier disappeared into the living room for a moment before striding into the kitchen. He was older than his comrade with a thick moustache that entirely obscured his upper lip, which only added to his stern and intimidating appearance. His gaze swept across every inch of the room and his nose twitched. The kitchen smelled of cooked onions and boiled cabbage. He made notes in a small notebook he carried. Irena and Krista exchanged uneasy glances.

'There are just two of you living here?' the older soldier asked, in heavily accented Polish. 'Two women?'

'Three,' said Irena, twisting a strand of hair around her trembling fingers. 'Myself and my husband and our friend.'

'My house was bombed,' added Krista, repeating the story she and Armin had come up with to explain her sudden appearance in town.

'Where is your husband?'

'At work. He works on the railway.'

'Papers?' the soldier demanded. The other soldier stood glaring at them from the corner of the kitchen.

After checking Irena's papers, he thrummed his pen repeatedly on the cover of his notebook while Krista retrieved hers from her bag. She held them out and he snatched them from her outstretched hand. Krista waited, watching for a flash of recognition to pass across the German's face as he read her name. Nothing. He thrust her papers towards his waiting comrade and scribbled something in his notebook.

The other soldier stepped forward, his heavy boots thumping against the floor. He dropped Krista's papers at his feet with a disdainful look. 'A German living with two Poles,' he spat out, his eyes gleaming with malice. 'You should choose your friends more wisely.'

Krista felt Irena's eyes land on her and knew her cheeks were colouring under Irena's gaze. She hadn't mentioned the fact she was German to her new friends. Why would she? Her nationality wasn't typically information she gave when introducing herself. But things were different now. Nationality mattered in a way no one could have seen coming. Her thoughts drifted to her grandparents. *They had seen it coming.*

The soldier smoothed his moustache down with a thumb and finger and strolled towards the pies cooling on the worktop. 'Who cooked these?'

'I did,' said Krista.

The younger man's nostrils flared and he lunged towards Krista, grabbing a fistful of her hair. She winced as he yanked her head back, causing her scalp to burn with pain. '*You're* cooking for *them*?'

A drop of sweat rolled down her neck and she bit down hard on her lip, refusing to cry out. She would not give him the satisfaction of seeing her terror.

His rage fizzled out as quickly as it arrived, and he released his grip. Krista dug her fingers into the edges of the table, willing herself to stay upright.

The other man stepped around his triggered comrade and stopped in front of Irena, who had retreated into a corner of the room, her body shaking with fear. 'Your house is being requisitioned,' he said. 'You have until noon to pack up. One bag each. Make sure everything is spotless and leave the keys.'

'I don't understand,' said Irena, her voice a quiver.

The soldier looked irritated and took a breath, scratching his moustache with the tip of his pen. 'Your house is being given to a German family.' He turned to glare at Krista. 'To a *suitable* German family. Pack up your things and be prepared to leave at noon. Make sure everything in the kitchen is washed and put away. Sweep all the rooms. Leave your keys by the door to make sure the new owner doesn't have any problems when they arrive.'

Irena stared open-mouthed at Krista. 'The new owner? But this is our house. Where do you expect us to go?'

'A transport will pick you up at noon. You will be relocated.'

'To where?' asked Irena.

The soldier closed his notebook, sliding it into the crisp, buttoned chest-pocket of his uniform. He straightened his posture and adjusted his cap. 'Not my concern. Just be ready to go at noon.' His voice was sharp and commanding.

The other soldier took a menacing step closer to Krista, his eyes once again blazing with anger. 'All of you,' he growled.

Krista flinched and a satisfied sneer crossed the soldiers face. In perfect unison, both soldiers pivoted on their heels and marched out of the house, leaving the door wide open behind them. Krista rushed to the door as quickly as her shaking legs could carry her. The soldiers marched out of Irena's garden and towards her neighbours house.

Krista closed the door and bolted it.

'Are you alright?' asked Irena.

Krista put her hand on the back of her head and

massaged her scalp in small circles, trying to alleviate the pain. She forced a tight-lipped smile. 'I'm fine.'

'What just happened? Have you ever heard of such a thing?' asked Irena.

She had. Anna had told her of people being suddenly evicted to provide accommodation for the arriving soldiers. But this was different. There was a plan in place. It was organised, and it wasn't about providing lodgings for soldiers. He'd said a German family would be arriving.

'They can't just take my home,' said Irena, still in disbelief.

Krista nodded. 'They can take whatever they like. We're in no position to stop them. I'll start cleaning. You should go and get Armin.'

14

———————

KRISTA FILLED THREE BOWLS WITH PORRIDGE IN CASE ANY OF them wanted to eat before leaving. It was cold now, but it would at least be something in their bellies. The thought of a German organised transport made Krista feel sick to her stomach. She'd seen firsthand how those could end. But this one was leaving at lunchtime. It would be daylight. That had to be safer. Surely.

She'd just finished washing the pot and returning it to the kitchen cupboard when Irena returned with Armin.

Armin stripped off his sturdy navy blue work jacket and tossed it onto a chair in the kitchen. 'I'll get the suitcases from the attic,' he said, wasting no time. 'Let's pack up all we can fit in them. Krista, we only have two suitcases. You still have your bag, right?'

Krista nodded. 'Yes, don't worry about me.'

'What if we don't go?' asked Irena. 'The entire street has been told to leave. If we all stick together and refuse to move, they won't have enough soldiers to physically drag us away.'

Armin shook his head, his jaw clenched. 'It's not that

simple. In Warsaw, a group of Jews fought back and killed a Nazi. The Gestapo retaliated by rounding up a hundred Jews. They shot every single one of them. Wives watched their husbands die; mothers watched as their children were slaughtered. We have no choice.'

Krista could feel the anger radiating off Armin's tense body as the muscles in his arms and shoulders twitched. Tears formed on Irena's eyelashes and Armin reached out for her. He wrapped his arms around her, pulling her close.

'It's just a house. We can get through this,' he said.

Irena and Armin disappeared into their bedroom to pack while Krista continued to clean. She scrubbed the inside and the outside of the kitchen cabinets. She wiped down all the surfaces and swept the floors. If the Germans inspected the house, she didn't want them to find a single crumb.

With only one bag each permitted, it didn't take long for Irena and Armin to pack. Armin stashed as many of their possessions as he could in the attic. There was no guarantee they'd ever be allowed to return to their home, but what else could they do?

Irena scrubbed the bathroom while Krista packed her few possessions into the bags she'd brought with her. Armin closed off the attic and left to see if his neighbours had gleaned any other details about what was happening.

When the cleaning was complete, Irena and Krista packed up the contents of the refrigerator.

'I just can't believe this is happening,' said Irena, wrapping a half-eaten jar of jam in newspaper.

'I know.'

Irena divided the food between the two suitcases. 'Put this one in your bag,' she said, handing Krista a parcel of food. 'I don't know if we'll be travelling together.'

Krista nodded, her eyes welling up as she tucked the parcel of food into her bag. She didn't want to think about being separated from her friends. Alone, again.

Armin returned soon after, a look of fury on his face. 'The entire neighbourhood are leaving. The Germans are making a mistake. Railway workers, factory workers, even some of the farmers have been told to pack up and go. The country will come to a grinding halt.'

'Does anyone want to eat the porridge?' asked Krista.

'Not really,' Armin said. He plucked three spoons out of a drawer and dropped them on the counter.

They each picked up a bowl and ate standing up, in silence.

As the minutes ticked towards noon, Irena asked the question that Krista had known for hours was coming.

'So, you're German?'

Krista glanced at Armin, but he didn't react. Irena must have already told him. She wouldn't have blamed either of them if they were angry. When the invasion started, there were rumours of Germans turning on Polish neighbours they'd lived peacefully alongside for years.

'I was born there,' said Krista. 'My parents died when I was ten and I moved to Poland to live with my grandparents.'

'That should be good for you,' said Armin. There was no anger or judgement in his tone. He looked down at her bulging bag, resting against the suitcases he had packed. 'Perhaps.'

At the stroke of noon, two military trucks rumbled into Irena's quiet street. Krista peered out of the window, her heart hammering in her chest like a drumbeat. The trucks parked at the end of the street, their imposing presence casting an ominous shadow over the residential neighbourhood. German soldiers poured out of the vehicle, barking orders for everyone to leave their homes immediately.

Irena and Armin looked around the house they'd moved to when they'd married two years earlier. This home, Krista knew, was the place they had hoped to start a family together. But now that dream was being torn away from them without warning. A lump formed in Krista's throat, and she averted her eyes as the young couple embraced for the final time in their home.

A single gunshot rang out, causing them all to jump. Armin rushed to open the front door. 'Stay together,' he said.

Irena looked at the keys in her hand. A tear slipped down her cheek as she reached out and dropped them on the table near the front door.

Armin picked up both suitcases and stepped out of his house for what Krista knew was likely to be the final time. Krista hid the bag from her grandmother under her coat. She strapped the other one across her body and followed them out.

Together they joined the steady stream of Poles walking towards the waiting trucks, their eyes downcast and their shoulders slumped in resignation. The occasional nod was exchanged between neighbours joining the queue, but there was little other interaction. The gunshot had brought an eerie silence to everyone. Perhaps that was its intention.

'One bag only,' Krista heard a soldier instructing in German. She peered through the crowd and saw a pile of suitcases discarded on the ground between the trucks.

'Irena, take one of the suitcases,' Krista said, keeping her voice low so as not to draw any attention to herself.

Irena took a suitcase from Armin just before they reached the front of the queue. A soldier looked the three of them up and down and motioned with his rifle for them to climb into the back of the truck. They did as they were told and climbed inside. They found space on one of the benches and Irena and Krista sat down. Armin tucked his suitcase in between them and hung around at the back of the truck, helping people to climb aboard.

Armin reached his hand out towards an older woman, her skin with deathly white and her cheeks streaked with tears. She reached for his hand, but she was batted away by the butt of a rifle. The soldier yanked something from the woman's neck and tucked it into his pocket with a sly grin. The woman let out a small squeal and her hand flew to her neck.

'Just come aboard,' said Armin. 'Arguing is futile, maybe even dangerous.'

The German responsible for the theft smirked and tapped the woman with his rifle to get her moving.

Krista stood up and offered the woman her seat.

'They can't do this,' the woman said. 'It's not right.'

'I know,' said Krista. 'Take this seat, please. Hopefully it will all be over soon.'

The woman sat down, and they all watched as people piled into the trucks, some clutching suitcases, some clutching babies, but everyone looking terrified about what was to come next.

15

THE TRUCK JOLTED TO A STOP AT THE TRAIN STATION, AND they were ordered to disembark. The station was swarming with Polish police officers and Nazi soldiers, their guns glinting in the winter sunlight. Two trains sat idling on the tracks, but these weren't meant for human passengers. They were cattle cars designed to transport livestock. The putrid stench of manure clung to the air like an invisible fog, wrapping itself around everyone and giving a hint as to the inhumane treatment they were about to receive.

'Where are we going?' multiple voices asked, all unanswered.

'Women and children go left. Men go right,' one of the soldiers instructed in fluent Polish. She recognised a bit of herself in him – a native German who spoke Polish without a discernible German accent. But she heard it. She suspected he had grown up here, too. Or at the very least spent a lot of time in Poland. Now here he was, tearing Polish families apart.

The murmur of voices grew louder as families were forcibly separated from each other. Children clung to their parents, tears streaming down their faces, while officers barked orders and pushed people into designated lines. Krista watched as Irena and Armin hugged each other tightly, each trying to hold back tears.

'I won't leave you,' said Irena, clinging to Armin. 'They can't make me.'

Armin's eyes darted around. 'They're looking at us. You must go now. Please.'

Krista put her hands on Irena's shoulders to peel her away from Armin, but Irena wouldn't budge. Like Armin, she felt Nazi eyes on their small group and feared drawing any further attention their way. She turned and made her way through the chaos towards the Polish-speaking officer. She could almost hear her grandfather scolding her. He would tell her to get in line and do as she'd been told. But if there was a way to help Irena then she had to do it.

'Excuse me, sir,' she said politely in perfect German.

The officer turned towards her, eyeing the bag strapped across her body and the empty space on the ground around her as if expecting a suitcase. 'Ja?' he responded.

Krista took a quick glance around her and lowered her voice. 'Where is everyone going?' she asked, still speaking German.

The officer's eyes narrowed into slits, their icy blue colour gleaming with suspicion. A faint twitch of his jaw and the slight tilt of his head conveyed his mistrust. 'You're German?' he asked.

Krista nodded. 'From Berlin, but I moved to Poland after my parents died.'

The officer's tense expression loosened, and he leaned closer, seemingly deciding she was different from everyone else. Krista resisted the urge to step back. 'The men are going to Germany for work',' he said. 'Everyone else is being sent to the General Government zone.'

'Danke,' said Krista. She offered him a smile with her thanks and prayed it looked genuine before rushing back to Armin and Irena.

The news that they were being separated would be devastating, but she had to get Irena to stop drawing further attention to their little group. 'We're going somewhere in the General Government zone,' Krista said, positioning herself between Irena and the officer. 'Armin is going to Germany for work.'

Irena's hand flew to her mouth. 'No.' She squeezed Armin's arm with both hands, her knuckles turning white. 'Please,' she pleaded with tears in her eyes. 'Don't go. Refuse.'

Armin prised Irena's hands off his arm and clasped them in his. His eyes were wide, betraying his fear, but his voice was steady and firm. 'We must do this. If I can get away, I will. But no matter how long it takes, I will come back for you. Go to Maja's if you can and stay there.'

Irena couldn't hold her tears in any longer. A gut-wrenching wail came from her mouth. Armin silenced it with a final kiss before a burly police officer grabbed him and shoved him towards a group of other men, their faces grim and angry.

'Will you take care of her?' Armin shouted to Krista over the screams and cries of families being forcibly separated.

'I will,' Krista yelled back. 'Come on, let's go.' She wrapped her arm around Irena's shoulders, trying to be strong for both of them. She steered her towards the crowd heading for the cattle cars. The future was more uncertain than ever, but Krista couldn't focus on that right now or she would fall apart too. There was no choice but to keep moving, one shaky step at a time.

Together, Krista and Irena joined the sea of other scared and desperate women and children, their arms linked tightly. They shuffled forward as best they could in the pile up of people. Two young girls, identical twins with wide eyes and curly hair, clung to each other as they sobbed. Their mother, a young woman with exhaustion etched into her features, desperately tried to soothe them while balancing a heavy suitcase in one hand and holding a squirming baby boy on her hip.

'Can I help you with your bag,' Krista said reaching for the woman's suitcase.

The woman gripped it tighter and swung it away from Krista. 'No, I can manage.'

Krista couldn't blame her. They had already lost so much in the last hour.

The Germans were vicious as they herded everyone into the cattle cars. Few of them spoke Polish, most of them barked instructions in German that they knew people barely understood. The seized any opportunity to jab their rifles into the crowd. Krista watched in horror as a woman who dared to protest was hauled from the line and beaten until she was bloodied and incapable of being anything other than compliant. It wasn't enough that they had taken these people's homes, and separated husbands from wives and children from fathers, they seemed intent on breaking their spirit too.

A soldier, seeming unhappy about the gap widening between the two girls and the women in front, took the butt of his rifle and shoved one of the girls forward. She stumbled, falling to her knees. Krista positioned herself between the soldier and the child. She quickly pulled the girl back to her feet. The soldier's eyes narrowed as he aimed his weapon at Krista, his finger hovering over the trigger. He smirked.

Krista felt the weight of the metal weapon pressing against her abdomen as he dared her to make a move. The metallic tang of fear filled her mouth, her saliva thick and difficult to swallow. She wasn't doing a great job of keeping out of the spotlight, but how could she stand back and do nothing? If her grandparents' death had taught her anything, it was that staying small, and hiding did not keep you safe.

'The line will move faster if you let me help the girl to the train,' said Krista in German, her words fluent but with an obvious tremor in her voice. A bead of sweat trickled down her back.

His eyes burned into her, but her flawless German accent seemed enough to prompt the soldier to withdraw his weapon. Without a word, he motioned for them to go and turned his back to her.

Krista's shoulders sagged and a long, shaky breath escaped her lips, sounding almost like a sob. She gripped the girl's hand and tried her best to calm the now screaming child. She looked across to the girls' mother and offered what she hoped was a reassuring smile. The woman was on the verge of tears, but Krista could see the determination in her eyes as she battled to stay composed for her three children.

'Take your sister's hand,' Krista told the little girl. 'Let's get on board the train then you can sit down beside your mama.'

Irena walked alongside the children's mother, talking to her and gently patting the mother's arm, seemingly putting her own feelings of anxiety on hold as she focused on helping someone else.

Krista climbed aboard one of the cars and, with Irena's assistance, she pulled the two little girls inside. They rushed to their mother's side as she boarded with the baby. The others in their car shuffled aside as much as they could to free up space in the back for the family to sit down on the floor. Krista and Irena slumped down beside them.

Once the Germans accepted that they couldn't ram any more people into their car, the wooden doors were slammed shut and the passengers were plunged into darkness. Only slivers of light leaked in through the gaps in the wooden walls. A steady pounding from outside pierced the silence, as if someone was hammering nails into the doors. No one dared to utter a word.

Krista's heart was heavy with doubt as she sat on the crowded train, wondering if she'd made a mistake climbing onboard. With her German papers, she could have talked her way out of boarding the train. She felt Irena's hand squeeze hers and her doubts were gone. She'd promised Armin that she would look after Irena. They had looked after her when she'd had nowhere else to go. For now, at least, this was where she was meant to be. Warsaw would have to wait.

The train finally moved, and people shifted and bumped into each other in the near darkness.

Krista checked her bag was still strapped across her body. It was. 'They're taking us to the General Government zone,' she said to no one in particular.

'Is that good?' someone asked.

'Sandwiched between the Nazis and the Soviets? Probably not,' someone else replied. 'It's still under German rule.'

'Are our men going there, too?' a third voice asked.

'They're going to Germany.' Irena's voice was like a wilted flower, drooping with defeat.

Her answer triggered a wave of nervous chatter as people talked about the implications. Everyone seemed most concerned about how long they would be away and how they would find each other again. But for Krista, the thought that plagued her mind was what awaited them at the other end of their journey. Dread settled in the depths of her stomach.

Hours passed and soft snores sprang up through the cattle car as the relentless rhythm of the train and the heat generated by so many people in such a small space sent some of the passengers to sleep. Krista closed her eyes and allowed herself to drift off too.

16

THE TRAIN LURCHED FORWARD, WRENCHING KRISTA FROM sleep. She opened her eyes, rubbing at them before remembering it wasn't sleep that clouded her vision, it was the darkness inside the cattle car. A shiver ran down her spine and she pulled her coat tighter around her body. The heat in the car was long gone. Chilly winter air had now seeped in through the walls and from the floor beneath them.

The train slowed and eventually stopped. As people shuffled around, Krista stayed rooted to the spot, not willing to give up her space in case they weren't yet getting off. Beyond their wooden cell, commands were shouted in German and dogs barked. Children around her cried with fear at the noises from outside. Rusty hinges groaned as doors were opened.

'They're loading more people,' said Krista.

'I hope they don't try to put anyone else in here,' someone said.

They didn't. Their car remained nailed shut.

By the time the train set off again, there was no light coming through the gaps in the wood. Krista guessed they were now into their second day of travelling, but she couldn't be sure. She shivered again as a cold burst of air swept past her. With numb fingers, she reached into her bag and dug through its contents until she found the hat, scarf, and gloves Anna had given her nestled together. She worked them free from the jumble of clothing in her bag, careful not to pull anything else out. After closing her bag, she shoved her hands into her gloves and let out a sigh of relief as the wool enveloped her fingers. She wrapped the scarf around her neck and pulled the hat over her head, making sure her ears were covered. Almost immediately, she felt the difference – she wasn't warm, but at least she wasn't freezing anymore. Beside her, Irena rustled around, and Krista suspected that she too was layering up to protect herself from the cold.

Someone relieved themselves in the bucket they'd discovered on board. The stench of urine turned Krista's stomach. She covered her nose with one hand and breathed through her mouth for a time.

Her stomach growled. The thought of eating made her feel queasy, but her last meal had been cold porridge, and she'd digested that long ago.

When Krista could face taking her hand away from her nose, she rummaged in her bag for the package of food Irena had given her before they'd left. Her hand closed around something soft wrapped in paper.

The constant din of the train trundling along the railway tracks beneath them was like a never-ending thunderstorm.

'Irena?' Krista whispered in the darkness, hoping her friend would hear her.

'Yes?' came the whispered response.

Krista leaned in the direction of Irena's voice. 'Have you eaten?'

'No. Everything is in my suitcase, and I've been too scared to open it.'

'I have something here. Give me your hand.'

Their hands met and Krista placed the small package into Irena's palm. The soft rustling of paper as Irena unwrapped the food prompted others to follow suit and retrieve whatever food they had brought with them. The gentle clink of metal clasps unfastening, and the crinkling of paper could be heard as everyone began to fill their empty stomachs.

People traded slices of bread for chunks of cheese or meat. Talk of food brought temporary relief from the misery of their journey. Behind Krista, someone bit into an apple. Her mouth watered at just the thought of it. She'd give anything to feel the juice of an apple sliding down her parched throat, providing relief from the desert-like dryness. It had been too long since she'd had anything to drink.

Irena's hand patted its way up Krista's leg until it found her hand. 'Eat this,' Irena said. 'I have half of it here.'

Krista took the paper and felt the familiar smooth pastry of one of the pies she'd made. She brought the pie to her mouth and took a generous bite, cupping her hand beneath her chin to catch any pastry crumbs. She was rewarded with a mouthful of onions, cabbage, and potatoes. It was divine. It didn't even matter that she was eating it cold. She took a second large bite and contemplated wrapping the rest for later while she chewed, but she was too hungry. After the final bite, she ran her fingers across the paper and smiled as she found a stray cube of potato. She popped it in her mouth, folded the paper up, and stashed it in the pocket of her coat.

'I would eat that dish war or no war,' Krista said, her

voice warm despite the dire situation. She imagined Irena smiling in the darkness as she devoured her half, a moment of comfort in the uncertainty.

Food perked everyone up and the atmosphere shifted from one of oppressive fear to something a little lighter. For Krista, at least. The baby beside her wailed, piercing the fragile calm, and his mother tried her best to calm him while also dealing with one of her daughters who seemed unnerved that her mother's attention was no longer fully on her.

'No, Mama, hold me,' the little girl demanded, her voice trembling.

'I'm still here,' her mother said softly. 'I have to try to feed your brother again.'

Sensing the growing unease, Krista cleared her throat. 'Has anyone heard the story of Magda and Melania?' Krista asked, raising her voice just enough to catch the girls' attention.

'No. Who are they?' asked Irena.

'They are two little mice,' Krista began, a playful lilt entering her voice. 'They're really quite famous.' She heard shuffling around her, and she hoped it was the children leaning closer, drawn in by the promise of a tale.

'Are they twins?' a small voice piped up, close enough that Krista could feel the child's breath on her face.

The simple question cut through the heavy air like a lifeline.

'I never asked,' said Krista. 'But they do look very alike.'

A hush spread through the carriage as everyone else listened. Even the baby had quietened down, presumably successfully feeding at last. Krista smiled into the darkness at the small but powerful reminder that stories mattered, even here.

'Magda and Melania can play the piano,' said Krista. 'They bounce from one key to another with such precision that they create the most beautiful songs. What else do you think these little musical marvels can do?'

'Can they walk on a tightrope?' a girl asked.

'Do you know what? They can,' said Krista. 'They're expert tightrope walkers. I've never seen them fall off. They're also pretty good on a trapeze. There was only one time when Magda didn't manage to catch Melania, but ssshhh, we don't talk about that.'

The girl's giggles could be heard above the din of the moving train.

'Can they fly?' another young voice asked.

'That is the one thing that they cannot do,' said Krista. 'But they have a friend called Chopin. Chopin is a cat.' This drew more giggles. 'And Chopin can fly so he allows his two little friends to climb on his back and fly around with him any time they want to.'

'Doesn't Chopin want to eat them?' someone asked.

'Well, he tried at first, of course. That's what cats do. But Chopin is also a music lover, and when he heard Magda and Melania play, he promised never to try to eat them again. No matter how tasty they smelled.'

For the next half an hour, Krista crafted tales of the mice walking tightropes, travelling around on the back of a flying Chopin, and diving so deep into the ocean that they had to hide on a shipwreck to avoid being eaten by a cantankerous shark named Hubert, a name suggested by a boy somewhere in the carriage. If eating had lightened the mood somewhat, creating stories had transformed it. For the first time since they'd been herded onto the train like cattle, people laughed.

The train lurched to a stop, jarring Krista awake. Scraping sounds on the outer doors of their carriage signalled their arrival at their destination. As each nail was removed, Krista's sense of dread grew. She held her breath, bracing herself for the opening of the doors and what awaited her on the other side.

The doors opened and blinding sunlight poured into the carriage. Krista shielded her eyes. Those who were standing wasted no time in grabbing their bags and scurrying off the train. Krista scrambled to her feet and helped Irena to hers. Irena grabbed her suitcase and that of the woman with the baby. Krista untwisted the strap of her bag and made sure it was hanging in front of her body, her smaller bag once again tucked securely beneath her coat. She followed the hurried footsteps of the others as they rushed off the train, eager for fresh air and an answer as to where they had ended up.

'Can I help you both to get off?' Krista asked, holding out her hands to the two little girls.

The girls glanced up at their mother who nodded.

Krista guided the children off the train and onto the bustling station platform. She scanned the chaotic crowd. Polish police officers roamed around and there was a wall of German soldiers. But neither group of uniformed men appeared to have much interest in the women and children streaming out of the trains. Instead, their focus was on a group of men on the other platform being marched, at gunpoint, into another cattle train.

Two young girls, no older than fourteen or fifteen, approached. 'Come with us, please,' one of the girls said. 'We have food and water and can help you to find a place to stay tonight.'

The young mother's weary eyes lit up with gratitude, as if finally seeing a glimmer of hope that she and her children would be alright. Krista smiled. The Nazis may have stopped the Guides from wearing their uniforms, but they couldn't stop them doing what Guides do best.

As Krista stood in the midst of Nazi soldiers and police officers, her posture straightened, and a burst of energy surged through her body. This was the most liberated she had felt since the Nazis had seized control of Zawica. Irena nudged her, urging her to join the others and find refuge before the Nazis changed their minds about letting them all go. But Krista was done with cowering behind walls. Her earlier dread was replaced by a fiery resolve that emanated from deep within her soul.

'Excuse me,' Krista said to one of the girls. 'Can you please tell me where I can find a telephone? I need to place a call to Warsaw.'

17

KRISTA REACHED OUT AND TOOK IRENA'S HAND IN HERS. THEY trudged towards the railway station carrying their luggage, their steps heavy with emotion. Only a week ago, they had arrived at this very station after enduring a gruelling two-day journey in a crowded cattle car. Now, they were back again, but this time they would be making their journeys alone.

As they neared the station, a woman's voice called out and a figure came into view. Her long blonde hair flowed behind her as she dashed towards them. She wore dark trousers with an emerald green woollen jumper, exuding confidence and effortless style.

'Irena!' the woman said, latching on to Irena and hugging her tightly.

'Maja!' said Irena, putting her suitcase on the ground and returning the embrace.

'You must be Krista,' said Maja, turning to face her and offering a delicate hand. 'I'm Maja, Irena's cousin.'

Krista shook her hand. 'It's good to meet you.'

'You too, dear Krista,' said Maja. 'Are you certain you won't come with us? I have an extra bedroom at the farmhouse and you're very welcome to use it.'

'Thank you, but no. I'm going to Warsaw.'

'Whatever for?' asked Maja. 'I hear the city is crawling with Germans.'

Irena nodded. She and Krista had barely left each other's side in the last seven days, and they had a deeper understanding of each other. Irena's priority was staying safe and awaiting Armin's return. Maja's farm was the best place to do that. But Krista could no longer hide indoors. She needed to feel productive.

She had reached out to Anna's cousin, Nelka, who had helped her to find a cheap apartment and a volunteer position at a canteen preparing lunches for the neighbourhood children. The bustling city of Warsaw held the promise of anonymity and an opportunity for Krista to do something good while the country was tainted by darkness. She imagined herself walking down the cobbled streets, her steps light and purposeful as she headed to work. Just one face among many. The thought of starting anew where no one knew her name filled her with a sense of liberation that she had missed so deeply since that awful day the Nazis had marched into her village. The loss of her grandparents was still a constant ache in Krista's heart, and the injustice of their death still fuelled her anger. But dwelling on that anger would only harm herself. Volunteering in Warsaw and assisting those in need felt like a step towards finding peace and that's what she needed right now.

'Look after yourself,' said Irena. 'Find a cute little cafe and have lunch where everyone can see you, but no one knows who you are.'

Krista laughed. 'I can't wait.'

Maja shook her head and shrugged. 'Well, if you change your mind, you now know where we are.'

'I do,' said Krista, patting the bag draped across her body. She had added Maja's contact details to the address book Anna had given her. It brought her comfort to know that she would be able to find Irena again when this ordeal was over. Carrying that book, with its beautiful pattern of clover leaves, made her feel less alone in the world.

Maja picked Irena's suitcase up off the ground. 'Now let's get out of here. All of these Germans are making my skin crawl. Do you know, until I arrived here, I hadn't seen a single German for more than a month? A pile of them camped overnight in one of my fields before heading north. I stayed downstairs all night with my shotgun trained on the door, but they didn't come near me. I used to wonder if the farm was too isolated, but now, I'm grateful for the isolation.'

Krista smiled. She couldn't see Maja living and working on a farm. Her fingernails were too clean and her porcelain skin too flawless for someone who spent a lot of time outdoors.

Krista wrapped her arms around Irena, squeezing her tight. 'Thank you so much for helping me,' she said.

'And you for helping me,' said Irena, her voice strong. The initial shock of being cruelly evicted from her own home and wrenched apart from her husband had faded, replaced by a fierce determination that Krista hadn't known she possessed.

Maja loaded Irena's suitcase into the trunk of her car, and the two women settled into their seats. Before they drove off, Irena turned to give Krista a final wave, and she smiled back as she watched her friend disappear from view. Krista had fulfilled her promise to Armin; Irena was now as safe as possible.

Krista made her way inside the railway station and purchased her ticket. Next stop, Warsaw.

She joined the bustling crowd flowing towards the platform, her heart fluttering with a mix of anticipation and trepidation. The platform was teeming with people – families bidding tearful farewells, uniformed guards, and weary travellers clutching their belongings. The air was thick with the sound of chattering voices, the clatter of suitcases, and the distant whistle of an approaching train.

She found an empty seat near the window and hurried towards it, grateful that this journey would not be spent sitting on a freezing wooden floor. Closing her eyes, Krista leaned her head against the cool glass, attempting to shut out the world around her for just a moment.

The rhythmic clickety-clack of wheels on the tracks reverberated in her ears as the train pulled away from the station, gaining momentum with each passing second. The landscape outside rapidly transformed into a blur of countryside scenery interspersed with small towns and quaint villages. From this vantage, Poland didn't look much different to how it had looked before the Germans had invaded.

A guard appeared at the other end of the carriage. 'Tickets and papers,' he demanded.

Everyone on board fumbled in their pockets and bags for their documents. When it was her turn to hand over her papers, her mouth went dry and bitter, as if she had just taken a sip of spoiled milk. She swallowed hard. There was no reason for her nervousness, she told herself, she had done nothing wrong. She'd paid for her ticket and her papers were legitimate.

The guard scanned her identity papers and glanced up at her before returning them. He didn't even bother to check her ticket. She thanked him, but he was done with her. He'd already moved on to the next passenger.

18

As the train approached the outskirts of Warsaw, evidence of the German invasion became increasingly apparent. The vibrant and bustling city that she recalled visiting now lay in ruins, its buildings reduced to crumbling remnants of their former grandeur. Smoke billowed in the distance, as if a symbol that the war raged on in Warsaw.

She disembarked the train, her eyes immediately drawn to the swastikas that adorned every available surface. German soldiers patrolled the platforms with an air of authority, their cold gazes scanning the crowd for any signs of resistance. Fear gripped Krista's chest as she navigated through the mayhem, desperately trying to look as if she knew where she was going to avoid attracting unwanted attention.

A man approached her, tall with a scraggly beard that made him hard to age. The scent of stale smoke clung to him. But there was also something else, a familiar aroma that she couldn't quite place. It reminded her of coffee, but with a slightly different edge.

'Krista?' he asked.

She nodded.

'Good. Come with me.' He turned and walked ahead of her. Nelka had said that someone would meet her at the railway station to give her keys to the apartment, but she didn't know who it would be. All she could do was trust that this man was who she was supposed to meet. She followed him out of the station and into the bustling heart of the city.

The man hadn't introduced himself and Krista thought she ought not to ask. He led her in silence through the remnants of bombed-out buildings, dodging the occasional group of soldiers. Warsaw looked less like the desolate landscape she'd viewed from the train. The city was severely damaged almost everywhere she looked, but there were also tiny signs everywhere that the Polish people were well, their spirit had not been broken. Paper swastikas torn in two littered the street, patriotic graffiti reminded everyone, including the Nazis, that Poland was fighting on.

The streets were teeming with activity. People working, people shopping, people walking. Citizens vastly outnumbered the German soldiers. She felt reassuringly invisible. No one seemed to notice her at all.

Before long, they arrived at a dilapidated apartment building. Krista looked up. Gouges large and small peppered the entire front, barely a brick had been left untouched, and the windows across the entire top floor had been boarded up.

'It's safer than it looks,' the man said.

Krista followed him up a set of steps tucked around the corner of the building and directly into what was to become her temporary new home. The door had been painted a dull brown a long time ago. It was ordinary and reassuring. It allowed the door to blend in with the end of the building. She liked that it had its own entrance. It would make it easier to come and go without bringing any attention to herself. There could be no awkward exchanges with neighbours in a hallway.

The apartment was small, but perfectly adequate for Krista's needs. It had a bathroom, a separate bedroom, and a main living area with a kitchen tucked in the corner. It weirdly smelled of paint, but nothing in the place looked new or freshly maintained. Nothing matched. There were three wooden chairs, each one a different shade, squeezed around a small round table. Two armchairs dominated the rest of the floor space. The most worn-out-looking one had a lavender floral pattern and the other was plain beige.

'Who lived here before me?' Krista asked, dropping her bags onto the worn carpeted floor beside her.

'A Jewish couple.'

'What happened to them?'

The man hesitated, as if reluctant to say. He pointed towards the bedroom. 'A friend tipped them off that their names were on a list to be arrested. They were old and knew they were too frail to survive whatever the Nazis had in store for them, so they took their own lives right in there, on the bed, the night before the Nazis were to come for them.'

Krista shuddered. 'That's... heartbreaking.'

'Is it? They lived as free people and died as free people. Together.'

Krista nodded. It was the single strand of good she held on to about the night her grandparents were killed: knowing they died together and neither of them had to live with the horror of what had happened to the other one. If they had been arrested, they likely would have been separated. If the rumours were true, about conditions in the Nazi camps, she couldn't see how either of her grandparents would have been strong enough to survive this war.

'It's a different bed,' the man said, studying her. 'The Nazis stole everything. Their dining table probably has a nice Aryan family sitting around it talking about how dreadfully difficult they're finding the war.' He made no attempt the hide the venom in his voice.

'That's probably where my grandparents' dining table is too. They were killed, shot, the same day the Nazis arrived in our town.'

'Jewish?'

Krista shook her head, an instinctive gesture. *The wrong kind of German*, she thought, echoing her grandfather's words.

The man nodded. He didn't offer any platitudes the way people usually responded when someone died. Death had become such an everyday occurrence that people had stopped saying they were sorry to hear about it. He handed her the key for the apartment.

'Thank you,' she said.

'If you need to get in touch with us, you know how?'

'Yes.'

'Then good luck to you,' he said, leaving her alone in the apartment.

Krista had never lived alone before. It had been coming someday, but she hadn't expected it to happen so suddenly. She'd had no time to prepare. No time to adjust.

Sinking into one of the unfamiliar chairs, she yawned. A folded blanket rested behind her head and she reached for it, wrapping it around her body. Memories of her grandparents' final moments muscled their way into her mind and

tears welled up in her eyes. She wondered what they would
have thought about her coming to Warsaw. The distant
sounds of explosions and gunfire echoed in her ears. It was
like the beginning of war all over again.

Suddenly, another noise broke through her exhausted
state. Vehicles rumbled past her building, screeching brakes
and clanging metal filling the air. Her heart thundered as
she listened for any sign of trouble outside her door. The
piercing scream of a woman and the desperate cry of a child
only added to her fear and uncertainty. She had traded one
danger for another, and now she questioned if this new life
was worth it?

'Sit down, now!' someone shouted, loud enough for
Krista to hear it clearly inside her apartment.

More voices chimed in. They all seemed to have questions without answers. Krista wiped her sweating palms on
the blanket. The charged tension in the air was palpable
even through the brick walls of her apartment. A loud
gunshot echoed through the building and Krista jumped,
huddling deeper under the blanket. She pressed a hand
over her mouth to muffle her gasps. She was safe inside. For
now, at least.

Twenty minutes passed before the sound of vehicles
faded away as the Nazis left her street. Krista rubbed at her
eyes, trying to block out the images of what could have
happened. As the silence settled in, she reminded herself
that it wasn't her who had been taken today. Guilt washed
over her as she thought about those who were not so lucky.
But there was nothing she could have done. All she could do
was cling on to each day of freedom, each day of life.

A tapping on her outside door startled her. She sprung
up from her chair and frantically looked around her. Her
first instinct was to run and hide, to pretend she wasn't

home, but a voice inside her told her to answer. Another tap. Her heart raced as she crossed the room to the door, her fingers tracing the bumpy plaster in the hallway to steady herself. Taking a deep breath, she grasped the handle and pulled the door open.

19

A YOUNG GIRL, NO OLDER THAN THIRTEEN KRISTA GUESSED, stood on Krista's doorstep with a smile and a bunch of carrots. She held the carrots by their leafy green tops and thrust them towards Krista. 'I'm Larysa. I've come to show you around the neighbourhood.'

The girl's bright blue eyes shone with an air of innocence. Krista leaned out of her door and glanced up and down the alleyway. She didn't know what she was looking for, but she also didn't know what to do with the girl, so she took the carrots and invited her in.

Dirt from the carrots transferred to Krista's skin. She suspected Larysa had pulled the carrots from the ground on her way over. 'Did you grow these yourself?' Krista asked.

Larysa beamed with pride, tucking a strand of dark hair behind her ear. 'I did.'

She stood a full head shorter than Krista, but with their similar colouring they might get mistaken for sisters on the street, a useful disguise to deflect any unwanted attention.

'We only have a small garden,' said Larysa, 'but we're trying to grow as much food as we can.'

'Thank you, that was very thoughtful of you,' said Krista, setting the carrots on the counter and turning on the water to wash off the grit from her hands. Krista took in the genuine smile on the girl's face and the kind glint in her eyes. 'I'm Krista, by the way.'

'Yes, I know,' said Larysa. 'Nelka told me your name.'

Krista gestured towards the sink, inviting Larysa to wash her hands, too. The girl crossed the room and rinsed her own hands under the running water. Blue sleeves of a woollen jumper peeked out from the arms of a coat that had been too small for her for quite some time.

Hearing that Nelka had sent Larysa filled Krista with a strange mix of relief and anxiety. On the one hand, it was thoughtful of Nelka to help Krista get her bearings. But on the other hand, having someone show her around meant facing the reality of her new surroundings, something Krista wasn't quite sure she was ready for. She took a deep breath and forced a smile, trying to mask her inner turmoil. 'So... you're going to show me around?'

Larysa nodded. 'Yes. This is my neighbourhood, and I know it really well. You need to know it too or you'll look like you don't belong here so I'm your guide.'

Krista had never met Larysa before, she was certain of that, but she'd met many other girls like her. 'Tell me, Larysa, are you *my* guide or are you *a* Guide?' asked Krista.

Larysa looked at Krista, a smile tugging at the corners of her lips.

Krista brushed a hand over the collar of her coat and flicked it up, revealing the trefoil pin that she kept hidden there.

Larysa turned her collar up to reveal her own trefoil pin. The young girl's grin was like a sudden burst of sunshine through stormy clouds. Krista smiled back. Coming to Warsaw had been the right decision.

Krista and her young guide ventured out into the bustling streets of the city. The air was heavy with the scent of vehicle fumes and the occasional burst of sizzling meat as they passed a handful of restaurants. Larysa was chatty and eagerly pointed out key places Krista needed to know, such as local stores and the canteen where Krista would be working alongside Nelka to provide hot meals for local children. Larysa also worked there, she said, her eyes lighting up with genuine enthusiasm and joy. She reminded Krista of her friend Olesia and her almost unbreakable positivity.

As they walked, a boy with dark hair and a sprinkling of freckles across his nose passed by them. His arm was adorned with a white band, marked by the distinctive star of David.

Larysa leaned in closer. 'All Jews over the age of ten have to wear those,' she whispered, her bubbly voice now filled with sadness and indignation for the injustice.

The boy glanced at them nervously before hurrying away, disappearing into the crowd.

The sight of the symbol and the hatred behind it left a bitter taste in Krista's mouth and a heaviness in her heart. How could such intolerance exist in their world?

Before long they were at the entrance to the Old Town and Krista paused in front of the Royal Castle. Its roof was little more than an empty frame charred by flames, the scent of which still clung to the air. Its majestic exterior now scarred by hundreds of bullet holes. She couldn't imagine what it now looked like inside. The Germans had ransacked galleries and museums, taking all the precious artwork with them. She doubted the Royal Castle would have been spared from this fate. Once a symbol of Poland's freedom, its tragic fate seemed to be a message to the Polish people that freedom was theirs no longer.

They continued their journey in silence, eventually turning onto a wide avenue lined with trees, their leaves long gone. Giant red flags emblazoned with swastikas hung from ornate lampposts on both sides of the street, stretching as far as Krista could see.

'Hitler himself paraded down this street,' said Larysa.

'Did you see him?'

She shook her head. 'No. We weren't allowed outside during his visit. My aunt lives in the building on that corner over there and she wasn't even allowed to open her window.'

As they continued down their walk through the neighbourhood, a procession of military vehicles rolled by in perfect formation. Three sleek motorcycles, their chrome gleaming under the grey sky, led the way followed by five muddy trucks carrying German soldiers. Their stiff postures and rifles pointed upwards gave off an intimidating presence. Krista couldn't help but shudder at the sight, feeling a sudden chill run down her spine.

'You get used to it,' said Larysa, her words laced with a hint of resignation and acceptance, as if this was just a normal aspect of daily life.

Krista wasn't sure she would. It was too stark a reminder of the day the Germans arrived in Zawica. The day her life changed forever.

'Let's find a different path,' said Larysa. 'There are fewer soldiers when you stick to the side roads.'

Following Larysa's lead, they took a left turn and entered a long narrow lane with uneven cobblestones. The ancient stones were worn smooth from centuries of footsteps. A little cafe, with a red painted sign bearing the name Cafe Róża, sat at the end of the lane. The sweet scent of freshly baked goods drifted out onto the street, tempting Krista's senses. She paused and took a deep breath, savouring the mixture of rich aromas. Turning around, she gazed back up the path they had just taken, committing it to memory. Two elderly men sat at one of the three small tables outside the cafe, their faces etched with lines of experience and wisdom. Sipping on their drinks, they shared stories and cursed the Germans and their incompetence on the battlefields.

'They lost one war, and they'll lose this one too.'

'Cowards, that's all they are.'

'But cowards with an endless supply of grenades. Our boys will need a lot of bullets to get rid of those Nazis for good.'

Krista surveyed their surroundings for any potential trouble coming their way.

Larysa placed a reassuring hand on Krista's arm. 'Don't worry. The Germans rarely venture this far into the Old Town. They tend to get lost if they stray from the main routes.'

It was a relief for Krista to have someone guide her through this unfamiliar and hostile environment. They continued, weaving their way through the winding streets and narrow alleys, avoiding the busy avenues that Larysa said were patrolled by German soldiers. But even in these secluded corners, they couldn't avoid the brutal reality of occupation for long.

A large military truck was parked in front of a house head of them, blocking the entire road. The flimsy canvas walls of the truck flapped back and forth in the cold wind. Soldiers marched out of the house carrying armfuls of possessions that seemed to belong to a family. A man dressed in dirty grey overalls followed behind.

'What are you going to do with our things?' the man asked, but the soldiers ignored him, shoving him to the side. 'What right do you have to do this?' he shouted, his expression a mix of anger and despair.

A woman stumbled into the doorway, her face swollen and blotchy from tears, her hand gripping her young daughter's. They watched helplessly as soldiers tossed the contents of their home onto the truck without any regard for their value or fragility.

The little girl, perhaps unable to comprehend the sudden upheaval, stood frozen in shock. But when the soldiers removed a piano from the house and hoisted it onto the truck, the girl's composure shattered. A heart-wrenching sob escaped her lips.

'Please,' the girl's mother pleaded, her voice trembling. She reached out her pale hand to touch the glossy black finish on the instrument. 'That piano means everything to her. It's her only solace in these troubled times.'

One of the soldiers, a large hulking man with a ruddy complexion, regarded her for a moment before responding with a slap to the woman's hand.

'Why are they taking it away?' the girl wailed. 'It's mine! I didn't do anything wrong!' Her sobs only grew louder as she watched the soldiers continue their heartless task. Her mother tried to turn her face away, but the girl wouldn't budge. Wouldn't shift her gaze away from her beloved piano.

'Don't you worry, girl,' said one of the soldiers in heavily accented Polish. 'Your piano will be given to a nice German family. To a girl who is worthy of playing such an instrument.'

The soldier laughed. He thudded his fist on the rear of the truck and the driver fired up the engine. As the truck drove away with its cargo of stolen goods, the little girl buried her face into her mother's arm, her sobs muffled by the fabric of the woman's dress.

Krista stood nearby, watching with more than a dozen other onlookers. A surge of anger bubbled within her chest. It pained her to witness such injustice and destruction. She had come to Warsaw hoping to help, but many injustices were beyond her control.

A propaganda poster on the opposite side of the street caught Krista's eye. A Wehrmacht soldier standing stony-faced in front of a Nazi flag with the words *Der Sieg wird unser sein!* Victory will be ours! The poster had been pasted onto the boarded-up door of an empty shop. Krista marched across the street; her gaze fixed on the soldier's painted blue eyes. Her fingernails clawed the top of the paper away from the wooden board. She tore the entire thing down and hurled it into the gutter that lined the road. Krista couldn't get the girl her piano back, but she refused to be someone who idly watched and did nothing.

20

THE FOLLOWING MORNING, KRISTA LEFT HER WARSAW apartment alone. With no one to guide her, this would be her first true test. Could she navigate the city without giving away her status as a newcomer? She buttoned her coat up to her neck and glanced around at the other passersby, trying to mimic their confident strides and casual glances at their surroundings. Every sound and scent seemed to come alive, and, despite the unfamiliarity, Krista felt a sense of belonging, knowing that this was where she was meant to be.

She'd been walking for only a few minutes when she noticed a lone soldier leaning against a building on the corner, his boot propped up against the wall. He took a bite of a sandwich, the thick meat filling peeking out between two crusty slices of bread. A bell chimed and a group of soldiers spilt out of the building, laughing and joking around. Without a word, the lone soldier tossed his unfinished sandwich onto the street and joined the others as they walked away. Out of nowhere, a young boy in a patchwork jacket rushed forward and grabbed the discarded sandwich, devouring it with desperate hunger. Krista's heart broke at the sight of such a young child scavenging for food on the streets.

Krista approached the boy. He tried to dart away, but she reached out and grabbed the back of his tattered coat.

'Hey,' she said softly, trying to calm his frightened brown eyes. 'I know where you can get some food.'

The boy stopped struggling against her grip and looked up at her with cautious hope. She released his coat, and he dashed a few paces away from her, turning to look at her, his gaze untrusting.

'There's a canteen nearby that gives out hot meals to children. It's free,' she explained, pointing down the street. 'I'll show you if you want.'

The boy's expression was a combination of desperate longing and deep scepticism.

'You can follow me and see for yourself,' Krista offered, pointing out the route they would take. 'I'll walk this way and make two left turns. You'll see a long building with big black doors. The doors will be open and lots of other boys and girls will be going inside.'

Krista turned and began walking towards the canteen, taking the same route Larysa had shown her the day before. She kept her pace slow, knowing the young boy was following behind her at a distance, the promise of hot food too tempting for him to ignore. Every now and then, she glanced back to make sure he was still there.

When they arrived at the canteen, its inviting doors were wide open, and a small group of children had already lined up outside. Krista hoped that the boy would gather enough courage to join them.

A young woman stood on the front steps surrounded by children who looked to be hanging on her every word. She wore a simple yellow dress, with her hair pulled back in a loose braid. A chunky green cardigan protected her from the winter air. Her face was kind, with gentle features and warm, inviting eyes. Krista walked towards her.

'Hi, I'm Nelka,' the young woman said, when Krista reached her.

She looked nothing like her normally raven-haired cousin. Nelka's light brown hair had a natural shine to it, catching glints of sunlight that gave it a warm, honeyed hue. 'I'm Krista.'

'I thought so,' Nelka said with a friendly smile. 'Come on in and I'll show you around.'

The children cleared a path for Nelka and Krista followed her inside the building.

The hall was laid out with enough tables to accommodate fifty children. A dozen other girls were busily filling jugs with water, stacking plates, and mixing trays of food, steam rising above the hot food. The sweet and savoury smell of caramelising onions filled the air.

Nelka led Krista behind a counter and into the kitchen, introducing her to the other volunteers who ranged in age from eleven to eighteen. She showed Krista where to hang her coat.

'How are your cooking skills?' Nelka asked, slipping a blue and white striped apron over Krista's head.

'Pretty good,' said Krista. She tied the strings of the apron behind her back and clasped her hands together. 'My grandmother was an excellent cook, and I like to think that at least a little of her skills rubbed off on me.'

'Wonderful,' said Nelka. 'I thought today you could help out front, so the children get used to seeing you around. Some of them are very anxious and it helps when they see the same faces every day.'

'I'm happy to go wherever I'm needed,' said Krista.

Nelka smiled. 'Great. Are we ready girls?' she asked.

The others all confirmed that they were and Nelka raised her hand to a girl hovering near the entrance. The girl turned towards the waiting children and, one by one, the children streamed inside and hurried towards the long counter where a row of girls were ready and waiting to serve up that day's lunch.

Krista stared towards the door, examining the face of each child scurrying in.

'Are you OK?' asked Nelka. Her hand gently rested on Krista's shoulder. Nurturing instincts flowed from her like sweet nectar and Krista could see why the children seemed so keen on her.

'Yes, sorry,' said Krista, aware that she was not yet doing any work. 'I found a boy on the street earlier and I told him to come here. He followed me. I'm just hoping he comes in.'

'He'll come in. The smell of food is usually enough to tempt even the most nervous child inside.'

Just as Krista was about to turn away, she spotted the patchwork jacket. 'Here he comes,' said Krista, grinning and practically bouncing with joy.

Nelka smiled. 'I'll go and show him how it all works. Why don't you help the girls to dish up?'

Krista breathed a sigh of relief at the sight of the boy who would very soon have a full belly. 'Thank you,' she said to Nelka, and hurried away to help wherever she could.

Each time Krista cleared a table, it filled up again with another dozen hungry children. It took two hours to feed everyone who arrived. In that time, Krista had served what felt like hundreds of meals, washed tables and dishes, and had chopped too many potatoes and onions to count. Her eyes still stung from the onions, but it had been worth every tear that had streamed down her face. She was contributing something worthwhile.

The bustling noise of the lunch rush faded, replaced by the contented hum of children's laughter and chatter. It was a beautiful symphony that she heard so rarely these days. Mindful of Nelka's wish for the children to get used to seeing Krista, she ignored the empty plates for the time being and wandered through the hall, chatting with the children. She engaged them in playful banter and making silly jokes that sent them in to fits of giggles, her heart swelling with admiration for their resilience despite the hardships they faced.

The boy in the patchwork jacket sat alone. Krista walked over to him, pulled up a chair and sat down.

'Are you enjoying your lunch?' she asked, seeing the remnants of it smeared around the boy's mouth.

He glanced up at her with his big brown eyes and nodded.

Krista reached for the discarded plates on either side of the boy and stacked them on top of each other. 'I'm Krista. I can't remember if I told you that. What's your name?'

'Armand.'

'Have you made any new friends, Armand?' Krista asked.

The boy shook his head, his eyes locking on to a chunk of bread that had been left on one of the plates.

Krista nudged the plate closer to him. 'Do you like stories?' she asked.

Armand nodded. He reached out with a dirt-streaked hand and snatched the bread off the plate.

Krista pointed to a table where two boys and three girls were finishing their food. 'That group there are telling stories about a magical land with talking animals and an enchanted forest. Stories with talking animals are my favourite. Do you want to go and listen in?'

Armand dipped the chunk of bread into the last of the gravy on his plate and stuffed it into his mouth. He shrugged, glancing over to the group of children.

Krista took Armand's now-empty plate, stacked it on top of the others, and stood up. 'Come on. Let's go over and I'll introduce you.'

The boy stood up. Krista took a handkerchief from her pocket and wiped the stray food off his face. She took him by the hand and led him towards the other children.

'Hi, everyone,' she said. 'This is Armand. It's his first time here today. Can he join you?'

One of the girls hopped out of her seat and offered it to Armand. 'Of course. Sit down.' She pulled out another chair and sat alongside him. 'What's your favourite animal, Armand?'

'An elephant,' he said, quietly.

'Oooh, good one,' said one of the boys. 'We haven't used an elephant yet.'

Krista listened in for a minute as Armand answered questions about his elephant and the others explained how the enchanted forest worked. She smiled. By giving up her seat, the girl had allowed Armand to feel included in the group, rather than sitting on the outskirts.

Satisfied with the outcome, Krista turned away, hoping that the boy would return tomorrow for another hot meal and stories with his new friends. She gathered empty plates from a nearby table and made her way to the kitchen. Nelka was standing blocking the entrance, her friendly expression now more serious and her gaze fixed on Krista.

21

KRISTA HELD ONTO HER STACK OF PLATES FIRMLY AS SHE MADE her way towards Nelka, who was standing in the archway of the kitchen.

'Is everything alright?' Krista asked, certain of a shift in Nelka's demeanour.

Nelka shifted aside to allow Krista to enter, her eyes following her every move. 'You're very good with children,' she said. 'Do you have younger siblings?'

A heavy silence hung between them before Krista finally answered. 'No. It's just me.' *No parents, no grandparents.*

Nelka followed Krista into the kitchen. 'I sense that you may be interested in contributing more to the war effort than providing meals to children, as worthwhile as that cause is.'

Krista lowered the plates into the sink and turned on the tap, watching as water spilt over the dishes and down the drain. 'I'm happy to do whatever is needed.'

'Glad to hear it. Come with me a minute.' Nelka led Krista to a storeroom tucked away at the back of the hall. 'I have a group of children that need an education. Their last teacher was… well, she's gone.'

Krista glanced around the room. Shelving units were piled high with boxes labelled with everything from forks and knives to rice. 'I'm not sure I'm following you. What is it you need me to do?'

'Teach them,' said Nelka.

Krista shook her head. 'I'm not a teacher.'

'We're all pulling together and taking on jobs we're not qualified for. I think you can help this group of children. Just until we get something more permanent organised.'

The Germans had closed so many schools down. They didn't see the point in teaching Polish children more than simple arithmetic and the ability to write their own names. Many teachers had been arrested and no one was quite sure where they had ended up.

'You know I'm German, right?' Krista asked. It was a fact she had shared during her initial conversation with Nelka, but she felt the need to remind her now.

Despite never meeting in person, they had spoken on the telephone multiple times before Krista's arrival in Warsaw. Krista had been completely honest. She didn't know how close the cousins were, but if Anna trusted her, then Krista felt that she could too. So far, Nelka had proven to be reliable – arranging for Krista's apartment and volunteer work at the children's canteen. But teaching children was very different from feeding them. Teaching had to involve an underground school. That could put people at risk of arrest or worse. Trusting Krista with its location and possibly even the names of others involved was big. If something went wrong, she didn't want to be accused of hiding her true identity.

'You told me,' said Nelka. 'You also told me that the

Germans had murdered your grandparents. A fact that Anna verified.'

Krista felt tears spring to her eyes at both the thought of her grandparents and hearing her friend's name out loud. Perhaps that's why Nelka was so quick to trust her. Anna had vouched for her in some way.

'You don't have to say yes,' said Nelka. 'There are risks. You know that. Take some time to think about it.'

Nelka turned to leave the kitchen. Krista plunged a pile of dishes into the sink and watched them disappear under the soapy water. What was there to think about? Hadn't she already decided that she wouldn't be the type of person to stand by and do nothing?

'Wait,' said Krista. 'I'll do it. I'll help in any way I can.'

Nelka smiled and joined Krista at the sink. 'You can start tomorrow morning. Go to Cafe Emilia on Targowa Street. Emilia is German, too.' Nelka leaned closer, the soft murmurs of her further instructions almost drowned out by the clinking of Krista washing and rinsing the plates as she listened intently.

One of the other girls came into the kitchen carrying more dirty plates. She placed the dishes beside the sink and turned to Nelka. 'Someone outside is looking for you.'

'I'll be right there.' Nelka followed the girl out of the kitchen, but before leaving, she turned back to Krista. 'Oh, and please don't go tearing down any more posters. Let's avoid any unnecessary attention coming our way.'

Nelka's lips curved upwards into a warm smile. Even her chastisement was delivered with a gentle touch, as if she wanted to soothe rather than scold. Krista nodded, looking contrite. Larysa must have tattled on her.

∾

With the dishes washed and ready for the following day's lunches, Krista left the canteen. As she turned the corner, she saw a woman with her young daughter being shoved to the ground by a soldier. He jabbed the butt of his rifle into their backs. The woman fell to her knees, tumbling forward. Another soldier in front of them jumped back as though being within a foot of a Polish woman was cause for alarm. He kicked the woman in the chest. The little girl screamed, and the soldier aimed his weapon at her. Her mother scrambled back to her knees and clamped a hand around the girl's mouth to silence her.

Other pedestrians in the street gave the group a wide berth and hurried past with their heads down. Nelka's warning echoed in her mind. *Let's avoid any unnecessary attention.* Intervening in some way would bring unnecessary attention. Krista clutched a hand to her heart. She didn't want to be that person who scurried away and did nothing, but sometimes there was no other choice. She watched on helplessly for another few seconds before she too turned and walked away. She couldn't bear to stay and see the fate of the woman and her child. She preferred to hold on to at least a sliver of hope that they had been allowed to stand up and walk away.

As Krista approached her apartment, two soldiers armed with rifles blocked the street ahead of her. She swiftly turned left onto another street, only to find it also blocked with trucks and more soldiers on guard. It was unclear who or what they were waiting for.

Krista hesitated before retracing her steps. She reminded herself that she was a German citizen, and there was no reason for her to be afraid of her own people. But of course, that wasn't true. She knew she had much to fear. Suppressing her emotions, she reached into her pocket and retrieved her identification papers. Slowly, she approached the barricade, holding out her documents for the soldiers to inspect. One of them lowered his rifle slightly while the other continued to keep his weapon trained on her. After a quick glance at her papers, the soldier waved her through without any further questioning or hesitation.

As she passed through the barricade unchallenged, Krista understood why her grandparents told her that her German heritage would protect her. The Nazis' hatred had spread far and wide, sparing only those who they thought were like them. She was nothing like them, but just the thought of it ignited an idea in her mind. The first lesson she would teach might not align with Nelka's expectations, but she was going to do it anyway. She was going to teach the children German.

22

THE SUN HUNG LOW IN THE WINTER SKY. KRISTA PULLED HER coat tighter around her body, trying to ward off the chilly morning air as it seeped through the fabric. Her breath escaped in small puffs of white, contrasting against the vibrant blue sky above.

She rounded the corner onto Targowa Street and her eyes immediately fell upon a group of German soldiers chatting and sipping their coffee at outside tables. More soldiers lounged at the tables inside the cafe, chatting and smoking cigarettes. She squinted at the sign above the door to confirm she had arrived at the correct place. The sign read Cafe Emilia in beautiful swirling cursive writing with gold paint. She knew that Emilia was German, but she hadn't expected the clientele to be German too. While she understood the need for discretion, she couldn't shake the feeling that Nelka would have mentioned this important detail beforehand. It almost felt like a test, to see how she would react when confronted with a room full of German soldiers without warning.

Krista took a deep breath and pushed open the cafe's

glass door. The aroma of coffee wafted towards her. It smelled real. It seemed impossible that it could have been, but so much of what was happening in the world seemed impossible not too long ago. Her heart thumped in her chest as she made her way to the counter. With each step, she felt the weight of stares on her, a lone woman among a swarm of uniformed men.

As she weaved through a tight cluster of soldiers, a woman with fiery red hair emerged from a nearby doorway, deftly balancing two plates in her hands. Krista's gaze fixated on the plates, her stomach growling. Each one held a chunk of fresh bread, two eggs with bright orange yolks, and a small whole fish whose smokiness tickled Krista's taste-buds as the plates glided by her.

'I'll be with you in a minute,' said the redhead.

The woman placed the plates in front of two Germans, pausing to talk. She threw her head back with laughter at a joke one of them appeared to have shared with her. Her hair cascaded down her back in loose waves. She left them to devour their breakfast and sashayed back towards Krista, her hips swaying in a dark green dress that hugged her curves and accentuated her figure.

'You'll be Krista, then?' the woman asked. Her face was flawless, with high cheekbones and full, ruby lips. 'I'm Emilia. Let's get you an apron. Believe it or not, the morning rush hasn't started yet. You can put your coat through the back.'

Before she could respond, Emilia ushered Krista through a doorway and into the cafe's kitchen. Another woman was hard at work managing multiple sizzling pans.

Emilia's eyes scanned Krista from head to toe before finally settling on her face. 'I thought you'd be older,' she said. 'You can put your coat in the office. It stops it smelling of whatever Diana is cooking.'

At the mention of her name, the other woman looked up and gave Krista a brief nod before turning back to her work and disappearing behind a cloud of steam from the stove.

Krista smiled politely, unable to muster any words as she followed Emilia into the office. She hung her coat on a rusty hook and smoothed down her hair. Her nerves were on edge as she surveyed the bareness of the room. The walls were a stark white, devoid of any decorations or personal touches. A lone desk sat in the centre, its surface neatly organised with only a pen and notepad resting upon it.

'Where is the school?' Krista asked.

'In the basement. The children will come in through the hatch in the alleyway behind the building, but there's a door you can use from inside the building when we're finished breakfast.'

'Breakfast?' Krista asked, fidgeting with the sleeves of her jumper.

'Yes,' said Emilia, her voice carrying a hint of weariness. 'My usual waitress hasn't turned up and I need your help.'

Krista's eyes widened and her breath hitched in her throat like a fish caught on a hook. It was one thing to teach a group of children in the relative safety of an underground school, but another thing entirely to wait on German soldiers. Krista let out a small cough to clear her throat. 'I can't do that,' she said.

Emilia blew out a sigh of frustration. 'It's the same every time. Did no one tell you that this cafe caters to Germans?'

Krista shook her head.

Emilia waved her hand dismissively. 'Well, now you know. And before I can show you the ropes, I need those Germans fed and out of here.'

'I don't understand. Why are we even teaching here if it's a German cafe?' Krista asked.

Emilia leaned against the office desk; her gaze fixed on Krista. 'This building holds secrets, my dear. The children who come here learn much more than just reading and writing.'

Krista waited for Emilia to elaborate on her statement, but she said nothing more. Instead, she raised a perfectly groomed eyebrow and waited for Krista to join the dots herself. Underground activities, Krista suspected. She'd heard rumours of children being used for this purpose, especially among Guides and Scouts who were not content with sitting back and doing nothing. Many of them were acting as couriers or carrying out surveillance on the Nazis. Children milling around and watching raised fewer suspicions. But that still didn't explain why they were being trained right under the noses of the Nazis.

'We were here long before the Nazis showed any interest in me,' added Emilia, as if sensing Krista's remaining question. 'And where better to hide from the wolf than in its lair?'

Krista would have preferred to hide from the wolf anywhere but its lair, but she had to trust that there was a reason for being in this particular location.

'When you said it's the same every time, how many times have you done this?'

Emilia's features softened, and a small grin tugged at the corners of her mouth. 'You're the fourth teacher. But don't worry, the others left for different reasons. The Germans haven't yet figured out what we're doing here.'

The word *yet* wasn't exactly reassuring.

With that, Emilia spun around and waltzed back towards the cafe. Krista had little choice but to follow behind her. As they re-entered the bustling cafe, Emilia handed Krista an apron with a wink. 'Just pour coffee and clear tables. Try not to attract too much attention.'

Krista nodded. She watched Emilia deftly manoeuvre through the tables, taking orders, and serving plates of food with ease. The German soldiers seemed oblivious to Krista's presence. All eyes had returned to the glamorous redhead.

Krista made her way towards a vacant table littered with empty plates and glasses. A well-dressed officer at the neighbouring table lifted his gaze to meet hers. His steely blue eyes sent a chill down her spine.

'More coffee,' he grunted in German, his tone impatient.

Emilia appeared beside her and handed Krista a jug of coffee. Krista forced a tight smile. A deep sense of unease settled in her stomach. Each step towards him felt like a betrayal to everything she believed in. As she reached out to refill the officer's cup, her foot caught on an uneven floorboard and she stumbled, watching with horror as a cascade of scalding coffee splattered onto his pristine uniform.

The room fell silent as everyone stared at Krista. The man's face turned crimson with fury and his jaw clenched so tight that it looked like he might shatter his teeth.

Krista stood rigid, every muscle in her body tense with fear as she braced herself for what would come next. Spilling coffee on a German, particularly a high-ranking one, would be punished in some way. Whispers rippled through the cafe like a gathering storm. He took a menacing step towards her.

'I-I'm so sorry, sir. It was an accident, I didn't mean to–' Krista stammered, her voice barely audible.

But before she could finish her sentence, the officer raised a hand to silence her. His icy glare bore into her.

Krista grabbed a handful of napkins and offered them to him. He took them and dabbed at the stains on his uniform.

'Hauptmann Schneider.' His name rolled off Emilia's tongue like drops of honey, sweetness coating every syllable. Emilia glided in front of Krista. Reaching out, she placed a hand on the Hauptmann's sleeve, smoothing down the damp fabric. 'Please excuse me. This one is new, but she's a loyal German girl. She just needs a little training. You understand that, don't you?'

Hauptmann Schneider loomed over Krista. But then, to Krista's surprise, his expression softened, and his rigid posture relaxed just a fraction. He looked down at Emilia's hand, still on his arm. 'Accidents happen,' he said.

Krista blinked in disbelief, unsure if she'd heard him correctly.

'Just don't let it happen again,' he snarled. With that, he turned on his heel and marched out of the cafe, leaving behind a lingering trail of bewilderment and relief in his wake.

Krista stood rooted to the spot, her heart still racing from the adrenaline of the moment. Emilia turned to face her, her expression shifting from calm to concerned as her brows furrowed, forming deep lines across her forehead. 'Are you alright?' she asked, prising the coffee jug out of Krista's shaky grip.

Krista nodded. 'I really didn't mean it.'

'Let's just call it a happy accident and get back to work,' Emilia whispered.

23

KRISTA MADE IT THROUGH THE REST OF THE BREAKFAST SHIFT without scalding anyone else and now stood in the dimly lit underground classroom, her eyes wandering over the faces of her small group of students. They stared back, uncertainty with a glimmer of curiosity etched on their young features. The musty scent of the basement hung heavy in the air, as if reminding them all of the constant danger lurking outside. Krista's mind was a blur of thoughts from her own school days. She took a deep breath to calm the chaotic jumble of memories and nerves. She wasn't a teacher, but right now, she was all that these children had.

'Good morning. Let's start by introducing ourselves. I'm Krista. My favourite subject at school was reading.' She stopped there. These days, sharing too much information with people could be dangerous.

Krista's hand extended towards a young boy with tousled hair, perched on an old barrel that creaked under his weight. He was ten years old, she guessed. His legs dangled off the sides of the barrel, and he fidgeted with a pencil in his hands.

'What's your name and what's your favourite school subject?' Krista asked the boy.

'I'm Oskar,' he said brightly. His skin was grubby, and his clothes were worn and tattered, a testament to the harsh realities he faced. But despite it all, he sat there ready to defy the Nazis and pursue the education they had tried to deny him.

'And your favourite subject, Oskar?' Krista prompted.

He swung his legs back and forth. 'I like reading, too.'

'Thank you, Oskar,' said Krista. 'Who's next?'

They went around the room with each child introducing themselves. Krista made sure to repeat each of their names as many times as she could in the conversation in the hope it would help her to remember them. She had the outline of a lesson plan scribbled in a notebook, but she decided against writing down any of their names in case she was ever stopped and her notes inspected. A girl named Olivia was the only child to say she liked arithmetic. The others copied Krista and Oskar by saying they like reading. It seemed the children were just as cautious about the information they shared with each other.

Once the introductions were made, Krista was ready to begin her first lesson. 'We're going to learn some German phrases.' She caught the children's nervous glances. 'That's our cover,' explained Krista. 'If we're ever caught, we'll say that I'm teaching you German.'

'Why?' asked one of the boys. 'They think we're stupid and shouldn't be educated so won't that get us into trouble?'

'If they find us together, we're in trouble either way,' said Krista. 'I think learning German gives us a chance to talk our way out of trouble.'

Some of the children looked sceptical, others looked horrified.

'Let's start with a simple greeting. Does anyone know the German word for hello?'

Oskar, the boy on the upturned barrel, raised his hand. 'Go on,' said Krista, inviting him to speak.

'My sister said hello to the Germans, and they beat her. They said Polish filth have no business talking to them.'

The children all shifted their gazes to Krista. She took another deep breath to quash the fury rising inside of her. Who could possibly think that beating a girl for saying hello was not only acceptable, but was required? How had Hitler got so many other people to participate in his madness? Would she have toed the line if she'd spent the last ten years in Germany? She hoped she wouldn't. And she hoped that there were people in Germany doing exactly as they were doing now – preparing to rise up and fight back against the Nazis.

'I'm very sorry about your sister,' said Krista. 'The Germans have said that Poles can learn German and basic arithmetic. Let's combine the two by counting how many Nazis we'll kick out of Warsaw when the fight back begins.'

The children grinned, even Oskar.

Krista held one finger in the air. 'Repeat after me. Eins, zwei, drei...' One, two, three... She raised her fingers with each number as she counted slowly from one to ten in German. The children, after some gentle encouragement, counted alongside her.

As Krista progressed through her lesson, she sensed a shift in the atmosphere. The initial scepticism had dissipated. The children began to ask more questions. They moved on from German and did a little reading, some arithmetic, and a history lesson as Krista tried to replicate what she remembered from a morning at her old school. For a brief moment in their day, the weight of their circumstances lifted, and they were just children learning together. Krista cherished the time, knowing it was a rare gem in their otherwise bleak reality.

'Krista,' said Oskar, following a particularly spirited discussion about historical figures who had fought for freedom. 'Do you think we can really make a difference? Can we really drive the Nazis out of our city?'

Krista paused, contemplating her response. She looked at Oskar, glimpsing the hope that burned within him. She reached out and rested a hand gently on his shoulder. 'Change always starts with individuals like us,' she said. 'We may be young, but our voices are powerful, and our hearts are resilient. For now, we educate ourselves, and when the time is right, we rise against the darkness that has invaded our country. The determination that I see inside each of you will inspire others to stand with us. So, yes, I believe we can make a difference.'

The children's faces were glowing, as if they now believed in their ability to make a difference. That, to Krista, felt like success.

Just as Krista was about to bring her first class to an end, a sudden commotion erupted from outside. The sound of scuffling feet and harsh German voices permeated through the walls. The children froze. Krista rushed to the tiny window near the ceiling, sneaking a glance outside.

She gasped as she saw a group of Nazi soldiers surrounding a young boy, no older than twelve. His trembling hands were raised in surrender and his face contorted in a mixture of fear and desperation. One of the soldiers barked orders at him in German while another rummaged through his bag. It didn't take long for them to find what they were looking for – a stack of banned Polish newspapers. The soldiers sneered and laughed as they tore apart the papers, throwing the scraps into the air like confetti. The boy's shoulders slumped, defeated, as the papers were trampled under the soldiers' boots. Krista's chest tightened with anger.

She turned back to the children, who were huddled together at the far side of the basement, eyes wide. 'Stay quiet,' she whispered. Oskar trembled with suppressed terror. The others nodded in silent understanding.

As the sound of the soldiers' boisterous laughter faded into the distance, Krista breathed a sigh of relief. They had let the boy go. He appeared shaken, but otherwise unharmed. She kept her class in the basement for another few minutes until the boy had moved on and she could be certain the soldiers were gone.

When it felt safe for them to leave, she watched the children cautiously slip away from the basement. Their innocence had been stolen at such a tender age. She understood then that her role as their teacher was about more than just education. Her job was to guide them through this oppressive occupation until the time came for all of them to join the Resistance movement and confront the Nazis directly.

As Krista prepared to leave through the door to the cafe, two students were blocking her path.

'It's safe to leave now,' she said.

'We know,' said one of the boys. 'We're staying here for our next lesson.'

'Oh, what will you be learning?' asked Krista.

'Explosives,' the boy said, rubbing his hands together, mustering more enthusiasm than he had shown during Krista's lesson.

The other boy elbowed him in his side and the boy's face fell as he realised he shouldn't have said that.

Krista felt a surge of curiosity prickling at her skin. 'You're going to learn about explosives? Here?'

The boy hesitated for a moment, exchanging a nervous glance with his friend. Finally, he spoke in a hushed tone, 'Not here, exactly. There's a tunnel in the back of the cupboard that connects to some of the other buildings on the street. It's how we move around without being seen by the Nazis.'

The other boy threw his hands in the air and exhaled a disgruntled sigh.

'What? She's one of us,' said the boy.

'It's alright,' Krista reassured. 'I don't need to know any more and I won't tell anyone. Just please be careful.'

She left the boys alone but couldn't shake off her unease. The pieces were coming together in her mind. Emilia's cafe was just one part of a larger operation. The mundane lesson she had just been teaching now felt insignificant compared to the mysteries lurking elsewhere in the building.

The word "explosives" echoed in her mind as she stepped out of the cafe. Explosives should have been something children read about in an adventure story, not taught to boys who couldn't have been older than twelve. But it wasn't something she could think about right now. The lunchtime rush would be about to start at the children's canteen. She was tempted to ask Nelka if she knew exactly what was happening at Emilia's, but she had promised the boys she wouldn't say anything. And, in this world, one could never be sure who was listening.

24

KRISTA CLOSED HER NOTEBOOK, PACKING IT INTO HER BAG AS the children left the underground classroom through the basement door. She pretended not to notice the three boys lingering in the room, waiting for her to leave so they could sneak along some secret passageway to another building and a lesson that would never appear on a school curriculum.

Three weeks had gone by, and Krista had settled into her new routine of teaching one group of children in the morning and feeding another group at lunchtime. She spent her evenings scribbling down everything she remembered from her own school days and coming up with lessons she thought might engage the children. She was an amateur, but she was still helping. And the work kept her occupied. It stopped her mind from dwelling on things she'd rather not think about. She hadn't yet mustered the courage to eat in a restaurant by herself as she'd told Irena she would. But today, she was determined to finally do it. Cafe Róża was calling her name.

As she left the classroom, Emilia was standing in the hallway, waiting for her.

'I need you to do something for me,' Emilia said. 'It's important.'

Krista waited, expecting to be handed an apron with a request to serve lunch in the cafe. Instead, she was handed an envelope.

'Can you deliver this?' Emilia asked.

'What is it?' asked Krista.

Emilia raised her eyebrows and gave a small smile which Krista took as a sign that it was best not to know.

Krista took the envelope and flipped it over, searching for an address. 'Where does it need to go?'

'Good,' said Emilia, taking this as a yes. 'Go to Szeroka Street. There's an alley behind the old bakery with only one door. Knock three times and wait. You must go quickly.'

Before Krista could even respond, Emilia pressed a finger to her lips. 'No more questions. You must go now. And be discreet – don't let anyone else see it. If you run into trouble, get rid of the envelope if you can.'

With that Emilia marched into the kitchen, leaving Krista standing alone with the mysterious envelope and a flood of unanswered questions swirling in her mind.

Krista left the cafe. Emilia's insistent voice echoed in her mind, urging her to deliver the envelope without delay. She boarded a busy tram and found a seat by the window. The envelope tucked securely in the waistband of her skirt felt like a weight pressing against her hip.

The tram rattled along the tracks, the worn seats squeaking in protest with each jostle and shake. Krista kept her gaze fixed on the passing buildings outside, trying to appear nonchalant, despite the turmoil inside her. What could Emilia possibly be entrusting her with? And how much trouble would she be in if the Germans got their hands on it? She fidgeted in her seat. The tram suddenly felt like a mistake. She should have crossed the city on foot, but she didn't want to be late for the canteen service. The number of children coming in for lunch was increasing, and every volunteer was crucial in ensuring that they left with their stomachs full.

Krista took a deep breath. The soldiers had their own carriage, she told herself. The worst that could happen was a papers inspection and that no longer worried her. Her papers were genuine and attracted no more than the occasional raised eyebrow from their inspector.

As the tram rumbled closer to her stop, Krista's stomach rumbled just as loud with hunger. She hadn't eaten since the platter of cheese and apple that Diana had slipped her at Cafe Emilia that morning. She distracted herself with thoughts of food. The girls usually ate together in the canteen after the children had gone. Today would be sausages, onions, and potatoes. The sausages never quite had enough fat in them to disguise their lack of meat and she hated to imagine what they'd been padded out with, but she would savour them anyway, just grateful for a hot meal.

Amidst frantic whispers from her fellow passengers, Krista's thoughts were interrupted, and a surge of panic gripped her heart. The tram lurched to a stop and two Gestapo men marched into view. A massive military truck pulled up alongside the tram, blocking its tracks. The Gestapo burst onto the tram and demanded everyone get off immediately. Krista's stomach turned over in fear. She touched her hand to the envelope hidden beneath her clothing. If she could get it out, she could drop it underneath the seats, but there was no way to retrieve it without being seen. She stood up and joined the mass exodus of bewildered passengers.

'Polish go left, Germans go right,' barked a particularly fierce-looking soldier as the passengers stepped down onto the street.

Krista's skin prickled as memories of arriving at the railway station with Armin and Irena flooded back to her. She stepped off the tram and went right. She tried to calm her breathing. They weren't looking for her. If they were, they would not have ordered everyone else off.

A third Gestapo man made his way up the line of people on the German side, checking identity documents. Krista pulled out her documents and handed them over. He snatched them from her grip, studying them for longer than anyone else's. Nerves gnawed at her from the inside.

'Why are you in Poland?' he asked her, in German.

'When my parents died, I was sent to live here with my grandparents,' she responded in German. Given her grandparents' insistence that only German was spoken in their home, Krista had never lost her native German accent. Her reply seemed to satisfy the soldier's curiosity about her. He handed her identification back before moving on down the line.

The man next to her handed over his documents. 'I'm Polish, but I work for the railway.' His documents were returned without any further questioning. Krista thought of Irena and Armin. The Germans had quickly realised their mistake and those working on the country's critical infrastructure were now often spared. If Armin could have avoided the first roundup, perhaps he and Irena could have stayed together during the war.

One of the other soldiers counted the Polish people standing on the opposite line. He started at seventy-eight and kept counting until he reached one hundred. Person one hundred, a frail woman with stooped shoulders and a face marked with age lines, was shoved in the direction of the other numbered individuals. She appeared to straighten up as best she could in a symbol of defiance against the oppressive forces surrounding her.

Those without numbers were herded into the waiting truck, its engine growling to life as soon as the last person stepped on. Krista stood still. Sweat sprung to her forehead, and her hair stuck to her clammy skin. She looked around with wide eyes, taking in the alarm of those around her as the truck accelerated away. Its destination was unknown, but she feared that the men, women, and children onboard were being taken to one of the horrific labour camps that people whispered about. Or worse – there were rumours that some of these camps were death camps in disguise. As much as it horrified her to believe it, Krista had witnessed enough brutality and senseless killings to know that such a place could exist.

'Go,' a soldier barked at the numbered Poles who had been left behind.

Krista watched in horror as they were forcefully led away, flanked by Nazis on both sides and marched along the street and out of sight. A cold shiver ran down her spine as she contemplated the fate of those innocent people. If they were not being sent to a camp, where were they going?

The soldiers dispersed and the tram moved on with the few passengers who had risked scrambling back aboard. Krista stayed still, choosing to walk the rest of the way. The street was oddly quiet like a fog had smothered all of the usual noises. Then, without warning, the silence was shattered by a deafening eruption of gunfire. The shots echoed off the nearby buildings, reverberating in Krista's ears.

Screams and shouts filled the streets as people scattered in all directions, desperate to find safety in the chaos.

A young boy rounded the corner, running from the direction the numbered people had been led. 'They're shooting everyone,' he yelled.

Panic spread through the people still standing around.

Krista reached out and grabbed the boy by the arm. He must have been about eight years old, too young to have witnessed what he had just seen. His clothes were dirty and torn, and his face was streaked with tears and dirt.

'What's happened?' she asked.

The boy was like a moth flitting around a flame, his movements full of nervous energy and his eyes constantly darting back to the source of danger. 'They said they were killing one hundred Poles for the beating of a German officer.' He quickly looked behind himself again, his movements jerky as if he expected to see someone chasing after him.

Krista released his arm. 'Go!'

He sprinted off, disappearing in a blur of movement. Krista stood there, rooted to the spot, unable to comprehend the brutality of what she had just heard. As the echoes of gunshots faded into the distance, her mind raced with a mixture of anger and grief. She couldn't fathom the senseless violence that had just unfolded. Twenty-three people who had been travelling with her on the tram were dead, their lives snuffed out, all in the name of retaliation.

25

WITH A HEAVY HEART, KRISTA TORE HER GAZE AWAY FROM THE corner around which the Poles had vanished. She had witnessed enough tragedy for one day. The only thing she could now do was keep going. Using shadows and side streets as her allies, Krista continued her way through the maze-like city, avoiding lingering German soldiers who still patrolled the area. When she reached Szeroka Street, she glanced around her to make sure no one was watching and approached the door in the alley behind the bakery.

She reached to the waistband of her skirt and carefully pulled out the envelope, its edges slightly crumpled from being pressed against her body. She held it out with trembling hands and knocked on the door three times. The door creaked open with a groan, the hinges protesting the movement. A hand snatched the envelope. Before she could react, the door slammed shut.

Krista pushed aside the nagging doubts that were creeping up inside her. She wanted to believe that whatever she had just done did would help to end this brutal war, but a part of her couldn't shake the fear that she had made a grave mistake. Was she really doing the right thing? Would her actions truly make a difference, or was it all just wishful thinking? The weight of her decision weighed heavily on her mind as she left the alleyway and hurried to the canteen on foot. Cafe Róża would have to wait; dining alone no longer felt like a significant accomplishment.

As she arrived at the canteen, a wave of relief washed over her as she saw the comforting sight of hungry children tucking into their lunch. The sound of chatter and laughter filled the air, mixing with the clinking of cutlery and the aroma of freshly cooked food. It was a stark contrast to the earlier horrors she had witnessed.

Nelka spotted Krista and rushed over to greet her, her delicate features creased with concern. 'Krista, are you alright? I was so worried when you didn't show up.' Nelka's arms enveloped Krista in a tight hug.

Krista sank into Nelka and returned the embrace gratefully. She had made it back to the canteen safely, and the relief flooded through her. 'I was caught up in something on the tram,' Krista explained, her voice betraying a lingering fear. 'There was a roundup... people were taken away. It was terrifying.' The images of their faces haunted her, their wide eyes filled with fear and helplessness as they were forcibly taken away. She shuddered at the memory.

Nelka released her. 'I heard about it,' she whispered. 'Come, we have enough people serving. Help me get started on the soup for tomorrow.'

They made their way to the kitchen and Nelka handed Krista an apron and a knife. 'You can chop the carrots. Did you make the delivery?' she asked. Her voice smooth and unbothered, like a stream flowing over smooth rocks.

That explained why Nelka had been so concerned when Krista was late. She had known about the envelope Emilia had asked her to deliver. Krista slipped on her apron and picked up the knife. For a few seconds, the only sounds in the kitchen were the crunch of carrots and the rhythmic beat of the blade hitting the wooden cutting board.

'I wasn't sure if I was doing the right thing,' Krista admitted.

Nelka paused her own task of cubing potatoes and faced Krista. 'You were,' she said. Her confidence wrapped around Krista, easing her wavering uncertainty. As they continued cooking together, Nelka asked, 'How's it all going over there?'

'OK, I think.' Krista pushed the chopped carrots into a pile on the board, her fingertips already stained by their vibrant orange colour. 'The children are great and, considering I'm not a teacher, I think they're learning a lot.'

Nelka cupped handfuls of chopped potatoes and transferred them to a large steel pot. 'I know you still have concerns about the school and its proximity to the Germans, but there are only so many places we can go. People are nervous and naturally suspicious when new people show up in their neighbourhood.'

'I was thinking about that,' said Krista. 'What about here?' She picked up the board of chopped carrots and joined Nelka at the stove, tipping the carrots into the pot. 'Children are already piling into the building. What's a few more? It must be less suspicious than the basement of a German-only cafe.'

Nelka picked up a stray carrot cube that had fallen on the stove and shook her head. 'That was one option we considered, but we didn't want to take the risk that the Gestapo find out and shut this place down completely.'

Krista nodded. There were too many children relying on the canteen for food. She fidgeted with the hem of her apron, her fingers twisting into the fabric. 'Do you trust Emilia?' It was a question that had been playing on Krista's mind, but there were too few opportunities to ask it. When Krista wasn't surrounded by hungry children, she was working alongside the other volunteers, and she didn't know how open she could be around them.

Nelka put her knife down and fixed her gaze on Krista. 'Emilia is one of us. She worked tirelessly to support her community after the invasion. She hid people in the rooms upstairs, provided free meals for local children, and arranged secret lessons when the schools were closed down. People coming and going in a cafe didn't raise any suspicions. Then the Germans took their fancy to her and decided to make the cafe their breakfast venue of choice. Emilia was all set to close her business down. She's German, but like you, she didn't want to serve them. She doesn't agree with what they are doing here, and she felt serving them food would make her complicit in that. But then we decided to see it as an opportunity. Emilia has eyes and ears on the Germans who can be loose-lipped when they're eating and drinking. It's proved helpful to have someone listening in.'

Nelka's certainty should have been reassuring, yet a seed of doubt lingered in Krista's mind. She had seen the ease with which Emilia waited on the Germans in her cafe. Being so close to the enemy made Krista's skin crawl, but not so for Emilia. Had Emilia just had more practise, or was it possible that she was playing a dangerous game of deception?

26

KRISTA STRODE DOWN THE CROWDED STREET, THE WAISTBAND of her skirt concealing Emilia's latest envelope. She had proven herself with the first delivery and now she had even more to make, all to the same address. The unknown contents of these envelopes weighed heavily on Krista's mind, but knowing that Nelka was aware of the deliveries reassured her that she was doing something good. As she walked, a bead of sweat formed on her forehead which she quickly brushed away with her sleeve. Carrying these mysterious packages was never easy, but today seemed especially difficult. There were more German soldiers than usual patrolling the area and streets were being blocked off one after the other. Knowing what she held in her possession, Krista didn't attempt to brazen her way through any of the blockades. She changed directions as often as she had to, eventually finding herself walking along the outer wall of the Jewish ghetto.

The towering wall loomed over her, its barbed wire casting sickening shadows on the ground. She couldn't bear to imagine the horrors on the other side. It was rumoured that people were dying from starvation and disease, perishing in front of their helpless families. Half a dozen guards clustered around the entrance, their hands gripping their weapons, as if expecting trouble at any moment. Krista quickly crossed the street, passing a young boy heading towards the ghetto.

The frayed edges of the boy's jumper stopped halfway down his mid-riff, while his trousers were stitched together rags and tied at the waist by a length of grubby string. With each step, his bare feet slapped against the road. His cheeks had lost any youthful fullness they might once have had, and his deep brown eyes were rimmed with dark circles, sunken further into his face than they should have been.

The boy slipped past the officers and disappeared into the confines of the ghetto. The officers stationed at the wall didn't even glance in the boy's direction. Perhaps they didn't care who wanted in. Their only concern was inspecting the permits of those trying to leave. Those who could be of use to the Germans. For now.

As she turned the corner, her body jolted at the sight of two burly German soldiers interrogating another young boy. The boy stood frozen, refusing to speak. Her heart sank like a rock into the depths of her chest as she recognised the face of the boy standing in front of her. It was Oskar.

One soldier grabbed his bag and rummaged through it, while the other kept his rifle trained on Oskar's head. Krista's instincts kicked in, her body moving to shield her student from harm. But her thoughts were in chaos – what if they searched her too? The envelope tucked against her body would only make things worse for Oskar. Despite her conflicted mind, she couldn't stand by and watch harm come to the boy.

She pushed herself between Oskar and the menacing weapon. 'Can I be of any assistance?' she asked in German.

The soldier with the gun glared at her. 'Who are you?' he spat.

'I'm this boy's teacher,' she said.

The soldier's eyes grew large, and Krista immediately realised her mistake. The other soldier stopped his search of Oskar's bag. The boy was small, but he could be of an age where he ought to be in secondary school. Only the Nazis had closed secondary schools down. After all, what need did the racially inferior Poles have for a higher education?

Krista pulled her identity documents out of her pocket and handed them over. 'I'm teaching him German. He's learning to be a messenger.'

The soldier tossed Oskar's bag into a puddle on the ground and took Krista's identity documents, inspecting them closely.

The other soldier smirked. 'Let's hear it then.'

Oskar looked up at Krista and she saw a brightness in his eyes where she had expected fear. 'Eins, zwei, drei...' One, two, three, he began, counting to ten.

The Germans laughed. 'So stupid.' The soldier pressed the butt of his rifle into Oskar's forehead. The boy straightened his shoulders and retained his balance.

'Let's go,' the other said, handing Krista back her documents. 'We're wasting time on nothing.' He seemed to be in charge and marched off without a second look at Oskar or Krista. The rifle-wielding soldier slung his weapon over his shoulder and marched off too. They clearly had somewhere else to be and had no time for questioning them further, which felt like a massive stroke of luck.

Krista watched the soldiers disappear into the distance;

her fists clenched at her sides. She turned to Oskar, feeling both relieved and worried at the same time.

'Are you alright?' she asked, her voice shaky.

Oskar nodded, though his face remained pale and tense.

They stood there for a moment, the weight of the encounter hanging heavily in the air. The envelope hidden against her body felt as if it were burning her flesh. She placed a hand on Oskar's shoulder, offering what little comfort she could.

'You were incredibly brave,' said Krista. 'And your German was excellent.'

Oskar smiled at that, and she was grateful to see a little colour return to his cheeks. She sent him home and continued through the streets of Warsaw, her senses on high alert. She couldn't shake off the encounter with the Germans. Why was there such an increased presence of German soldiers on the streets? And why did they let Oskar and Krista go so easily? These questions kept nagging at her as she quickened her pace towards her drop-off point. Something was surely brewing, and that was never good.

Her chest was still tight with tension as she arrived at the door in the alley. She readied the envelope, feeling the rough edges of the paper between her fingers, and knocked on the door three times. The door opened and a hand reached for the papers. As Krista was about to turn and leave, the door creaked open a little wider, inviting her inside. She hesitated, her mind at war with itself. A part of her wanted to run away, but another part was curious about what awaited her in the dimly lit room. Nerves tingled up her spine as she stepped over the threshold.

27

Once inside, Krista put her hands in her pockets to hide their trembling. She'd frequently wondered what was in the room behind the old bakery and now she was inside of it. An oven dominated the room, its large stone structure standing tall and imposing. Its interior was dark and empty now, but the walls were marked with deep burns and scorch marks, evidence of its past use. The surrounding walls were bare and grey, devoid of any decoration or signs of life. The lingering scent of wood smoke lingered in the air, mixed with the musty smell of abandonment.

The man who had taken receipt of the envelope stalked across the room and tossed it onto a large wooden table in the centre. He scraped a chair along the concrete floor and sat down. Two other men were already seated at the table, their eyes scrutinising her. She suddenly felt like a mouse being watched by a group of hungry cats.

'Krista Schulz,' said one of the men, his voice low and gravelly.

Hearing her name on his lips when she knew nothing of

him unnerved her. His hair was a messy mop of black, and his clothing was plain and unremarkable, yet there was an air of power around him.

He clasped his hands together and stretched them out in front of him, cracking his knuckles. 'You're German,' he said.

It wasn't a question or an invitation to explain. Something told her that this man already knew her story. His companions sat on either side of him, their cold eyes never leaving her.

Movement behind them caught Krista's eye and she looked up to see Emilia, with her unmistakable red hair, gliding through a doorway carrying a tray loaded with a coffee pot and a collection of mismatched mugs.

'Krista! Good, you made it,' said Emilia, setting the tray down on the table.

Emilia's presence caught her off guard. If she was already here, why did she ask Krista to deliver the envelope?

'I see you've met everyone,' said Emilia. 'So, you'll help us?'

Krista's gaze shifted between Emilia and the men. 'Help you with what?'

Emilia stepped away from the table and raised one eyebrow. 'A little retaliation of our own,' she said.

Krista bristled at the word *retaliation* and its connotations, but Emilia's tone was almost breezy as if she'd just offered Krista a drink in the cafe.

Everyone's eyes were on Krista and they didn't all feel friendly. She shook her head. 'I don't want to be responsible for more killing.'

The man who seemed to be in charge leaned forward and picked up the coffee pot. He poured steaming dark liquid into one of the mugs and set the pot down again.

'This isn't killing,' he said, taking a gulp of his drink. 'This is hitting them where it hurts – the railways. The Germans have been stealing our belongings for too long. Thanks to Emilia's eavesdropping, we've found out when the next train loaded with our possessions is leaving. We plan to stop it.'

Krista's mouth felt dry, and her stomach turned at the thought of being part of such a plan. Even the mention of it left a sour taste in her mouth. 'And then what?' Krista asked. 'How many people will the Gestapo murder in retaliation?'

Emilia's face fell, and Krista sensed the disappointment radiating from her. She had apparently expected a more enthusiastic response.

The man to her left scoffed, as if her response was the one he had expected. 'So, we should allow you Germans to take your haul of stolen goods to Berlin?'

'That's wrong,' said Krista, choosing to ignore the *you Germans* part of his question. 'But what good can come from returning a piano that no one would dare to play? I've seen them march people away to their deaths. One hundred people slaughtered for the beating of one German soldier. How many lives will be lost in this case until the Nazis feel that vengeance has been served?'

The man thumped his fist on the table. 'I told you it was a mistake to involve more Germans.'

Emilia let out an obviously exaggerated sigh. 'Do be quiet, Jan.'

A vein in Jan's neck bulged; from the admonition or the use of his name Krista couldn't tell.

The man in charge held out his hand as if trying to calm the brewing tension. 'You're right, Krista,' he said. 'There will be consequences. But this isn't about pianos and paint-ings and fur coats. The train is also carrying an arsenal of weapons. I don't think I need to tell you why that is valuable to us.'

Weapons. Just the word made her shudder. But she knew that the war could not be won without them. Krista touched a still-trembling hand to her churning stomach. This time, her gut reaction was clouded with uncertainty.

Emilia caught Krista's eye and waved her aside, away from the others who immediately entered into a heated discussion. As they stepped into the corner, Emilia spoke in a low tone.

'Krista, I know the thought of stopping a train and stealing weapons is daunting. But the Resistance need weapons and the only way we're going to get them now is to steal them.'

Krista reached up to her hair and pulled it to one side, exposing the back of her neck. Cool air from the room brushed up against her skin. 'It feels impossible. How can we do this without getting caught?'

Emilia shrugged, looking unconcerned. 'They've done it before. Let's leave the finer details to them. All you would have to do is watch for the train and signal when you see it. This isn't about violence. It's about ensuring our survival.'

Krista hesitated, torn between her fear of getting caught and her desire to help the Resistance. 'Will you be there too?' she asked.

Emilia's expression faltered for a moment before a shadow of guilt crossed her features. 'No. They prefer to keep me on the sidelines to avoid any suspicion falling on me or the cafe.'

Signal a train's arrival. Such a simple task, but what would be the consequences? The Nazis would retaliate against the Polish people with unimaginable horrors. Still,

Krista knew that fighting back was the only way to end this brutal war, and the Resistance needed weapons.

With a heavy heart, Krista straightened her stance and turned to face the men gathered around the table. 'Alright,' she said. 'I'll do it.'

28

KRISTA STOOD AT THE EDGE OF THE DARK FOREST, SHIVERING despite her thick coat and the collar turned up to shield her neck from the chill. Standing still, even a slight breeze felt like a blast of arctic air. She squeezed her hands around her flashlight, wishing she could turn it on for some warmth from the bulb, but it wasn't time yet.

There will be consequences. Zygmunt's words reverberated in Krista's head. As soon as she had agreed to help stop the train, introductions had been made. Whatever the consequences, Krista would have to live with them. The Resistance needed weapons. She wished there was another way, but no one was coming to Poland's aid. They were going to have to fight their way to freedom.

The haunting call of an owl sent chills down her spine. She thought about the track in the darkness beneath her, rigged with explosives, and someone waiting for her signal. The others, Jan and Kazim, were still unsure of her, but Zygmunt seemed to trust her quickly. Perhaps he'd had no choice. His team was small, and he needed them trackside to set the explosions and load the weapons into the waiting vehicle before the Nazis had time to react. All Krista had to do was listen for the train and watch for three bursts of lights from someone further down the track. When she saw it, she was to flash her light three times to signal the train's approach. She'd been warned to give her signal and leave the area as fast as possible after the first explosion rang out.

The rumbling of the oncoming train pierced the quiet of the night, growing louder and more intense with each passing second. She was on the wrong side of the bend in the tracks to see the train. She readied her torch and peered down the tracks and into the darkness, not daring to blink for fear of missing something. Her breathing deepened. One, two, three flashes of light. In response, she gave her own signal – one, two, three – and quickly gathered her things, strapping her bag across her body and scanning around as best she could so as to leave nothing behind.

As the train curved around the bend, blinding lights dazzled her eyes. The first explosion was so close that it shook the ground beneath her feet. In quick succession, more explosions followed until they all blended into a deafening crescendo. The night sky illuminated with a furious orange glow, surely visible for miles. It was an explosion like no other she had ever seen.

She should have been gone by now, but she was transfixed by the colours in front of her. War was so bleak. From bland food to her drab woollen coat and the assortment of brown nylon clothing that made up her second-hand wardrobe. It was all depressingly dull. But nothing about tonight had been dull. Any reservations she'd had were gone, replaced by a deep satisfaction for striking back at the Nazis. It was a small step towards ending this dreadful war.

Suddenly, German voices tore her gaze away from the inferno raging in front of her. They were getting closer.

Krista closed her eyes and tuned in to their direction. They were to her left. It was too late. Stealth was no longer an option. She turned right and ran as fast as she could.

She hadn't made it far when strong arms locked themselves around her upper body, anchoring her to the spot. She was spun around, coming face to face with the polished buttons on his uniform. His arms remained clamped around her body, and she lifted her gaze to meet his for the briefest of moments before he suddenly whipped his head around at rustling in the bushes behind him. Releasing her, he placed a heavy hand on her shoulder and shoved her hard to one side. She stumbled and fell. Her hands instinctively flew towards her head to protect it as her body hit the ground with a thud.

Her breath caught in her throat, and she held it in seeing two figures cloaked by the darkness of the forest. Mumbled words were closely followed by the crackle of gunfire somewhere in the distance and one of the figures took off.

Krista lay on the ground, her ragged breathing loud in her ears as she struggled to comprehend the events unfolding before her. Her gaze settled on a fallen tree branch nearby and she reached out and scooped it up. The German soldier loomed over her and her puny weapon, the flames from the explosions casting eerie shadows on his face. She dared not move, every muscle in her body tensed with anticipation, waiting for his next move. As he leaned closer, she felt his hot breath on her skin. Confusion clouded her mind as she tried to make sense of the familiarity in his eyes. Her eyes must have been deceiving her.

'Marcin?' she whispered, unable to hide her shock.

He nodded solemnly, a mixture of guilt and sadness in his expression. 'Krista, I can explain,' he started, his voice barely above a whisper. 'I never wanted this. The Germans forced me to join their army.'

Krista's mind swirled with emotions as she struggled to process Marcin's words.

'They said my grandmother was German,' Marcin continued, his voice tinged with bitterness. 'That was enough for them to come after me. They are desperate for men, and they threatened Olesia and my mother. I had no choice.'

Tears welled up in Krista's eyes and she reached out a hand towards him. He was no longer the skinny boy she remembered. He was still thin, but his shoulders had broadened, and his jaw held a hint of stubble. She laid her hand on his chest. Seeing him in that uniform shattered her heart.

The distant sound of gunfire brought her back to reality, reminding her of the danger surrounding them.

'I understand if you hate me,' said Marcin, his voice heavy with emotion. 'My loyalty lies with Poland. You must know that.'

He reached into his coat and Krista braced herself. For what, she didn't know. Despite the uniform, he was still Marcin. Her friend's brother. Her friend.

Marcin knelt beside her and handed her a crumpled stack of papers that had been tucked inside his coat. Her hand trembled as she took them, unfolding them slowly with one hand, her other hand still gripped around the tree branch. Her heart sank as she scanned through the familiar faces, Zygmunt, Jan, Kazim, plus a few she didn't recognise. Their images were accompanied by names, descriptions, and other details known to the Gestapo. She flicked through them again. Her image was not there. No Emilia, either.

'They don't know about you,' Marcin said in a gentle voice.

He stood up and extended a hand towards her, offering to help her up from the ground.

Krista hesitated for a moment then, without a word, took his hand and allowed him to pull her to her feet. She looked up at him, searching his face for any hint of what his intentions might be. He stared back, revealing his inner turmoil. His shoulders were slumped and his whole body exuded a sense of shame.

She wanted to tell him that it was OK, that she understood. But how could she say that? The brutality she had witnessed since the war began had been at the hands of men wearing that same uniform. But then she thought of Olesia. Her cheerful features, the innocent spring in her step when she walked.

'Olesia?' she asked. Her voice came out shaky and unsure, but she held Marcin's gaze.

'She's OK.' Marcin looked around. 'We need to get out of here.'

Krista heard a rustling behind her and she turned to see Jan emerging from the trees over her shoulder. He inched towards her aiming a pistol at Marcin. She caught a glimpse of Jan's hand, red and blistered with patches of scorched skin.

'Wait,' said Krista. She put her hand on the barrel of Jan's gun and forced it down. 'I'll do it.'

She approached Marcin and whispered, 'Cafe Róża.' Clearing her throat, she spoke louder, 'Turn around.'

Marcin obeyed, turning away from her. Krista steadied herself. Her fingers were still gripped tightly around the tree branch as if it were a tennis racket. She inhaled deeply and swung it at him with all her might. It collided with the side of his head, and he fell to his knees with a pained groan. She hoped it was hard enough for Jan to be convinced that she meant it, but not so hard as to cause Marcin more than a headache.

Jan aimed his gun once more, this time at the back of Marcin's head. But a loud snap of branches nearby caused them both to jump. Jan spun around, pointing his weapon in the direction of the noise.

'Let's get out of here,' he whispered.

Krista tossed the branch aside and they ran off, fleeing as fast as they could.

29

———

THE FOLLOWING MORNING, KRISTA MADE HER WAY TO THE room in the back of the bakery and knocked three times on the door. She had been tempted to go straight to Cafe Róża, hoping that Marcin had heard her murmurs and would show up there. She longed to see him again. However, they had agreed to meet at the bakery at dawn and she couldn't miss it, especially after what had happened the night before.

Zygmunt opened the door and Krista slipped into the dimly lit room. Jan and two others were already there. She hadn't met the others, but she recognised them from the images she had tucked in her pocket.

'Wazim?' Krista asked as soon as she entered.

Zygmunt shook his head. Jan clenched his fist as if to punch something, but then winced in pain. He tucked his hand behind his back, hiding his raw flesh. It wasn't clear if Wazim had been arrested, or if he was injured, or dead. She decided that she would rather not know.

'They were there too soon after the explosions,' one of the men said, as if continuing the conversation they had been having before Krista arrived.

Zygmunt ran a hand across his stubbled jaw. 'We think someone tipped the Wehrmacht off.'

Krista nodded. She pulled the papers containing their images from inside her coat and handed them over to Zygmunt. 'They knew who they were looking for.'

Zygmunt's face twisted in anger as he let out a string of curses, his foot connecting with one of the chairs and sending it skidding across the concrete floor. 'How did you get these?' He tossed the papers into the middle of the table.

Jan snatched them up, flipping through them with a look of intense concentration. His eyebrows furrowed together as he studied the images. 'The only photos they don't have are you and Emilia,' he noted, his tone sharp and accusatory. 'That can't be a coincidence.'

The other men in the room exchanged wary glances.

Krista felt her cheeks colour and feared it would make her seem guilty of something. 'One of the Germans gave them to me.'

Zygmunt slowly bent down to pick up the chair, lifting it off the ground with ease. 'Why would he do that?' His jaw was clenched as if trying to contain his rage.

'You knew him, didn't you?' spat Jan. 'Is that why you stopped me putting a bullet in him?'

Zymund and the others stared at her, waiting for her answer.

She rubbed her thumb over a splinter lodged in the pad of her middle finger, a reminder of the branch she had swung at Marcin. She hadn't intended to hit him so hard, but it had been the only way to prevent Jan from shooting him dead. 'He let me go. I thought I should do the same for him.'

Jan gave a sharp laugh, like a burst of air escaping through his clenched teeth. She knew how that must have sounded to his ears, but even in the sobering reality of daylight, she still believed that she had made the right decision. Marcin was more than his uniform. Whatever he had done, she could not have stood back and allowed Jan to shoot him.

'Or maybe you gave him information,' said Jan. 'Traded your life for our secrets. Is that how it played out?'

Krista took a breath before answering. 'There's nothing I can say that will make you trust me. But it doesn't matter. What matters is that the Germans know about all of you so what happens now?'

'It does matter,' said Jan, not backing down. He stepped towards her and shook the papers in her face. 'Why isn't your photograph in here?'

'I don't know,' said Krista. She held her ground, forcing herself not to shrink away from him. 'Maybe because all I've done so far is serve food and teach children. Can you say the same?'

Zygmunt took the papers from Jan and sat down. 'She's right. It's no surprise that we're on their radar. But if someone tipped them off, why didn't they get there before the explosion? Why not stop the train?'

One of the other men shrugged then said, 'Perhaps they didn't trust the intelligence. Or maybe they didn't know exactly where we would be, so they sent patrols all along the line.'

'That makes sense,' said Zygmunt. 'They weren't heavily manned. That's the only reason why we're all still here.'

'Not all of us,' said Jan.

Zygmunt looked up at him. 'No. Not all of us.'

A heavy silence settled over the room, broken by the sound of footsteps approaching from outside. The group exchanged uneasy glances. Suddenly, the thick wooden door burst open with a loud thud as someone kicked it in. Blinding sunlight flooded the room, quickly followed by the sound of heavy boots as the Gestapo stormed in with weapons at the ready, shouting orders and demanding their hands be raised. Krista threw her arms in the air and followed the others as they were herded out of the building and onto the street.

Fear pulsed through Krista's body. Her ears burned at the sound of imaginary gunfire, and she desperately wanted to cover her ears, but she dared not move her hands. They turned the corner and emerged out of the alleyway to find a truck waiting for them. She stepped up into the truck. She ought to feel relieved that she wasn't about to be gunned down in the street, but the heat intensified under her skin as she braced herself for how much worse this could still get.

They travelled in silence. Not that there was any other choice with two Gestapo men sitting with them. Krista kept her eyes focused on the floor of the truck knowing that at least Jan's eyes were trained on her. He thought her a traitor. He probably even suspected that she'd revealed the address of their safe house and set herself up to be arrested with them.

The driver of the truck slammed on the brakes and the group thudded into one another as they each fell forward. A hand gripped Krista's wrist and hauled her out of the vehicle. A sea of grey-green uniforms swarmed around her, and she couldn't see anything beyond them. The uniforms dragged her into a building. She stumbled along a narrow corridor and was shoved into a room barely bigger than a cupboard. Early morning sunlight streamed through the bars on the tiny window, providing some warmth in the otherwise cold and cramped space.

'Sit!' a savage voice called out from behind her.

She squeezed her way through the gap between the table and the wall and sat on a wooden chair. The uniform closed the door behind him and left her alone in the room. She hadn't heard the door lock. As footsteps faded in the hallway, she contemplated opening it to see if there was a way out. The truck hadn't travelled far so she was confident she could get her bearings if she could sneak a peek outside. Voices on the other side of the door – German – made her quickly reconsider that plan.

The door reopened and an officer marched in with eyes so dark they were almost black, and a scowl that told her not to mess with him. He pulled a chair away from the table and sat down.

'Your name,' he demanded, in confident Polish.

'Krista Schulz.' Her only defence was to stick as close to the truth as possible.

The man retrieved a small, black notebook and pen from his uniform pocket and scribbled something down. 'You're Polish?' he asked.

'German, actually,' she said. His hand halted for just a beat before he continued writing.

'What are you doing in Poland?' This time he asked his question in German. A test, she figured.

Answering in fluent German, she explained her story, leaving out the fact that the Nazis had slaughtered her grandparents. The man put his pen down as she spoke, taking no further notes. She wasn't sure if that was a good sign or not.

Seemingly satisfied with her history, he probed into her connection with the others who had been arrested. They didn't have her photograph, and she had to trust that Marcin hadn't mentioned her. The only thing connecting her to the others was the location of her arrest.

Krista took a breath before answering. 'I don't know them. I was going to work and one of them, the tall one,' she added, knowing that they were all tall, 'ran out into the street looking for a doctor. I'm not a doctor, but I am trained in first aid and I asked if I could help.'

The man raised a bushy eyebrow. 'What exactly did you do to help?'

'I followed him to his house. There was a man inside who had a badly burned hand. I barely had a chance to examine his wounds before the Gestapo burst in.'

He put his elbows on the table and crossed his hands in front of his face. 'Did you know they were bandits?'

'I'm not sure what you mean,' said Krista, trying to keep her voice light and innocent.

'You knew they were Resistance?' He spat the words with venom, his voice dripping with disgust.

Krista's heart beat a little faster. 'Well, I didn't at first. But once I arrived at the house, I suspected the man's injury wasn't caused by an accident.'

'Yet you treated him anyway, yes?'

Krista shook her head. 'I didn't get a chance to.'

His eyes roamed over Krista features, searching for signs of deception. 'How long have you worked with the Resistance?' he asked, his voice laced with suspicion.

Krista stood her ground, holding out her hands in a gesture of innocence. 'I'm just a girl who offered to help an injured man. That's all.'

The man let out a scoffing laugh and pushed back his chair back, rising to his feet. 'I know you're lying,' he said bluntly. 'But you're also of no use to me. A silly young girl like you will know nothing.' He turned to leave, reached for the door handle and paused. His head twisted around, and his gaze roamed across her face once more. 'Where do you work?' he asked.

'Cafe Emilia,' she said. Krista felt bile rise in her throat as he left the room. It was the first place she thought of, and her mind was now too full of fear to think through the consequences.

30

KRISTA ROLLED HER SHOULDERS BACK AND FORTH TRYING TO ease out some of the knots that had built up. She was facing her second night sleeping on the cold, hard floor of a cramped cell. Around her were a dozen other women who had been arrested for offences including purchasing black market meat and possessing a single copy of a Resistance newspaper. One woman's only crime had been daring to say no to a Nazi who had told her to hand over her engagement ring. The woman had been arrested and the ring yanked from her finger anyway. And now she faced an uncertain future at the mercy of the occupiers. When the others had asked Krista why she was there, she had lied, sticking to her story about doing nothing more than offering help to an injured man.

The clanging of metal echoed through the narrow corridor as a guard marched towards their cell. He unlocked the door and ordered everyone out. They were forced to march on foot to the railway station, their tired feet pounding against the hard ground. Krista heard murmurs of fear from the other women about their suspected destination.

Unshed tears filled Krista's eyes as she saw the waiting cattle cars, their heavy doors looming like ominous gates to hell. Something sharp jabbed her in the back. She flinched and turned around, coming face to face with Hauptmann Schneider, a man she hadn't seen since she'd spilt coffee down his pristine uniform during her first morning at Emilia's cafe.

His cold blue eyes bore into hers, sending shivers down her spine. She could see a ripple of satisfaction in his expression as he looked upon her plight. But Krista refused to let him break her spirit. She straightened her back and met his gaze with defiance.

He laughed. 'The only German among this filth. Perhaps you'll get a job as a guard in the camp, you traitor.' He laughed again and prodded her in the stomach with the butt of his rifle, pushing her towards the train.

Her heart pounded wildly in her chest as she stepped into the cattle car, her eyes scanning the faces of the men already inside. Jan and Zygmunt stood together, their expressions grim. The men had been treated differently, that much was clear. Fresh cuts and bruises marred their flesh, bearing witness to the brutality they had endured at the hands of their captors. Krista's heart ached for them.

The air inside the cattle car was stale, a mixture of fear and resignation clinging to the walls. The passengers shifted uneasily, eyes darting around the confined space as they braced themselves for what was to come. Krista found an empty corner and pressed herself against it, trying to make herself as small as possible amidst the sea of bodies.

'Schultz!'

She straightened up. Had someone just called her name?

'Schultz!'

She heard it again and inched her way to the front of the car.

'There she is,' said Hauptmann Schneider, pointing in her direction.

'You are Kristian Schulz?' a man asked, his voice stern and commanding.

For a second she thought he had said Kristian, but she knew it was her sleep-deprived brain playing tricks on her. 'Yes,' she confirmed.

The man wore a dark suit rather than a uniform but exuded enough power and control that even Hauptmann Schneider stood a little straighter in his presence.

'What do you want with her?' asked Hauptmann Schneider. 'She's nothing. Just a girl who can't keep coffee in a pot.'

'You're probably right, Hauptmann. But I'll have a word anyway. Follow me.'

As Krista jumped down from the train, she glanced over her shoulder and saw the hard lines of suspicion etched on the faces of the others. Jan's accusing glare burned through her. She had no idea who this man was or why he was taking her off the train, but it was clear that he had planted seeds of doubt in even Zygmunt's mind.

The man ushered her into a small office just inside the train station. He took a seat behind the desk and motioned for her to sit opposite him. The desk was cluttered with piles of paperwork. He looked unimpressed. He pushed them aside with his elbow to create space to rest his forearms.

Leaning forward, he said, 'Kristian Schulz.'

'Krista Schulz,' she corrected.

A small smile tugged at his lips and he nodded. 'I was certain he would have changed your name.'

A chill coursed through Krista's body. Who was this man and how did he know who she was?

The man leaned back in his chair, resting his fingertips on the edge of the desk. His gaze grew distant, as if recalling memories long buried. 'I knew Kristian Schulz. Your grand-father, correct?'

Krista nodded.

'He's still alive?'

She shook her head, swallowing hard.

The lines on the man's forehead deepened, and his eyes clouded with a sadness that seemed genuine, though laced with an understanding that suggested he was not at all surprised.

'What about Ilse?'

Krista's heart clenched at the mention of her grand-mother's name. Just hearing it spoken out loud after so long brought tears to her eyes. She lowered her gaze, biting her lip, and shook her head. 'Who are you?' she asked, her voice trembling.

The man hesitated, as if weighing his next words care-fully. Finally, he looked her in the eye, his expression soften-ing. 'My name is Konrad Klein. I worked with Kristian many years ago in Berlin. We were friends.' He paused, studying her face as if searching for traces of the past. 'When did you come to Poland?'

Krista shifted uncomfortably in her seat, her thoughts swirling. She didn't see the point of lying. She'd survived this long by sticking to the truth, mostly. Besides, she suspected Konrad Klein already knew much about her. 'When I was ten years old.'

Klein nodded, as if he had already known the answer before she spoke.

'Why are you here?' Krista asked.

'Because of you. I saw your name on a list. Well, I saw the name Kristian Schulz on a list and hoped it was my old friend. It appears it was a spelling error. You are accused of providing aid to someone in the Polish Resistance.'

It was the first confirmation she'd received that the Gestapo had believed her story. Had Hauptmann Schneider seen her and confirmed she worked at Cafe Emilia, unwittingly supporting her version of events?

'When did Kristian die?'

Krista straightened up in her chair and stared at him. 'When the Wehrmacht marched into our village, pulled him and my grandmother out of their home, and shot them in the back of the head?'

Klein winced. His eyes, which had been stoic and unflinching, showed signs of sorrow. His hands trembled ever so slightly, betraying a turmoil within him. After everything he must have seen in this war, and perhaps the horrors he may have committed himself, it was clear that he was deeply affected by the thought of her grandparents' execution.

He rubbed the back of his neck with his hand. 'Krista, I'm truly sorry to hear that.'

If he was telling the truth, Konrad Klein was the only person Krista had ever met who knew her grandparents when they lived in Germany. 'Why did you say that you were certain he would have changed my name?' she asked.

'It's so similar to his own name. Kristian knew the danger. Did he really believe Poland took him away from that?' Klein looked to the ceiling as though he were thinking through the answer to his own question.

'Why was he in danger?' Krista asked.

He crossed his arms loosely over his chest and leaned in. 'You really don't know?'

Gertz, the lawyer, had believed it was because her grandfather was Jewish, but that wasn't information she was going to volunteer. She shook her head.

Klein glanced behind her towards the door, as if making sure it was still closed. He leaned further across the desk, his voice low. 'Krista, your grandfather was a Nazi.'

31

KRISTA'S WHOLE BODY STIFFENED, HER MUSCLES COILING LIKE a tightly wound spring ready to snap. She squirmed in her seat, the weight of Klein's accusation pressing down on her. 'No, it can't be true. My grandfather could never have been a Nazi.'

She shook her head frantically, refusing to believe the unthinkable. Her grandfather was a kind and gentle man who had fled Germany to stop his granddaughter from being indoctrinated into the Nazi ideology. She shook her head again, but deep down, a dark sense of doubt began to creep in, filling her with an icy fear.

The lines etched into Klein's aged face seemed to deepen as he spoke. 'Kristian really said nothing of his life in Germany?'

'He rarely spoke about his past,' Krista said. 'He told me he was the wrong kind of German.'

'Yes, he was,' said Klein, his tone solemn.

'You must be mistaken,' said Krista. There was a hint of desperation underlying her words, as if she was trying to convince herself that the man in front of her was wrong.

'My grandfather would never have supported such atrocities.'

'I know it's hard to reconcile the man you knew with the party you have experienced during this war, but many members of the Nazi party did not want war. It wasn't always like this.'

'What was it like?' asked Krista.

Klein's gaze seemed to drift off, lost in memories of a different time. 'When the Nazi party seized power in 1933, Kristian and I were both civil servants. Back then, anyone working for the government had to swear loyalty to Hitler. Party membership wasn't explicitly mandated, but those who did not join were viewed with suspicion and often ostracised. We both chose to join the party.'

Krista felt her world tilt on its axis. The idea of her grandfather being associated with the Nazis felt like a betrayal of everything she knew about her family.

Klein sighed heavily; his gaze distant as if lost in memories of the past. 'I thought it was just a necessary evil to stay employed in a time with mass unemployment, but Kristian thought differently. He was right. In the months that followed, we watched the party destroy all political opponents and abolish labour unions. Then they went after the arts and pressured young people to join the Hitler Youth movements. Kristian couldn't do it anymore. He feared he would lose himself to the darkness if he stayed. He left the party and, consequently, his job, a position senior enough that his departure was noticed.'

The story echoed the brief account her grandparents had given her. They made it clear that they did not want Krista to join the League of German Girls. The Hitler Youth organisations had one goal: to raise young people who were loyal to the Nazi party. So Kristian had left his job and then been handed the responsibility of raising his granddaughter. And rather than see her indoctrinated into the Nazi party, he had reinvented himself as a quiet country farmer. It was all conjecture. With her grandparents dead, she would never know for sure.

She looked at Klein. This man before her may be the only chance she would ever have to find out more. 'So they murdered him because he left the party?' she asked.

'No. He didn't just leave the party. He stood up against it and became a vocal critic. The Gestapo had a policy to aggressively pursue and silence dissenting voices. Shortly after Kristian's betrayal, as they saw it, Kristian's son and his wife were killed.'

Krista's pulse raced; the throbbing sensation palpable in her fingertips. 'Killed?' The word appeared to have a different meaning from simply "*died*".

His head bobbed in a small nod, as if acknowledging a painful memory. 'I'm sorry. This was your parents.'

'Are you suggesting that my parents were murdered?'

Klein shrugged. It seemed such a small action to accompany such a big accusation. 'I don't know,' he said. 'All I know is that Kristian did not believe it was an accident. He disappeared without another word. I always wondered what happened to him.'

'He came to Poland and became a farmer,' said Krista.

Klein smiled. 'I'm glad. It was the best way to protect you and Ilse. For a time, at least.'

Krista sat in stunned silence, struggling to grapple with the story unravelling before her. Her grandfather had been entangled in a web of political turmoil and moral conflict. That he had once been part of a regime now responsible for unspeakable atrocities was a bitter pill to swallow. She had asked her grandparents about their past so many times. If

Klein was telling the truth, the past was far more complex and painful than she had ever anticipated. Her vision clouded with tears.

Klein placed a hand gently in the middle of the table. 'I knew your grandfather for many years, and I believe the guilt of what has transpired would have haunted him until the end. But, Krista, he was a good man. A good friend. And brave. He tried to do the right thing. I could not.'

Krista dabbed at the corners of her eyes with her fingertips and pushed her shoulders back. She would not cry here. 'What happens to me now?' she asked.

'You'll be transported to a prisoner of war camp,' Klein said, louder now.

'Back on the train?'

With a sharp scrape against the wooden floor, he pushed his chair back and rose to his feet, beckoning for her to do the same. The door creaked open as soon as he stood, revealing a stern-faced soldier on the other side who seemed to have been awaiting movement. She eyed him warily, wondering what he had heard. A moment later, Hauptmann Schneider appeared, strutting into view with confidence and authority.

Klein let out a derisive snort and nodded towards Krista. 'You were right, Hauptmann. Completely useless.'

Hauptmann Schneider's expression twisted into a snarl, his lips curling back to reveal crooked teeth. He straightened his shoulders and puffed out his chest, as if taking credit for a job well done, too arrogant to see that she might be someone other than the girl who served him coffee.

The soldier by the door produced a set of metal cuffs from his uniform pocket and stepped towards Krista.

Klein waved him away. 'Please. Look at her. I think I can handle her.'

The soldier looked uncertain. Klein grinned and slapped the man on the back. The man looked Krista up and down, laughed, and tucked his cuffs back into his pocket.

'Follow me, girl,' said Klein. His tone noticeably gruffer than it had been when they were alone.

Krista followed Klein from the room. Her skin crawled as all eyes were on her. The prisoners had all gone, but the station was still teeming with soldiers and guards, and they all watched her every move. As they left the station, Konrad signalled for her to get into his car – a boxy, old model that had seen better days. The paint was chipping, the windows were tinted, and the interior was worn. It seemed a strange choice of car for someone who appeared to be so senior that he had been allowed to remove a prisoner from an already packed train.

Krista squeezed into the cramped backseat, folding herself into the corner. The upholstery was stained and smelled stale, like the dust and grime from years of use. The engine rumbled to life, and she felt the vibrations of the car shake her to her core.

As Klein drove away from the station, Krista tilted her head back and looked up at the sky. Daylight had faded into a deep indigo. Twinkling stars peered down at her making her feel small and unimportant. Klein's voice broke through her thoughts.

'Where can I take you?' he asked.

Krista blinked, momentarily confused. 'Excuse me?'

'Right now. Where can I take you?'

Krista leaned forward in her seat, studying the side of his face. 'I thought you were taking me to a prisoner of war camp.'

His eyes were focused on the road ahead. 'No, I'm not. You can come with me to Germany.'

He took a sharp right turn and Krista reached her hand out to grasp the door handle for stability. She recoiled at his suggestion of accompanying him to Germany. After everything that had happened and what she'd heard from Klein himself, she had no desire to ever step foot in Germany again.

'No, I can't go there,' she said. 'I won't go there. Just stop here. I can walk.'

Klein shook his head. Krista feared she had misunderstood, and he wasn't actually planning to let her go. She feared Germany hadn't been a suggestion after all. 'You can't be on the streets in the dark. A patrol will spot you and you'll end up right back in Schneider's clutches. If you won't come with me to Germany, I'm taking you to wherever it is that you call home.' He must have seen her hesitation and added, 'You'll just have to trust me not to tell anyone else where that is.'

'Turn left at the end of this road,' said Krista. She contemplated giving him random directions and jumping out in front of any old building, but she got the sense that Klein was particular. Despite the condition of his vehicle, he seemed the type to wait until she had physically opened her door before he drove away. And he appeared to be setting her free instead of transporting her to a prison camp. She had no choice but to trust him. She gave him accurate directions and took a deep breath as he came to a stop outside of her building.

Klein's head swivelled towards her with a slight jerk, his eyes catching hers. 'You'll be alright from here? It's probably better if your neighbours don't see who is dropping you off.'

'Yes,' Krista agreed.

'It was good to see you,' he said. 'I'm sorry about the circumstances.'

The sadness returned to his eyes as he sat across from her, baring his vulnerability. It made her heart ache for both him and her grandfather. She wanted to say something to comfort him, but what was there to say?

Krista swung open the car door.

'You look like your mother,' said Klein. 'I expect you've been told that many times before.'

'I haven't, actually,' said Krista. No one in her life, besides her grandparents, had known her mother. She had so many questions for this stranger in front of her, but she knew now wasn't the time. But she had to know one thing. 'Have we met before?'

A small smile played on Klein's lips. 'A very long time ago. Now, keep your head down. And stay away from Schneider,' he added. 'You cannot be his waitress any longer. Perhaps we'll meet again once all of this is over.'

Krista climbed out onto the pavement. She put her hand on the top of the car and leaned her head back in. 'Thank you.'

Klein smiled at her again and she shut the door. He waited in the car until she had unlocked the door to her apartment. She closed her door with practised silence then heard the low rumble of his engine as he drove off. It had been hard to hear what Klein had said, but something about him made her want to trust him. He had seemed genuine, and he had kept his word. She was free again, or as free as anyone could be living under occupation. As she undressed and crawled into bed, she thought about the countless injustices she had witnessed throughout the war and the times when she had turned a blind eye. Everyone was just trying to survive. She couldn't judge her grandfather or Marcin for the impossible choices they'd had to make.

32

THE NEXT MORNING, KRISTA STEPPED OUT INTO THE SOFT patter of raindrops, hoping the drizzle would create a blurry veil between herself and the world around her. She headed to the canteen, lingering in the street for only a few minutes before Nelka arrived. Nelka's eyes widened at the sight of Krista and they both hurried inside the building. As Nelka bolted the door shut behind them, the sound of rain on the roof intensified.

They sat down at one of the lunch tables and Krista blurted out the entire story. She told Nelka about the train, her arrest, Hauptmann Schneider, and KIein's role in setting her free. She left out any mention of Marcin. Finally, she finished her tale and fell silent, her breath coming in ragged gasps. She searched Nelka's face for any hint of disbelief or scepticism.

Nelka leaned across the table, her hand gently covering Krista's. 'I don't know what to say. I'm so sorry you had to go through that.'

Tears sprung to Krista's eyes. 'I can't go back to Emilia's.

If Hauptmann Schneider spots me there then suspicion will fall on the cafe.'

Nelka's eyes were slightly downcast, avoiding Krista's gaze. She bit her lip. 'I don't think you should work here anymore either.'

'But why?' asked Krista, her voice rising slightly in pitch. The thought of Nelka believing that Krista had betrayed them made her heart ache. 'I'm telling the truth. I never gave any information to the Germans, whatever the others think.'

'I know that,' said Nelka, squeezing Krista's hand. 'What we have here is all that some of these children have. The Gestapo have come sniffing around before. They've never found anything questionable here, so they mostly leave us alone. But I can't take the chance that they come back and one of them recognises you.'

Krista's jaw ached as she tried to suppress her emotions. She knew that Nelka was right, but it was still devastating. Working with the children had been the one good thing she'd had recently. The thought of losing that was like losing a piece of herself. But she had no choice. The children's safety had to come first.

'There are other ways you can help,' Nelka said softly. 'You have a kind heart and a quick mind. There are many ways you can make a difference without putting yourself or others at more risk.'

Krista leaned in. 'Do you have any suggestions?' she asked, her voice tinged with hope.

Nelka's eyes scanned the ceiling, deep in thought. A small smile spread across her face as an idea seemed to form in her mind. She turned to Krista, a glimmer of satisfaction in her expression. 'I do, actually. You have first aid skills, right?'

'Basic ones,' said Krista.

'You can be a first-aider. There are lots of girls moving around the city, assisting those who can't go to the hospital for whatever reason. I know a doctor who's co-ordinating this effort discreetly. I'll talk to him and see if he can use your help. For now, you should go home and keep a low profile.'

Krista's gaze swept over the canteen, taking in the empty tables and chairs where the children gathered to share meals, tell stories, and find moments of joy that, for a couple of hours each day, made life feel normal again. A lump formed in her throat at the thought of not saying a proper goodbye.

She turned to Nelka, grateful of her friend's guidance and unwavering support. 'Thank you.'

As Krista left the canteen for the final time, the grip of sadness was almost physical, as if someone had their hand tightened around her heart. Outside, the rain had stopped, and the damp air it left behind wrapped itself around her like a cloak of uncertainty. She could be a first-aider, but would the doctor trust her enough to let her help? Nelka believed her, but she knew how improbable her story must have sounded to anyone else. There was only one place Krista wanted to be now, and it didn't involve going home and keeping a low profile.

Cafe Róża was a quaint little establishment tucked away at the foot of a narrow cobbled lane. It had been three days since she'd whispered its name to Marcin. She had first stumbled across it with Larysa during her tour of the city and she hoped it was still a place that few Nazis ever stumbled upon. As she approached the cafe, her heart fluttered with anticipation. She knew he wouldn't be there, but it brought her some comfort to think that he might have come. That he might have wanted to see her again. Even just the thought of him being in Warsaw and that their paths might cross once more made her feel less alone.

She pushed open the door and was greeted by the slightly woody scent of chicory coffee and the murmured conversation of those who drank it. She made her way to a table in the corner, a cosy nook with a view of the door, and settled into a chair. It was a small and intimate space, decorated with warm tones and mismatched wooden tables and chairs. A large painting of a rose garden hung on one wall, its canvas dusty and dull.

A woman with waves of silver hair approached her table. Her smile was warm and inviting, and the scent of jasmine followed her every step. 'Waiting for someone?'

Krista shrugged. 'Probably not.'

The woman smiled, her blue eyes sparkling with a playful glint. 'You never know. Coffee?'

'Yes, please.'

The woman stepped away, returning a minute later with a mug of steaming hot coffee. Krista sipped it down, wincing at its bitterness. She barely remembered what a real coffee tasted like. Her grandfather had been the coffee drinker in their house and Krista had swiped the occasional sip growing up. Her grandmother had scolded her every time.

'Don't rush to grow up,' she would say to her.

Nothing forces a person to grow up faster than a war.

As Krista reached the bottom of her cup, she sighed softly. Despite knowing that Marcin was unlikely to be there, she still felt a twinge of disappointment. She signalled to the woman for one more coffee. If Marcin hadn't shown up by the time she finished her second cup, she would give up. For today, at least. She wasn't yet ready to give up completely. He must surely be as eager to see her again as she was to see him. There was so much to talk about.

Krista leaned back in her chair, gazing out of the window at the passersby. The cafe bustled around her. The clinking of crockery and snippets of conversations blending into a comforting hum. She closed her eyes, pretending for a moment that life was normal.

'Still waiting?'

Krista opened her eyes to see the woman standing over her with a fresh coffee in her hand. 'I'm Róża,' she said. 'I don't think I introduced myself earlier.'

'I'm Krista.'

Róża's face lit up with a radiant smile, her eyes crinkling at the corners. Her hands are steady as she sets the cup down, her movements graceful and precise. She leaned in closer, as if sharing a secret. 'Don't go too soon. Sometimes the people we're waiting for are just around the corner.'

Krista's heart fluttered at the possibility.

She was halfway through her second cup of coffee when Róża caught her eye and nodded towards the door. Krista turned her head, curious to see what had caught Róża's attention.

Through the cafe's window, she caught a fleeting glimpse of a man with his head down and collar turned up against the cold wind. He hesitated for a moment outside before pushing open the creaking door and slipping inside. Róża moved towards him eagerly, her silver hair catching the light as she glided across the room.

Krista's heart leapt as she watched the scene unfold before her. She felt a surge of hope rising within her, daring to believe that maybe, just maybe, it would be Marcin. The man turned to face her table, his eyes searching until they locked onto Krista's.

For a moment, time seemed to stand still. Krista felt her breath catch in her throat as she held his gaze, every fibre of her being willing it to be true. And then, Marcin began to make his way towards her table with slow deliberate steps, each one feeling like a thundering heartbeat in her chest.

33

As Marcin drew closer, Krista could see the lines of worry etched into his face and the broken and bruised skin from where she had struck him with the tree branch. He stopped at her table, shifting from one foot the other. A flood of emotions washed over her. She stood up slowly, her body trembling. Marcin's gaze was intense, as if trying to convey a thousand words without speaking a single one. She threw her arms around him in a tight embrace, tears welling up in her eyes.

Marcin's arms wrapped around her, holding her close, his strong presence grounding her in reality. They stood there for what felt like an eternity, lost in the simple comfort of each other's embrace. Finally pulling back slightly, Krista searched his face, taking in every detail.

'Marcin,' she whispered, the name carrying so much weight – memories of Olesia, and of their childhood together, of shared laughter and dreams now shattered. Marcin's eyes glistened as he spoke, his voice hoarse with emotion.

'Krista...' He began, but the words seemed to catch in his throat.

Róża appeared behind Marcin, nudging them apart. 'Perhaps you two will be more comfortable in the back room.'

'Yes, sorry, Róża,' said Marcin. He wrapped his arms around Róża and embraced her. 'Thank you.'

'I'm just glad it all worked out.' Róża turned to Krista. 'For both of you.'

'Who are you?' Krista asked her.

Róża smiled. 'Just a hopeless old romantic.'

The tips of Marcin's cheeks flushed, and he reached for Krista's hand. He guided her to the rear of the cafe and into another room, striding confidently as if he knew the layout by heart. They entered a cosy sitting room tucked away behind the cafe. The curtains were drawn, casting a warm glow over the floral wallpaper.

Marcin removed his coat and hung it over a nearby chair. Krista was relieved to see that he wasn't wearing a German uniform.

'You know Róża?' Krista asked.

Marcin smiled. 'As of three days ago. I came here looking for you. I assumed you must have known Róża, but she said she hadn't heard of you. She was kind to me, and I found I couldn't contain myself. I blurted out my entire story to her and I've come here every day since that night in the forest hoping to see you.'

Krista took a seat at one end of the sofa. Marcin sat at the other end.

'I still can't believe that you're here.' Krista gestured to the side of his face. 'And I'm sorry about that.'

Marcin laughed. 'You've got quite the swing on you.' His

playful grin faded, and his eyes narrowed. 'It wasn't a coincidence that I was in the forest that night.'

Krista felt her blood run cold as she waited for his confession that he was the one who had led the Germans to them.

'I told you that the Germans arrived and told me I had been conscripted. My grandmother being born in Germany was apparently enough for me to be declared a citizen of the Reich. I refused to go, of course, but then they grabbed Olesia by the hair and put a pistol to her head.'

Krista gave a sharp intake of breath and tears sprung to her eyes as she thought of her sweet, cheerful friend being put in that dreadful situation.

'She's OK,' Marcin added. 'I had to go with them. Any other choice would have been unbearable for me to live with. For a while, I kept my head down. I did what I was asked to do. But then I began working with the Resistance. Passing them information mostly. That doesn't make up for my betrayal, but I had to keep my family alive.'

Krista nodded. 'I understand.' And she did. She had no doubt that the Nazis would have put a bullet in Olesia's head if Marcin had refused to go. She had witnessed them do exactly that to her grandparents.

'I was posted to Warsaw six months ago and I've been doing the same here.' He ran a hand through his hair, the strain of the past few days etched in his features. 'Passing information to the Resistance. By the time I found out that the Nazis knew of the plan to stop the train, I was too late to warn Zygmunt.' His voice tightened with regret. 'But I knew that you would be in that forest, and I had to try to try to help you. As it turned out, you were the one who helped me.'

Krista's eyes widened, her hand gripping the edge of the sofa beneath her legs. 'You know Zygmunt?'

'Yes. He had heard that a trainload of weapons was being sent to Berlin. I found out which train and when. The Nazis didn't know where the Resistance planned to strike so they had small units stationed at points along the railway tracks.' He paused, scanning the room as if searching for threats even here. 'I hoped I could find you before they did.'

'Do you know who revealed the location of the safe house?' Krista's breath hitched, her heart hammering as she held her breath, hoping he did not say Emilia's name.

Marcin shook his head. 'I didn't hear about that until after it had happened, or I would have warned Zygmunt.'

Krista listened intently as Marcin detailed the many other hardships he had faced at the hands of the Germans and the narrow escapes from danger he'd had while supporting the Resistance.

In turn, Krista shared her own experiences – the struggles, the losses, and the flashes of hope that had kept her going. She spoke of her grandparents' bravery and sacrifice, and of the small acts of kindness that had sustained her during the darkest days.

Their conversation weaved through newfound revelations and shared memories. They laughed together at stories from their childhood, finding solace in each other's company.

'So, what happens now?' asked Krista. 'Can we keep seeing each other? We can meet here or find someplace else that's away from Nazi eyes.'

Marcin's face fell, like an invisible weight pressing down on him. He shook his head, his voice heavy with resignation. 'I'm leaving Warsaw.'

'With the Germans?' Her eyes narrowed as she searched his expression.

'No. With the Resistance. The Nazi's orders are more brutal than ever, and I can't do it anymore. Olesia and my mother haven't been visited by the Gestapo for a long time now. They've gone to stay with my aunt, and I can only hope that the threat to them is gone.' His voice dropped, a note of fear creeping in. 'But the Gestapo are already looking for me. They've labelled me a deserter. I have to leave the city.'

'When?' Her heart raced.

'Tonight.'

'So, if I hadn't come to the cafe today?' Her voice wavered, the reality of how close she came to missing him sinking in.

Marcin turned in his seat to fully face her, his knee pressing against hers. 'Then we would have missed our chance. That's why I was so desperate to see you and why I blurted everything out to Róża before I even knew if I could trust her.' His eyes held a mixture of sadness and urgency.

Krista couldn't believe that their brief encounter was coming to an end so soon. He had to leave, the Nazis executed deserters no questions asked, but Krista suddenly couldn't bear the thought of not seeing Marcin again.

'We will see each other again,' said Marcin, as if reading her thoughts. 'I found you once, I'll find you again. If you want me to, that is.'

His fingers tapped nervously on his knee.

Krista couldn't help but smile at his discomfort. 'I want you to.'

A small grin appeared on Marcin's face, and he leaned closer to her, their faces barely a breath apart. 'Will I ruin our reunion if I kiss you?'

Krista felt a flutter of excitement in her stomach. She shook her head, unable to form words.

Marcin closed the remaining distance between them. His lips brushed against hers and a jolt of electricity shot through her body, igniting something wonderful inside of her. She wrapped her arms around him and held him tight, lost in the moment of their reunion and the happiness it brought.

34

4 years later

Krista cycled towards the doctor's apartment to top up her medical supplies and get her orders. She gripped her handlebars tight to keep the bicycle steady as she bumped her way along the cobbles. The quieter streets were more challenging to cycle, but they were the best way to avoid the Nazis and unwanted inspections of her papers. And they were cooler. Cycling the narrow lanes between buildings providing at least a little shade from the stifling summer sun.

Two young boys played in the street ahead of her, their faces grimy, and their bodies skinny. One of them climbed on top of a burned-out car, grabbed the edges of his open jacket as if pretending it was a parachute, and flung himself off the top of the wreck. He landed with a thud, his eyes wide as if shocked to learn that his non-existent parachute hadn't opened. His friend wasted no time and shot at him with a stick and eerily realistic gunfire noises. *Had young boys always played soldiers or was that another consequence of war?* The boy with the failed parachute clutched his chest, threw himself to the ground once more, and pretended to die a painfully loud death. Krista hoped he was playing the Nazi in their little war game.

Memories of Oskar and the other children had stayed with her. Being a first-aider gave her purpose, and the additional training she received from the Polish Red Cross allowed her to pass through checkpoints and crisscross the city with ease. While she tended to civilians in need, she also discreetly assisted the Resistance, quietly patching up their injuries, couriering information, and smuggling food and medical supplies to wherever they were needed. Her contribution was valuable, but she missed her underground classroom.

The door to the doctor's apartment was always unlocked, so she walked straight in and wheeled her bicycle into the hallway with her. She never dared to leave it unattended outside. Nelka had sourced it for her and had stressed how difficult it had been to find. She didn't want to go back to the days of crossing the city on foot and she avoided the trams whenever possible. There were too many inspections. The thought of handing her papers over and the possibility that someone would recognise her name and drag her back to Hauptmann Schneider filled her with dread. It had been years since she'd seen him. She didn't even know if he was still in the city, but she wasn't prepared to take the chance.

The doctor's apartment was the same as hers – a ground floor apartment with its own entrance on the side of the building. She called it the doctor's apartment, but she was almost certain he didn't live there. The apartment had less furniture inside than hers. A large wooden table dominated the living space, but there were no chairs and the only decoration on the walls was a large map of the city.

'I've always wondered why you don't keep that door locked,' said Krista.

'No point in hanging around outside waiting for an invitation,' said Doctor Kowalski. 'The longer you're outside, the more people who will see you. And if the Gestapo want to come in, they're coming in whether the door is bolted or not.'

Doctor Kowalski was a tall thin man who wore glasses that always sat too far down the bridge of his nose to be useful. He was standing in his usual position behind a well-stocked table that looked like it should have been in the supply room of a hospital rather than a dingy room in a rundown apartment building.

He rattled off an address and gave Krista brief directions to a farmhouse on the outskirts of the city. 'It's a fourteen-year-old boy who has been injured in a farming accident and needs stitches in his arm,' he added.

Krista nodded, knowing that there was more to the story than she had been given, but she'd learned by now that the less she knew about people's circumstances, the better.

The doctor strolled into the kitchen and opened a cupboard. It contained a single stack of papers, which the doctor picked up and brought to the table.

He placed the papers onto the table and slid them towards Krista. 'The boy is expecting this,' he said.

Krista flipped through the stack of papers with her thumb. It was a hundred or so copies of the underground newspaper. She emptied her bag and removed a false base hidden at the bottom. She carefully placed the papers inside and pressed the base back into position. Some months before Krista had spotted a scrap of nylon at the market that matched the lining of her first aid bag. She had immediately purchased it and, with using a square of cardboard, she'd created a new base for her bag by stitching the nylon around it. As long as what she carried was flat, like the newspapers, the new base slotted into place perfectly. Only a Nazi diligent enough to unpack her bag completely might find it.

Krista unwound a length of thread and used one of her needles to stitch the corners of her false base to the bag, a habit she had recently adopted. Kowalski rolled his eyes as he did every time but said nothing. She suspected he considered it a waste of valuable resources. Krista, on the other hand, felt it was a precaution worth taking after she had witnessed the Gestapo inspecting someone's bag by tipping it up and dumping the contents onto the street.

'Help yourself to this lot.' Kowalski gestured to the array of medical supplies on the table. 'But use only what you need. Supplies are dwindling.'

Krista repacked her belongings and loaded up with fresh supplies of bandages, dressings, surgical tape, and antiseptic.

'Thank you.' Krista grabbed the handlebars of her bicycle and pushed it backwards along the short hallway. 'See you next time.'

Kowalski grunted something indecipherable. She closed the door behind her and cycled straight to the city's border.

It was almost as far as she could go without requiring a travel permit. She spotted the farmhouse and turned onto the farm track. She pedalled slowly towards the house, a two-storey building with a dilapidated barn to the right-hand side. A trailer blocked the barn doors and a muddy car that looked as though it hadn't moved for quite some time sat nearby. Everything looked normal, but the delivery in her bag confirmed that at least one member of the family inside was somehow involved with the Resistance.

A woman opened the front door. Her stance was tense and her shoulders hunched, as if carrying a heavy burden. Krista smiled, got off her bicycle, and leaned it against the outside wall of the house. It should be safe enough this far out of the city.

'Thank you for coming,' the woman said, her voice tight with tension. She glanced over her shoulder, then turned and began walking up the hallway. 'My son is in the kitchen.'

Krista followed; the sound of their footsteps muted on the carpeted floor. The hallway was dimly lit, lined with family photos and a faint smell of disinfectant hung in the air.

The woman paused at the entrance to the kitchen. 'The nurse is here,' she said to her son.

Krista didn't correct her. Her first aid training was a far cry from a nursing qualification, but usually people were so grateful for her help that they didn't care about her lack of formal credentials. Besides, Polish doctors and nurses were prohibited from helping the kinds of people she often helped, so she, or someone like her, was their only option.

The boy sported a bruised eye, a burn on one hand, and what looked like a cut on his upper arm given the blood-soaked rag tied around his arm. An older woman was sleeping in an armchair beside the stove, snoring softly with a blanket tucked over her legs.

Krista stepped into the kitchen and gave the boy what she hoped was a reassuring smile. 'I'll start with the cut,' she said, not bothering to introduce herself. Names were rarely exchanged in situations such as this.

Krista opened her bag and laid out a bottle of alcohol, two clean rags, and a bandage. She peeled the bloodied rag away from the boy's skin. The cut was deep and the skin a raging red. Blood dripped down his arm.

'What caused this?' Krista asked, not really expecting an answer. Her eyes narrowed as she examined the wound, her mind running through possibilities. She guessed a knife. It wasn't a hole like she'd seen before with bullets, nor was it ragged like the shrapnel wounds she'd treated in the past. It was a long, straight cut, clean but deep. She gently turned the boy's arm to check the back, but the skin there remained intact, unmarked by the violence that had torn into the front.

'I'm afraid this is going to hurt,' she said, her voice soft but steady.

The boy's mother, her face pale and tight with worry, came behind him and pressed her hands firmly onto his shoulders, as if trying to transfer some of her strength to him. The boy's eyes darted to Krista, a trace of fear in them, but he remained still.

Krista doused the wound in alcohol. The boy's body convulsed, a sharp gasp escaping his lips, but he held his breath, clenching his jaw against the pain. Working quickly, she plucked a needle from her first aid kit and doused that in alcohol too. She threaded the needle and pierced it into the boy's flesh with steady hands. The boy winced, a low grunt escaping his lips as she pulled the thread through his skin, his knuckles turning white as he gripped the edge of the table. Krista continued to work methodically, closing the gaping wound with each careful stitch, her focus unbroken by the occasional tremor of pain that passed through the boy's body.

After Krista had stitched up the wound as best she could, she lingered, taking her time now to inspect her stitching. It had improved. She cleaned the burn on his hand and applied a layer of the burn ointment that she carried in her kit.

'Do you have something else for me?' the boy asked once she'd finished. His voice held a timid tone that didn't quite match his obvious bravery.

Krista paused, her hand hovering over her first aid kit. She shot a glance towards his mother.

'It's OK,' said the boy, sensing her hesitation. 'She knows what you're bringing.'

Krista nodded, then unpacked the rest of her first aid kit onto the kitchen table. She took her small scissors, their blades gleaming under the kitchen light, and snipped away at the stitching inside her bag. Her fingers worked deftly as she wiggled loose the false base, a tiny knot of tension building in her chest as it came free.

She reached inside, scooping out the underground newspapers hidden beneath, and handed them over.

The boy gave a smile that brightened his pale features. 'Thank you,' he said. He glanced at his mother before disappearing out of the room, to hide the papers she suspected.

Krista fixed the base of her bag back into place and repacked it with the same care she had taken to unpack it. Her hands lingered for a moment before she smoothed out the lining of her bag, as if sealing away her secret once more.

'Clever,' the boy's mother said, gesturing towards the bottom of Krista's bag.

Krista looked up and smiled. 'I don't like the look of that cut. I'll be back tomorrow to check it.'

The mother nodded and Krista left without seeing her patient again.

35

THE FOLLOWING DAY, KRISTA RETURNED TO THE FARMHOUSE to clean and redress the boy's cut. As she cycled up the track, her throat clogged up with the sour taste of smoke. It took her a moment to realise that the smoke was coming from the barn, which now lay in ruins with smouldering wood scattered around.

The farmhouse door was swinging on its hinges and a Nazi soldier emerged, reaching for his pistol as he spotted Krista.

Krista froze, her eyes locked with the barrel of the soldier's gun. His cold, calculating gaze raked over her, his finger twitching on the trigger.

She forced herself to swallow and dismount her bike, trying to appear calm. 'What... what happened here?' she managed to choke out, her eyes darting between the soldier's face and the gun pointed at her.

'What business is it of yours?' the soldier spat back.

Krista took out her first aid identification and held it towards him. He tucked his pistol back into its holder on his side and took her papers.

'I treated someone here yesterday. A boy. He'd cut his arm in a farming accident.'

It was the truth as she knew it and she delivered it without hesitation despite the pounding in her chest.

The soldier narrowed his eyes as if trying to work out if her story was true. He handed her papers back and gestured to her bag. 'Show me!'

Krista held her bicycle steady with one hand and opened her bag with the other. The soldier leaned in to inspect its contents. There was nothing that ought not to be there, but she still held her breath, hoping he was one of the lazy ones who couldn't be bothered to inspect her bag properly.

He took his gaze from her bag, and she quickly zipped it back up. The soldier fished a cigarette out of his pocket and lit it, blowing smoke directly into her face.

'They were... arrested,' he said, disdain dripping from his words. 'Along with the Jews they were hiding.'

A gasp escaped Krista's lips as she processed the news. The cruel satisfaction on the soldier's face when he said the word *arrested* left Krista in no doubt as to what had happened to them. The Nazis didn't arrest Jews and their protectors, not in Poland anyway. They executed them.

'You won't be needed here again,' he said, flicking his hand to shoo her away.

Krista tucked her papers back inside her coat, mounted her bicycle, and pedalled away from the farmhouse. A tear rolled down her cheek as painful memories threatened to overwhelm her – the farmhouse, the Nazis, death. It was all too familiar. If her grandparents hadn't sent her away, she would have been dead too, of that she had no doubt. She wiped away her tears and took a moment to think about the boy and his family. And the others that she hadn't even known were there.

A rustle in the cornfield caught her attention. There was a breeze in the air, but this sound was different. She slowed down on her bicycle and the rustling slowed. It was as if something was following her, hidden from view but keeping pace with her movements. She looked back to make sure the soldier at the farmhouse was still there. He was walking around in the yard, his back to her. She picked up her speed to get out of his sight and turned onto the main road, hopping off her bicycle.

The corn twitched in front of her as a small figure shoved their way out of the field. Krista's mouth gaped as a young child stood before her, no more than six years old. The girl wore a navy blue coat that was at least a size too small for her, with skinny wrists poking out of the sleeves and scratched bare legs. A hat covered her head with a slick of jet-black hair poking out of the rim and framing her face. She wasn't exactly dressed for a hot July day.

Krista scanned the deserted road, her eyes darting from side to side, alert for any sign of movement. 'Let's keep walking,' she told the child, her voice gentle but firm. 'Stay back from the road.'

The girl turned and walked on in silence; her small shoulders hunched as if trying to make herself invisible. Krista kept a careful watch on the road as they moved, the crunch of their footsteps the only sound accompanying them.

Once Krista felt they were far enough away from the farmhouse, she stopped. She glanced around one last time, ensuring they were alone before crouching down to the girl's level.

'What's your name?' she asked. The girl didn't answer,

her gaze fixed on the ground. Krista softened her voice. 'My name is Krista. I'm going to help you, OK?'

The girl nodded; her eyes still downcast.

'Were you living in the farmhouse?' Krista asked, her heart sinking as she braced herself for the answer that she knew was coming.

The girl shook her head. 'The barn,' she whispered, her voice shaky, almost breathless, as if the words themselves were too painful to speak. Krista heard the fear in her tone, the sound of a child on the verge of tears.

Krista reached out and gently took the girl's hand, her fingers warm and steady around the child's cold, trembling ones. 'I'm so sorry. I lost my family, too, so I know how awful that is. You've been very brave.'

The girl looked up at her then, her dark eyes filled with a depth of sorrow that seemed far too much for someone so young. 'My name is Ayala,' she said, her voice still barely more than a whisper.

Krista smiled. 'Thank you, Ayala. That's a beautiful name.' She held Ayala's gaze, feeling the girl's grief gripping her own heart as she glimpsed the trauma the girl had endured at such a tender age. 'I'm going to take you to my apartment and then we'll figure out what to do next. Is that alright?'

Ayala nodded. 'I think we should take your hat and coat off. You must be very hot under there.'

Ayala reached up with one hand and gripped her hat, holding it in place.

'OK,' said Krista. 'We can do that later.' Krista gave the girl's other hand a reassuring squeeze before they started walking again, side by side, away from the horrors of the farmhouse.

Krista pushed her bicycle and led Ayala deeper into

Warsaw, their pace quickened as they manoeuvred through the throngs of people. She kept her head down, her eyes darting around warily, hoping to not draw any attention to herself and the young girl by her side. The weight of their situation pressed heavily on Krista's shoulders, but she maintained a facade of composure for Ayala's sake. The girl was Krista's niece visiting her from the countryside, that was the story she would give if they were stopped. Any other scenario – a neighbour or a friend's child – was too easy to check and would require a made-up address that might inadvertently bring trouble to someone else's door.

Finally, they arrived at Krista's apartment building. Krista rested her bicycle against her hip and fumbled with the keys in her pocket. The incessant thumping of her heartbeat seemed to vibrate through every inch of her body as she unlocked the door and ushered Ayala inside.

The curtains were still closed from the night before and the small space was dimly lit, filled with a musty smell that clung to the air.

'Make yourself comfortable,' said Krista, her voice soft and reassuring.

Ayala hesitated for a moment before sitting on one of the chairs, her eyes wide with uncertainty. She tugged off her hat, revealing matted black hair clinging to her head. She clutched the hat in white-knuckled fists and hunched deeper into her frayed coat.

Krista moved around the apartment, lighting candles to chase away the shadows that lurked in every corner. She poured a glass of water and prepared a plate of food, placing the plate on the arm of the chair beside the girl. It was the only comfort she could offer in a city torn apart by hatred and war.

'You're safe now, Ayala,' Krista said, hoping that was true.

36

Krista woke in the morning to the soft light of dawn filtering through her curtains. She stretched her limbs, trying to shake off the remnants of a fitful night's sleep. She sat up in the chair and glanced over at Ayala curled up on the bed, her chest rising and falling rhythmically in sleep.

She couldn't keep the girl hidden away in her apartment forever. It was too risky for both of them. Rubbing her tired eyes, Krista considered her options. She couldn't risk taking Ayala outside without a plan in place.

Krista quietly dressed and slipped out of the bedroom, padding her way to the kitchen to prepare some breakfast for Ayala. She had just finished grating a potato and forming small pancakes when Ayala appeared, her black hair sticking up in all directions.

'Good morning,' said Krista, trying to sound cheery and in control.

Ayala's eyes drifted towards the pancakes.

'Are you hungry?' Krista asked.

Ayala nodded.

Krista turned on the stove and placed a small piece of fat

in the frying pan. As it melted, she carefully added the potato pancakes, stepping back as the oil sizzled and spluttered.

'I have to go out for a little while, Ayala. You'll be safe here until I get back.'

The girl's eyes were like two moons, bright and wide, but filled with fear.

Krista flipped the pancakes over. 'I'm going to see a friend who helped me when I first came to Warsaw after losing my family. This friend helps lots of children every day.'

Once the potato cakes were cooked to a golden brown, Krista slid them onto a plate and led Ayala to the small dining table. 'You can eat now, and I'll be back very soon.'

Ayala sat at the table, picking at her plate of food with a fork. She pointed towards Krista. 'What's that?' she asked. 'On your coat. Is it a flower?'

Krista touched her hand to her coat, feeling the trefoil pin nestled discreetly under her collar.

'It's like clover,' Krista said softly. She crouched down so Ayala could see the pin up close. 'It's a symbol of the Girl Guides. To me, it represents friendship, loyalty, and taking care of each other. It's forbidden to wear this badge now. But I keep mine hidden as a reminder of the friends who have helped me through tough times.'

Ayala reached out with wonder and gently traced the smooth metal edges of the pin with her finger.

'I'll be back soon,' said Krista. She gave Ayala a final smile before she slipped out of the door.

❧

The streets of Warsaw were bustling with activity as Krista made her way towards Nelka's canteen. The cobbled paths echoed with the footsteps of passersby and the voices of street vendors hawking their wares.

Arriving at the canteen, Krista went around the back of the building hoping Nelka would be in the kitchen preparing for the day ahead. She spotted her and tapped on the window. Nelka turned around from where she was kneading dough. Her face broke into a wide smile when she saw Krista standing outside. She hurried over and opened the back door.

'It's been too long,' said Nelka, her voice filled with her usual warmth. 'Is everything alright?' Krista shook her head and Nelka ushered her inside the kitchen.

As she entered the kitchen, Krista received warm and welcoming smiles from the three other girls cooking. They seemed to sense that her unexpected return to the canteen was not for socialising. One of them turned off the heat under a pan of sizzling onions and signalled for the others to leave the kitchen with her.

'I have a young Jewish girl who needs a place to hide,' said Krista, getting straight to the point. She filled Nelka in on the events of the previous day.

Nelka ran floury hands through her hair. 'I don't know how to help. It's been such a long time since we got anyone out of the city.'

Krista nodded. 'I thought you perhaps knew of a family the girl could hide with.'

Nelka bit her lip, deep in thought. After a moment, she let out a heavy sigh. 'No, I'm sorry. I think we have to get her out of the city somehow. But how? Where?'

The large front doors to the canteen swung open with a bang. Krista and Nelka turned in shock to see a group of

Nazi soldiers marching in, their boots clanking loudly against the floor. The leader of the group, a tall man with a cold expression, scanned the canteen with his steely gaze, his eyes settling on Nelka and Krista. He strode towards the kitchen.

'What is going on here?' he barked, his voice sharp and authoritative.

Krista felt panic spread its way up her body.

Nelka stepped forward, her voice steady despite the fear in her eyes. 'We are just preparing food for the day, sir. Is there anything we can help you with?'

The Nazi soldier sneered, his lip curling in disdain. 'We need to search the premises.'

'Please, go ahead,' said Nelka.

The soldiers fanned out, causing havoc in the food hall, knocking over chairs and flipping up tables. The man in the kitchen rummaged through cupboards and drawers, leaving a mess behind him as he tossed spoons onto the floor and tipped up a bag of flour.

Nelka moved towards a pan of soup bubbling on the stove and stirred. Krista slipped an apron over her dress, plucked a potato from a pile that one of the other girls had been working on, and chopped it into cubes. Nelka had always been strict about keeping Resistance activity away from the canteen. She believed that providing a safe place and a hot meal for the children was too important to put at risk. There would be nothing incriminating for the Nazis to discover. Nothing except Krista's unexpected presence.

The soldiers continued their frenzied search, inspecting every corner of the canteen. Krista stood frozen, tensing the muscles in her legs to stop their uncontrollable trembling. She glanced at Nelka, who was staring into the pot of soup, her knuckles turning white around the ladle. Krista forced herself to cube more potatoes, blocking everything else out.

Just as it seemed like the soldiers would turn the entire canteen upside down, their leader called out, 'There's nothing here. Move out.'

Relief washed over Krista as the soldiers filed out of the building. When they had gone, one of the girls closed the doors behind them and they hurried into the kitchen. Nelka dropped the ladle onto the worktop with a loud clatter.

'This is my fault,' said Krista. 'I'm sorry. I shouldn't have come here.'

Nelka shook her head. 'It isn't your fault. They came last week too. Something is going on, but it has nothing to do with you.'

Krista grabbed a broom to clean the floor, but Nelka put a hand on her arm. 'You need to leave,' she said, a slight waver in her voice. 'We were lucky they didn't inspect our papers. Your name...'

Krista shifted her weight from one foot to the other, suddenly feeling like an unwelcome guest. Ever since Konrad Klein had released her, she had done her best to avoid her papers being inspected. No one knew if the Germans had realised that Klein had failed to deliver her to the work camp as intended, or if her name was on some list of escapees. And when she was asked for her identification, she always handed over her first aid worker credentials first, which seemed sufficient in quelling any suspicions. That would not have worked today, though.

Krista brought the apron over her head and handed it to Nelka. She crossed the kitchen and slipped out of the back door, guilt gnawing at her for bringing her troubles to Nelka's door. Ayala was her responsibility, and she could only think of one place where the girl might find safety.

'Wait,' said Nelka, following Krista out. 'What are we going to do about the girl?'

Krista paused. 'Don't worry about that. I have an idea. I just need a telephone.'

Nelka let out a sigh, her tense shoulders slightly loosening. Krista saw the relief in her eyes that she wouldn't have to get further involved. 'Emilia has a telephone.'

37

KRISTA HEADED BACK TO HER APARTMENT WHILE SHE WAITED for Emilia's breakfast rush to calm down. The last thing she needed was to be spotted by Hauptmann Schneider during his daily breakfast at Emilia's cafe. On her way, she took a detour to a small community garden. It appeared neglected, with overgrown trees and weeds taking over the path. Krista walked along the grassy edge of the path; her eyes glued to the ground as she searched for what she needed. After a few moments, she smiled and gently plucked a clover from the earth, brushing off a speck of dirt that clung to its stem. She left the garden and hurried back to her apartment.

As soon as Krista opened the door, she was greeted by Ayala's tear-stained face. Guilt washed over Krista as she quickly slipped inside and shut the door behind her, knowing she would have to leave again soon.

'Are you OK?' Krista asked.

Ayala rushed towards her and buried her face in Krista's dress. Krista's hand glided over the girl's back, moving in gentle, rhythmic motions in attempt to soothe her. Finally, Ayala stepped back and gave a small nod.

'Good. You're being very brave. I'm sorry, but I have to go out again soon.'

Ayala's face fell and she grasped Krista's hand, her raggedy nails digging into Krista's flesh. 'Your friend couldn't help me?'

Krista retrieved her address book from a drawer in the kitchen. 'She did help. And now I need to speak to someone else so I can get you out of the city.'

Ayala dropped Krista's hand and sank down onto a chair. 'I can stay here with you.'

The suggestion tugged at Krista's heart, but she knew it wasn't safe. Krista knelt. She flipped the book open to the decorative inside cover and passed it over to Ayala. 'Do you see these pretty clovers?'

Ayala stroked the clover-printed fabric.

Krista leafed through the pages for her. 'Do you see all these names? They are people we can trust to help us. I would like you to stay here with me, but it isn't safe. There's nowhere to hide if you need to.'

The girl's lower lip quivered, and her shoulders hunched, her small frame seeming to deflate with the heavy weight of sadness. 'Hiding isn't safe either.'

Krista wrapped her arms around Ayala and hugged her close. That was why she had to get the girl out of the city. She had probably been hiding with her family in the same barn since the beginning of the war, but it was too close to the city, which meant too many Germans. Krista could only think of one location where there were few Germans around. She hoped that was still the case.

'I have something for you.' Krista released Ayala from her embrace and opened her palm to reveal a delicate stem of clover nestled in her hand. She picked it up and held it towards Ayala. 'You're a clover girl now, too.'

Ayala grinned and her eyes lit up as she took the clover in her fingers. Krista was grateful the girl was still capable of a smile despite all she must have seen and the fear that still lingered within her.

Krista pocketed her address book and left the apartment once more, heading straight to Emilia's cafe. Her heart raced with anxiety. She hadn't stepped foot in the cafe since the operation to intercept the train. And she hadn't seen Emilia since then either. Nelka trusted Emilia, but Krista still wavered with her own trust seeing how easily Emilia interacted with the Nazis who frequented her cafe. And after what had happened with the train, Emilia had every reason to be suspicious of Krista.

A young boy was drawing with chalk on the corner of Emilia's street. Krista glanced at his artwork – an anchor with a loop at the top, the emblem of the Armia Krajowa, the Home Army. This powerful symbol of resistance had been painted all over the city, fuelling rumours that the uprising was imminent. If she had any chance of getting Ayala out of the city, she had to act fast.

The clear blue sky was reflected in the windows of Cafe Emilia, obscuring her view. She peered through the glass door, hoping there were no Gestapo officers inside looking back at her. Emilia emerged through the doors at the back of the empty cafe. Her face lit up as she saw Krista and she rushed towards the door. Unlocking it, she waved Krista inside and steered her towards a table tucked away in the corner.

Krista took a seat while Emilia fetched two cups of coffee from behind the counter. She placed one in front of

Krista. 'How have you been? Is everything alright?' she asked.

'I need to use a telephone,' said Krista. She pushed the cup away. The smell of the coffee brought back memories of Hauptmann Schneider, and she'd rather not think about him right now.

Emilia looked as radiant as ever, her red hair pinned up in a loose bun with a few stray strands framing her face. She took a sip of her drink. 'May I ask why?'

'I'm helping a friend,' said Krista. She could see the disappointment in Emilia's eyes but couldn't bring herself to explain further.

Emilia stood up. 'You can use the telephone upstairs.' Her voice was slightly high-pitched, and Krista suspected she was trying to mask her hurt feelings at Krista's secrecy.

She led Krista to a bedroom upstairs. The room was cosy and warm, with soft yellow walls adorned with paintings of flowers. Sunlight streamed in through lace curtains, casting the room in a peaceful glow. A small telephone sat on a bedside table.

'It's a different line from the one in the cafe,' said Emilia. 'The Germans don't know about this one. I've heard them talking about wiretapping. I don't know what it is or how it works, but they can somehow use it to listen in on telephone calls. You should be fine here, but just be careful what you say.'

Emilia left the room and Krista sat on the edge of the bed. She reached into her pocket and pulled out the address book, flipping through the pages until she found the number she needed. Her hand hovered over the telephone. What if the Germans were somehow listening in? The only other working telephones she knew of were in public buildings, which were crawling with Nazis. She clenched her fingers around the telephone. It was a chance she had to take.

The call connected and a wave of familiarity washed over Krista as she heard the voice through the line, a gentle and warm tone that brought comfort to the nerves rattling around inside of her. 'Hello?'

'Irena? Is that really you?'

'Krista?' Irena's voice held surprise and genuine joy.

'Yes, it's me,' said Krista. 'It's so good to hear your voice. Are you alright? Is Maja alright?'

Irena laughed down the line, a bittersweet melody that had Krista yearning to see her friend in person. The sound was crystal clear, free from static or interference.

'I can't believe you're calling. We're both good,' Irena assured her. 'Are you alright? Are you coming to stay? Oh, please come and stay with us. I've been so worried about you all this time.'

The offer was tempting. Krista thought about how it would feel to say yes. To say that she was going to Maja's farm. She would be safe. Alive. No more checkpoints. No more fear that she would run into Hauptmann Schneider and be arrested again. She looked down at the tiny scratches on her hand from Ayala's grip. The poor girl was terrified. She had lost everything and everyone, and Krista couldn't bear to think of what might have happened to her if Krista hadn't gone to the farm that day.

'No,' said Krista, choosing duty over her desire for safety and peace. 'I have work to do here. But I'm hoping that you can help a friend of mine.'

Krista was mindful of Emilia's warning about the Germans potentially eavesdropping on telephone conversations, but she couldn't ask Irena to help without telling her exactly what she would be risking. She briefly recounted

Ayala's story following which Irena offered to help, without hesitation.

'Thank you, Irena. Let me look at travel plans while you talk to Maja. I'll call you back tomorrow at the same time.'

As she disconnected the call, she heard the faint creaking of a floorboard behind her and turned to see Emilia standing in the doorway, her expression unreadable. Krista's breath caught in her throat. She waited, riding out the thick and uncomfortable silence between them. Perhaps this was the moment when she would get some certainty about where Emilia's true loyalties lay.

38

Breaking the heavy silence, Emilia spoke in a low and steady voice. 'How do you plan to get the girl out of the city?'

Krista's skin prickled and she clenched her jaw. Had Emilia heard every word of her phone call to Irena? 'I'll find a way.'

Emilia's gaze flicked back along her hallway, as if ensuring they were still alone. 'Let me do it. I'll take the girl wherever you need her to go.'

Krista's eyes narrowed. 'No, you can't.'

Emilia's unwavering gaze held hers, as if searching for something. 'I know you don't trust me.'

Krista's breathed caught in her throat. She looked away, focusing on a crack in Emilia's bedroom wall. 'It's not that,' said Krista, knowing that wasn't entirely true.

Emilia crossed her arms, her shoulders stiffening. 'You struggle to understand how I can serve them every day.'

After a moment of tense silence, Krista's gaze returned to Emilia, and she nodded slowly. It was difficult for her to comprehend how Emilia could willingly work for men of such cruelty.

Emilia's gaze softened with understanding and just a hint of hurt. 'I could have shut my business down. I wanted to but was persuaded otherwise.' A trace of regret passed through Emilia's expression before it hardened.

That was true, at least. Nelka had told Krista the same thing.

She ran a slender hand down the wooden door frame, avoiding Krista's gaze. 'I want to tell you that it isn't easy, but if I'm honest, it is easy. They come to eat, and I serve them. It's what I did before the war. Only now my customers speak German. Like me. Like you.'

A twinge of remorse stirred inside Krista. Was she unfairly judging Emilia for being German, just as Jan and the others had judged her? She thought through her interactions with Emilia. Had Emilia ever given her any reason not to trust her?

Emilia's fingers curled tightly around the door frame, and she looked at Krista once more, certainty etched on her face. 'The Germans think I'm one of them so they're nice to me. And then they forget I'm there and they talk to each other. Information I have overheard during these unguarded moments has saved lives. Resistance networks have been protected. An underground printing press was successfully relocated the morning before a raid. Countless Gestapo operations have been sabotaged. The Nazis are being thwarted by my eavesdropping skills and their own carelessness. No one has connected the dots back to me. It hasn't occurred to them that the woman who serves them breakfast is capable of spying on them.'

'I'm sorry, Emilia,' said Krista. 'You're right. I wasn't sure about you, and I had no reason to feel like that.' Her apology sounded hollow and insincere, even to her own ears.

Emilia stepped into the room and sat down on the bed

beside Krista. 'You had reason,' she said. 'I know what people think of me. I see the looks they give me on the streets. That woman who collaborates with the Germans. But the whispers are worth it because I'm doing good. I'm helping my friends and neighbours in the best way I can.' She bit her lip and glanced away, her self-assurance wavering. 'That's what I tell myself, anyway.'

Emilia's body trembled slightly and the light in her eyes dulled, as though she was burdened enough by her own doubts without Krista casting further suspicions towards her. Krista sank down further onto the bed, weighed down by her conscience. She reached out and clasped Emilia's hand. The warmth of Emilia's skin on hers was a reminder of the human connection between them. 'You *are* doing good, Emilia. And I truly am sorry.'

Emilia nodded and straightened her posture. 'So, how are we doing to get your friend out of Warsaw? You're going to need my help. You will never get a travel permit.'

Krista stretched her arms out in front of her to bring some energy back to her body. 'I know.' She'd spent all this time avoiding the Gestapo. She could hardly now march into the heart of their operations and apply for a travel pass. 'Do you know anyone with a vehicle who might still be able to smuggle her out?'

Emilia shook her head. 'All informal routes that I knew of are gone. We must hide this girl in the city or travel with her legitimately.'

Krista smiled, appreciating Emilia's use of the word "we". Seeing Nelka earlier and now Emilia made her realise just how isolated she had been feeling lately. Doctor Kowalski had become the person she saw most often, but he wasn't exactly known for his engaging conversations.

'Does she have papers?' Emilia asked.

'No, but I think I can get some.'

'Good. Do that. We'll say she's my niece and I'll take her.' Emilia looked down at her hands and her cheeks turned crimson. 'Hauptmann Schneider likes me. He can give me travel passes.'

Krista's body stiffened at the mere mention of his name, her mind flooded with memories of the fear he had instilled in her.

Emilia looked up again, her cheeks still flushed. 'He asked me about you after the train incident. Nelka told me what had happened to you, and I told Schneider that you had inexplicably stopped showing up for work. He seemed pleased and made no mention of his role in placing you onboard a train bound for one of those terrible camps. I brought you up again a week later and he dismissed it, telling me to forget about you and hire someone new. From that, I gathered he had forgotten about you too. I can't be sure, of course, but it didn't seem as though he realised that you never made it to the camp.'

The constant fear of sneaking around every day momentarily lifted from Krista's shoulders. Schneider had been so certain that Krista was nothing. It hadn't stopped her from being herded onto the cattle car with the others, but it perhaps explained why Zygmunt and the others had been covered in bruises and Krista had none.

'I can get the travel permits as soon as you have the documents,' said Emilia.

Krista bit her lip, her mind racing with the logistics. 'What about the cafe?' she asked. 'Will you have to close?'

Emilia shook her head, tucking a loose strand of hair behind her ear. 'No. Diana's niece has been helping in the kitchen. Sometimes she helps me with the service, and she hasn't spilt a pot of coffee over Schneider yet, so I think he'll tolerate my absence for a couple of days.'

Krista's gaze softened as she studied Emilia, noticing the subtle lines of fatigue around her eyes. As she witnessed the benefits of Emilia's relationship with the occupiers, she regretted ever judging her for developing it. 'I am sorry, Emilia.'

Emilia inhaled deeply and rose from the bed. 'Let's put it behind us and concentrate on helping our young friend.' She paused, her gaze meeting Krista's with a sense of solidarity. 'We both have work to do, and this time it's something good.'

Krista left Emilia's cafe and headed towards the doctor's apartment, her fingers crossed that he would be there. She had designated days for restocking her medical supplies and receiving orders, but today was not one of those days. But she had treated so many members of the Resistance under his direction that surely he must have connections with someone who could help her obtain forged papers.

She arrived at the apartment and tried the door. Unlocked, as usual. She entered and found Doctor Kowalski behind his large wooden table meticulously lining up glass bottles.

He gestured to the supplies on the table. 'Take a pack of bandages and one bottle of antiseptic. It's all I've been able to get. No extra deliveries.'

There were a dozen packs of bandages and bottles of antiseptic on the table, and she wondered who they were for. In all her time coming to this apartment, she had never once seen anyone else.

Kowalski's neutral expression suddenly contorted into a scowl, and he pushed his glasses up his nose, squinting at her through thick lenses. 'Wait. Why are you here?' he asked, his voice low and guarded.

'I need to get identity documents for someone,' said Krista. She knew it was a risky request, but couldn't see any other option. 'Do you know anyone I could talk to?' Her stomach churned as she waited for an answer, unsure if she would be met with understanding or judgement.

Kowalski's eyebrows knitted together, and his glasses slid further down his nose. 'For you?'

She shook her head. 'A child. She needs to travel out of the city, but needs new documents first.'

Kowalski brought his hand up and pushed his glasses back into position. His gaze grew more intense. 'Are you going somewhere?'

'No,' she said. 'Someone else is ready to escort her. I'm staying here.'

He let out a heavy breath. 'Good. Because very soon we'll need all the help we can get.'

Krista wondered what he knew. There was no point in asking him, he rarely answered questions. Rumours had been circulating for weeks that the Resistance were preparing their fight back. Perhaps that time was finally coming. But with that thought came conflicting emotions – hope, fear, and doubt. Were they truly ready for what was to come?

Kowalski crossed to the kitchen and opened a drawer. Krista stood on her tiptoes to sneak a peek inside. It was empty except for a few scraps of paper and a solitary pen. The doctor reached for piece of paper and the pen, offering them to Krista.

'Give me the child's details and I'll see what I can do.'

Krista scribbled down fake details for Ayala, keeping only her first name and year of birth. 'Thank you,' she said, sliding the paper and pen across the table.

'No promises,' said Kowalski, his tone laced with uncertainty. 'And you'll have to take what you get. Come back on Thursday morning for an update.'

On her way out of the apartment, Krista crossed paths with a girl, perhaps sixteen years old with pale skin and dark circles under her eyes. The girl nodded and gave her a knowing smile, as if they shared some secret bond. But Krista couldn't handle any more secrets. She prayed for the war to be over, so she could finally stop hiding. She dreamed of being able to stroll down the street without looking over her shoulder. This yearning, however, only served as a painful reminder that she had no place to call home and no one waiting for her to return.

39

A WEEK LATER AND EVERYTHING WAS IN PLACE. DOCTOR Kowalski had secured convincing documents for Ayala and Emilia had approached Hauptmann Schneider for permission to travel outside of Warsaw. Golden rays of sunlight filtered through Krista's window, bouncing off Ayala's glossy, black hair, making it almost sparkle. Ayala was bathed and immaculately dressed as one would expect a child accompanying Emilia to be. She looked beautiful and Krista clung to the possibility of new beginnings amidst the fear that lingered in their lives.

At exactly eight o'clock, there was a knock on the door, and Krista opened it to let Emilia in. Emilia's autumnal hair cascaded down her back in soft waves, and her skin glowed with a pale perfection accentuated by bold red lips. She wore a figure-hugging green coat that stopped at her knees. She looked exquisite, and so out of place in German-occupied Poland. Krista smiled, thinking that their plan might actually work. With Emilia as a distraction, the Nazis would have no reason to focus on Ayala. Emilia would attract plenty of attention, but Krista doubted anyone could tear their eyes away from her long enough to give Ayala's papers more than a cursory glance.

Ayala stood with her back pressed against the wall, her eyes wide. Her gaze followed every move Emilia made with a mixture of awe and trepidation.

Emilia handed Krista the travel permits for her and Ayala.

Krista inspected them. 'Any problems?'

'None. Schneider even sympathised with my desire not to be burdened by my poor little orphaned niece.' Emilia's face twisted in a look of disgust and contempt that mirrored Krista's own.

Krista handed back the permits.

Emilia tucked them inside her bag and turned to Ayala. 'Are you ready?'

The girl shook her head, her eyes darting around the room as if searching for an escape route. 'I... I don't want to go,' Ayala stammered.

Krista stepped forward, but Emilia put out a hand and stopped her. Emilia approached Ayala and knelt on the floor in front of her.

'Ayala,' said Emilia, her tone calm and even. 'I'm scared too, but I promise to take care of you. Let's try to push our fear away and pretend we're going on a trip. Soon we'll be in a place where you don't have to hide anymore. You can feel the warmth of the sun on your skin and run around outside as much as you like. Maybe you'll even make a friend there. Doesn't that sound good?'

Ayala nodded, but her lips were still pressed together in a worried line.

Emilia took the girl's hand. 'Let's say goodbye to Krista.'

Ayala wrapped her arms around Krista's waist and squeezed her tight.

'My friends will take very good care of you,' said Krista. She looked at Emilia and whispered, 'Good luck.'

Emilia gently removed Ayala's arms from around Krista and took the girl's hand again. 'We can do this,' she reassured, though it seemed like her words were meant just as much for herself as they were for Ayala.

They left the apartment, with Krista trailing behind them a few seconds later, not yet ready to leave them alone. She kept her distance. The streets of occupied Warsaw seemed to hold their breath as Emilia and Ayala walked through them, like two shining stars amidst dilapidated buildings and wary onlookers.

Turning a corner, they came face to face with a group of Nazi soldiers blocking their path. One of the soldiers stepped forward and Emilia stopped, still holding Ayala's hand. Krista sat down on the steps of a nearby apartment building as if waiting for someone. She watched; her hands clasped tightly in front of her. Emilia touched the soldier's arm, and Krista imagined her eyelashes fluttering with practised innocence. She was too far away to hear the conversation. The soldier smiled, a trace of humanity softening his stern features. His gaze lingered on Emilia for almost a full minute before he stepped aside. As they stepped past him, Krista saw that Emilia was still talking to him. The soldier laughed and nodded his agreement to whatever tale Emilia had been giving him. Emilia flashed a final bright smile and she and Ayala breezed past without further scrutiny. And without the soldier casting a single glance in Ayala's direction.

Krista felt a surge of relief as she watched them continue down the street and disappear from view. She stood up, wiped the dust off the back of her coat, and circled back to her apartment. Their journey was far from over, but she had done all she could. Ayala's safety was now in Emilia's hands.

~

As Krista approached her building, she spotted a figure sitting against the cold stone and clutching a weathered suitcase. Fear gripped her for a moment quickly followed by relief as she recognised Róża. Róża's warm smile put Krista at ease, and she motioned for her to come closer.

'There's someone waiting for you at my cafe,' Róża whispered, her eyes darting nervously around the deserted street. Her breath came out in short, anxious puffs.

'For me?' Krista's voice barely rose above a whisper, her pulse quickening as she scanned Róża's face for answers.

Róża put her hand out and allowed Krista to pull her to a stand. 'My door is unlocked. I have a train to catch.'

Krista's brow furrowed in confusion, a knot of unease forming in her stomach. 'What's going on?'

'I'm going to stay with my sister until this is all over.' Róża's voice wavered as she straightened her coat. She leaned in, her tone urgent. 'You should heed his warning and leave, too.'

Krista's heart began to beat faster still, her thoughts racing just as fast. There was only one person she could think of who would go looking for her at Cafe Róża, but surely it couldn't be.

But before she could ask any questions, Róża grinned and grabbed the handle of her suitcase. Without another word, she gave a final hurried wave and disappeared around the corner of the building, leaving Krista standing alone with a jumble of thoughts swirling in her mind.

With a mix of hope and caution, Krista hurried towards

Cafe Róża as fast as she could without drawing any attention to herself. She reached the narrow cobbled lane and glanced around, making sure no one was watching her. Then, unable to contain herself any longer, she sprinted down the lane, her breath catching in her throat with each step.

The door was unlocked, just as Róża had said it would be and a little metal bell above it tinkled as Krista entered. Her gaze immediately landed on a familiar face. Sitting at a corner table, bathed in the soft glow of a flickering candle, was Marcin.

Marcin's gaze met Krista's as she stood frozen in the doorway, her heart throbbing in her chest. Without a word, he rose from his seat and crossed the room to envelop her in a tight embrace.

She sank into his body, feeling a surge of conflicting emotions; relief at seeing him alive warred with the fear of what his sudden appearance might mean. She hadn't allowed herself to think of him much during these last four years. She had been too afraid of the dark paths that those thoughts might drag her down.

He loosened his grip, and Krista took a step back. She could see the toll that time had taken on him – the weariness in his young features. She wondered if that was what he saw too when he looked at her.

'Krista,' Marcin's gaze bore into hers, his voice low and urgent. 'The uprising is imminent. You must leave Warsaw before it's too late.'

Her stomach tightened and twisted, as if trying to contain a swarm of panicked bees. She had known this day would come, but she suddenly felt unprepared. Marcin's presence was a reminder that she still had more to lose.

Krista took a deep breath, steadying herself. 'Where will you be?' she asked.

Marcin hesitated for a moment, his expression grave. He glanced toward the window. 'I'll be here. I have to fight.'

Krista clenched her fists at her sides, her nails digging into her palms as she tried to suppress the fear rising within her. 'Then I'm not leaving either.'

He clasped her hands in his, squeezing them tight. 'But Krista, it's too dangerous. You should–'

'I should stay here.' She lifted her chin, her voice steady and unwavering. 'I've been training for four years to provide first aid to those who need it. People will need it now more than ever. I can't abandon them.'

She searched his face for a hint of understanding, but all she saw was hesitation.

Marcin's shoulders slumped slightly, the tension in his posture breaking for a moment. He shook his head. 'The dangers that lie ahead are unimaginable.'

'I don't need to imagine them. I've witnessed them first-hand. I'm staying.'

In that moment, time seemed to stand still as they both grappled with the gravity of their decisions.

Finally, Marcin broke the silence. He placed his hands on her shoulders, his eyes softening. 'Your strength and courage continue to astonish me.'

He reached out and gently brushed a lock of hair from Krista's face, his touch sending a jolt of warmth through her. She closed her eyes for a moment, savouring the sensation before meeting his gaze once more. The intensity in his eyes mirrored what was going on inside of her.

Words seemed inadequate as they stood locked in a

moment of unspoken understanding. The faint scent of chicory coffee lingered in the air, mingling with the raw emotions swirling between them.

Without breaking eye contact, Marcin leaned closer, his hand cupping Krista's cheek tenderly. Her heart raced with anticipation, knowing that this moment could change everything between them.

Their lips met, hesitant at first, like a tentative exploration of lost moments and buried emotions. But as they deepened their embrace, the weight of the past years lifted and Krista allowed herself to be swept away by the passion that had simmered beneath the surface for so long. Their kiss spoke of love, of loss, of hope for a future beyond the shadows of war.

They clung to each other, their bodies pressed close, neither willing to break the connection that had ignited between them.

40

A SUDDEN, DEAFENING ROAR OUTSIDE JOLTED KRISTA AND SHE instinctively pulled away from Marcin's embrace. The street outside the cafe's window was now filled with frantic people running in all directions, panicked screams blending with the sound of rapid gunfire reverberating down the lane. Marcin's eyes widened in alarm, and he quickly grabbed Krista, shielding her behind him.

'It's happening now?' Krista asked, fearing what that might mean for Emilia and Ayala.

Marcin stepped towards the window and peered out. 'No, that's not us.'

The din of gunshots was replaced by boots pounding against the cobblestones like a menacing drumbeat.

'We need to go,' said Marcin, his tone leaving no room for further questions. 'Now!'

He grabbed Krista's hand and pulled her towards the back door of the cafe. She caught a flash of Gestapo uniforms marching past the cafe's window. Marcin produced a set of keys from his pocket, unlocked the door, and pulled it open. Bright sunlight streamed in and Krista suddenly wished it was nighttime and they could slip away into the darkness.

Marcin leaned a little past the door frame to investigate the alleyway behind the building. 'It's clear,' he said.

Krista followed Marcin out into the narrow alleyway. It looked deceptively normal, with washing hung out to dry in the sunshine. The stomping of the Gestapo making their way down the street on the other side of the building faded into a muffled backdrop. But Krista's hand still quivered in Marcin's firm grip, the oppressive heat of the midday sun beating down on them seemed to intensify Krista's fear.

They hurried through the maze of back streets, finally emerging onto a wider street, flanked by old buildings with faded facades and shuttered windows. As they turned a corner, their path was abruptly blocked by a large military truck, its metal bulk casting a long shadow across the cobblestones.

A lone soldier spotted them and readied his rifle, his gaze fixated on Krista. 'Halt!' he called out.

Krista spun around, her eyes scanning the surrounding buildings as she tried to get her bearings. Everywhere she looked, the buildings seemed to blur together in a dizzying maze.

'Halt!' she heard again, more insistent this time.

She closed her eyes and took a deep breath, letting the air fill her lungs and calm her racing thoughts. Larysa had taken her down these very streets on her first day in Warsaw and she'd used the shelter of the lanes ever since to navigate her way around the city. She knew these lanes better than the Germans. When she opened her eyes again, the blur was gone, her mind refreshed. There was a passageway between two crumbling structures on the opposite side of the street and she knew exactly where it led.

'I know another way,' Krista said, her voice steady despite the fear that still clawed at her insides.

They darted across the street towards the passageway. The soldier's voice rang out as he gave chase, yelling orders to stop. They slipped between the two old buildings. It was even narrower than it had looked, barely wide enough for one person to pass through at a time.

Krista rushed through, Marcin followed closely behind her, their footsteps echoing off the dilapidated walls and the thud of boots on cobblestones growing ever louder behind them.

The passageway seemed to stretch on endlessly, twisting and turning like a labyrinth, but they pushed on.

Finally, they made it clear of the walls and found themselves in a small courtyard hidden from the prying eyes of anyone on the street. Krista paused, gasping for breath. Her ears strained, listening for any signs of pursuit, but all she could hear was the thunderous thumping of her own heart.

The crunch of footsteps grew louder as someone scurried along the passageway behind them. There was no time to catch their breath. They ran towards a shell of a building on the other side of the courtyard, climbing over the debris that partially blocked the entrance, and headed for daylight on the other side of the building.

They emerged back onto the street, Krista moving so quickly she barely noticed the old man until it was too late. She barrelled into him, nearly knocking him off his feet. His walking stick clattered to the ground as his body, hunched over, teetered dangerously.

Marcin's quick reflexes sprang into action. He lunged forward, clasping both hands on the man's frail arms, steadying him before he could fall.

'I'm so sorry,' Krista said, her voice breathless with both exertion and guilt. 'Are you alright?'

The old man's wrinkled face creased into a mild smile, his eyes twinkling with unexpected kindness. 'Why such a hurry?' he asked, no hint of annoyance in his tone.

Krista glanced behind her, the urgency returning as she scanned the building, ears straining for any sign of pursuit.

'The Germans?' the man asked, his voice dropping to a conspiratorial whisper.

Krista exchanged a look with Marcin, the tension of their predicament hanging between them. She nodded, a single, tight motion.

The old man's smile faded into a serious expression. He straightened as much as his aged frame allowed. 'Well, go,' he said, waving them on with a shaky hand. 'Hurry.'

Marcin's brow furrowed with concern as he gently released his hold on the man. 'You're sure you're alright?' he asked, scanning the man's face.

Before the man could respond, a clanging rang out from behind them, sharp and jarring against the quiet street. The sound of metal striking metal sent a jolt of adrenaline through Krista.

'Go, go!' the man urged, his voice rising with a newfound urgency. He bent down with surprising agility to retrieve his walking stick, holding it like a weapon. 'I'll deal with him.'

Krista and Marcin took off again, sprinting up the street. Before they rounded the corner, Krista glanced back and saw two Gestapo men spring from the building onto the street. The man stuck out his walking stick, pointing down the street in the opposite direction. The Gestapo wasted no time in running in the direction he had steered them in; the opposite direction from where Krista was peering around the corner. She waved her thanks to the man and she and Marcin walked off.

Marcin wiped the back of his sleeve across his sweaty forehead. 'I'll walk you back to your apartment before I go.'

'I'll be fine on my own,' said Krista, catching her breath, her eyes still darting around them.

Marcin nodded. 'I know you will be. I'm just not ready to leave you.' His voice softened, and for a moment, the tension in his shoulders seemed to ease.

Krista smiled, resisting the urge to reach out and intertwine her fingers with his. She longed to walk beside him as if everything were normal, but the knowledge that it wasn't pressed heavily on her chest. They needed to get indoors, before the Gestapo realised they'd gone off in the wrong direction.

'They were very keen to catch us,' Krista murmured. 'Do you think they know the uprising is coming?'

'We were just unlucky,' said Marcin, shaking his head. 'I think they thought we were part of whatever was going on in that street.'

They arrived at Krista's building. 'This is me here,' she said.

Marcin's hand found hers, his grip warm and reassuring as they took those final steps into her apartment together. The door clicked shut behind them and Marcin pulled her into his arms. Krista felt a rush of emotions swirl within her as Marcin's lips met hers. In that moment of blissful connection, the urgency and fear she had felt melted away and she allowed herself to forget about the world on the other side of her door.

∾

Marcin sat on the floor in the apartment and patted the space beside him.

Krista pulled a blanket from the back of the chair and sat down, draping the blanket across their legs. 'Do you have something against chairs?' she asked.

Marcin laughed and rested his hand on her leg. 'No. They're just too far apart.' His eyes lingered on her face. 'Just imagine sitting like this in front of a crackling fire. The dancing flames creating shadows on the walls and the sweet aroma of burning wood filling the room.'

Krista closed her eyes and pulled the blanket towards her chin, seeking comfort in its warmth. She tilted her face, letting the gentle sunlight streaming through her shaded window brush her skin. 'I can almost feel the heat.'

Marcin leaned closer, his fingers tracing a tender path along her cheek. 'Do you think you'll go back to Zawica after the war?'

Krista opened her eyes, the peaceful moment giving way to a rush of painful memories. She shook her head, the motion small but resolute. 'I've thought about it,' she admitted. 'But I don't think so. There are too many memories. And Gertz...' Her voice wavered as she spoke the name, bitterness creeping in. 'How can I look at him knowing that he was the one who put my grandfather's name on that horrible Nazi list?'

Marcin nodded, his jaw tightening as he listened.

Krista searched his face, looking for any sign of what he might be feeling. 'Will you go back?' she asked.

Marcin's gaze dropped to the blanket, his hand pausing mid-stroke on her cheek. 'I don't know,' he said, his voice low and uncertain. 'It depends on my father and if he...' His words trailed off, the sentence hanging unfinished in the air.

Krista reached for his hand, squeezing it firmly. She knew the unspoken words on his lips – *survives the war.*

'If my mother and Olesia go back then I'll make sure they are settled. After that, I don't know.' He shifted in his seat to look at her. 'I want to go wherever you are.'

Krista's heart skipped a beat at Marcin's words, her eyes meeting his. The warmth of his hand in hers sent a shiver down her spine, not from fear but from the thrilling realisation that perhaps she wasn't as alone in this world as she had believed.

The thought of a future with Marcin, one where they could sit by that crackling fire enveloped in each other's company, felt like a distant dream. She wanted to hold onto that dream, to grasp it firmly in her hands and never let it go.

'I want that, too,' Krista whispered. 'I want to be wherever you are.'

Marcin's eyes lit up with a mixture of relief and joy, his thumb gently tracing circles on the back of her hand. 'The thought of being with you is what has kept me going all these years. I can't imagine a future without you in it, Krista.'

She snuggled into the gap under his chin. The sunlight continued to stream in through the window, casting long shadows on the walls, as they both held onto each other, drawing comfort from the warmth of their connection in a world that had grown so cold.

Krista shifted slightly in Marcin's arms. 'The uprising,' she said. 'Do you really think we can win?'

Marcin's arms tightened around her, drawing her even closer. 'We have to,' he said. There was no hesitation or doubt in his voice, only a fierce determination.

Resting her head on his chest once more, Krista felt his

heart beating in harmony with hers. In that moment, surrounded by echoes of the past and the uncertainty of the future, Krista couldn't help but smile, treasuring every second she had left with Marcin at her side.

41

The uprising began at five o'clock. Krista sat alone in her apartment listening to gunfire explode across the city and watching from her window as smoke billowed up into the sky. She clutched the edges of her curtains, feeling the tremors of distant explosions beneath her feet. This was the day everyone had been waiting for, the day when the simmering unrest of the city boiled over into full-blown revolution. Another explosion rang out and Krista jumped. Knowing this day would come did not make it any less frightening.

There was a sudden hammering on her apartment door, sharp and insistent. Krista sprung to her feet, her heart racing. She hurried away from the window, her footsteps almost silent on the floor, and pressed her ear to the door, hoping to hear Marcin.

'We need your help,' a strange voice called out from the other side, low and commanding, as if he knew she was there, listening.

Krista's breath hitched, and she jumped back, a shiver of fear running down her spine. But her curiosity was stronger than her fear. She reached for the lock, hesitating for just a moment before undoing it. She pulled open the door.

Two men stood on the other side; their faces shadowed by the dim light of the alleyway. The taller of the two wasted no time in speaking, his words rushed and urgent. 'I apologise for the lack of warning,' he said, his eyes darting past her, already surveying the space behind her. 'But we need access to your apartment.'

Before Krista could react, both men pushed past her, their presence imposing as they entered her apartment. They moved swiftly, as if they had a clear purpose, stopping at the bumpy wall in the hallway, their eyes fixed on it.

'Close the door,' the other man ordered, his tone leaving no room for argument. He glanced back at her, his expression intense.

Krista swallowed hard. The door creaked as she slowly pushed it shut, her mind racing with questions and a growing sense of unease.

One of the men rummaged in a bag he'd placed on her floor. He produced a hammer and wasted no time in aiming it at her bumpy wall. The wall crumbled away piece by piece, filling the air with dust clouds and a musty smell. With a final swing of the hammer, the wall gave a resounding crack. The plaster fell away to reveal a hidden compartment filled with weapons glinting in the dim light.

Krista's eyes widened in disbelief as she took in the sight before her – an array of guns, knives, and ammunition neatly arranged within a hole in her wall. Her mind raced with questions, but before she could voice them, the men reached into the compartment and began loading the weapons into their bag. Once they were done, the men headed out of her apartment. The taller of the two paused, his broad shoulders filling the doorway. He turned back to her. His eyes held a fiery intensity as they looked on to hers.

'Be safe,' he said, yanking her door closed with a thud and leaving her alone once more.

The following morning, Krista stood in front of the hole in her wall, staring at it. She had cleaned up the debris and piled it into the hole, but the air was still heavy with dust. For now, it would have to stay that way. Her orders were to report to the hospital in the Old Town. Help in any way you can had been her only instruction. A sudden burst of gunfire outside shattered the silence in the apartment. It was time to go.

She took a few minutes to pack a bag of clothes before looking around at the apartment. There was no way to know what would happen as soon as she stepped outside, but a feeling in the pit of her stomach told her she wouldn't be returning any time soon. She picked up her address book, its pages filled with names of people who had helped her along the way – Olesia, Anna, Irena, Maja, Nelka, Emilia. She whispered a prayer for each girls' safety before turning to the inside cover, admiring the delicate clover leaves etched in different shades of green. The corner of Ayala's drawing peeked out from the pages of the book. Krista slipped it out and smiled at the charming illustration of a house surrounded by vibrant green clovers, each one with four leaves. Emilia had given it to Krista. She turned it over in her hands and traced her finger along the lone sentence written on the back: "Your package has arrived safely" with a tiny love heart at the end. It was unsigned, but there was no mistaking Irena's swirly handwriting. With a smile, she tucked the book and the drawing into her bag. From now until the war was over, she vowed to keep the book with her. It was too precious to risk losing.

Krista crossed the city on foot taking in all of the changes in just one day. Symbols of defiance and unity had sprung up all over as Polish flags were hoisted high on the tops of buildings and hung from residential windows. They billowed in the warm breeze, their edges curling from the light drizzle that brought some relief from the sweltering August heat. Warsaw was a flurry of activity as the Polish army emerged from their underground hideouts, determined to reclaim what was rightfully theirs. Guns were loaded and homemade catapults and carts filled with rocks had been wheeled onto the streets. Even the children were poised to help. Boys and girls huddled in small groups, pouring gasoline into empty glass bottles, ready to use them as makeshift weapons. The fight back had begun, and the mood was jubilant, as if Poland had already won.

As Krista rounded the corner, she saw Emilia outside her cafe, hammering nails into wooden boards covering her windows. Each blow of the hammer was like a crack of thunder, echoed by the shattered glass beneath Krista's shoes as she approached.

'It's futile, I know,' said Emilia, her voice heavy with resignation as she caught sight of Krista approaching.

Krista glanced at the shattered window, the glass glittering on the ground. 'What happened?'

'Someone put a rock through the window last night.' She crossed her arms, rubbing them as if warding off a chill. 'They didn't come inside, but that's only a matter of time.' She turned to Krista. 'My business is gone.'

'Oh, Emilia!' Krista stepped forward and touched her hand to Emilia's arm, her heart aching for her friend.

A green silk scarf framed Emilia's face; her fiery red hair concealed beneath it. Her eyes glistened with unshed tears, which she blinked away stubbornly. 'It's OK,' she said, her voice steady despite the trembling of her lips. 'If this is what is needed to finally be rid of the Nazis then so be it.'

'What are you going to do now?' asked Krista.

Emilia sighed; the sound filled with sorrow. 'I'm leaving the city,' she said, a note of finality in her tone. 'I can't stay here. People only see me as the German woman who served the Nazis. It's not safe for me, anymore.'

A sharp voice cut through the air, filled with venom. 'Traitor!' a voice yelled from behind them.

Krista turned just in time to see a glass bottle filled with a flaming rag being hurled towards the cafe. She dragged Emilia out of the way and watched in horror as the bottle smashed against a wooden panel, igniting a blaze that spread quickly up the front of the building.

'No!' yelled Krista. 'You've got it all wrong.' But the street was empty. Whoever had decided that Emilia should be punished was already gone.

Emilia's sobs mingled with the crackling of fire. Krista watched helplessly as the flames devoured the cafe. She felt numb. Emilia was being branded as a collaborator when all this time she'd risked her life to steal information from the Germans. But few people knew that.

Emilia dried her eyes. 'I must go now.' She tossed the hammer she had been clutching into the flames. 'I'll see you on the other side.'

As Krista watched Emilia walk away from her business and her home, her heart twisted in anguish. But there was no time to dwell on her sadness. The uprising had only just begun, and she was needed elsewhere. She pressed on towards the hospital. The streets near the hospital were filled with groups of heavily armed fighters. Suddenly, an explosion rattled through the air, its deafening sound reverberating in Krista's bones. Fear pulsed through her as she heard the echoes of war all around her. Every step felt like walking on hot coals, each moment fraught with the possibility of burning through her shoes and searing into her flesh. But she couldn't turn back now. She squared her shoulders and kept her gaze focused on the hospital building ahead of her.

42

ONCE INSIDE THE HOSPITAL, KRISTA WAS IMMEDIATELY PUT TO work, alongside a dozen other girls. Their first task was to set up makeshift beds in a nearby hallway. One of the girls brought over a pile of sheets and blankets and they got to work, swiftly pulling up crisp linens and tucking them tightly beneath thin mattresses. As the girls moved from bed to bed, Krista focused solely on the task at hand and tried her best to block out the explosions that were now ringing out across the city. The Germans were not going to hand their city back easily.

Before long, wounded fighters were pouring into the hospital at a rate faster than the medical teams could handle. The atmosphere quickly turned tense as doctors shouted orders and nurses hurried back and forth, their once-white aprons now covered in blood stains. The reassuring scent of antiseptic was replaced by the stench of blood and despair. Krista and the other girls weaved their way through a maze of stretcher-bearers and patients as they did their best to locate and deliver whatever the hospital staff asked for.

A tall, authoritative nurse marched through the double doors at the end of the ward, her uniform crumpled and sleeves rolled up. Her eyes scanned the room as she took in the scene. 'Listen up,' she said at the top of her voice. 'Has anyone here stitched wounds before?'

Krista and two others raised their hands.

'Good. Come with me.' The nurse spun around, her heels clicking sharply against the floor as the double doors swung shut behind her with a loud thud.

The three girls exchanged a brief, nervous glance because hurrying after the nurse, their footsteps quickening to match her pace. They moved through rows and rows of weary patients. Krista caught glimpses of the suffering all around them. Some men lay with limbs mangled by shrapnel, their faces pale and etched with pain. Others stared blankly ahead carrying the heavy weight of loss in their hollowed eyes.

The nurse came to an abrupt halt and pointed towards another set of double doors.

'Everyone in that corridor is walking wounded. They need their cuts cleaned, stitched, and dressed. Can you girls handle that?'

'Yes!' all three replied in unison, their voices firm despite the uncertainty flickering in their eyes.

Krista took a deep breath, squaring her shoulders, and led the others through the doors. The hallway ahead was lined with makeshift beds and bleeding patients. The air was thick with the metallic scent of blood and the low moans of pain. Distant explosions rumbled through the walls, a constant reminder of the danger just outside.

The girls each grabbed a tray of medical instruments from a nearby trolley, chose a patient, and set to work.

Krista approached a boy who sat hunched on one of the

beds, his uniform soaked through with blood. The fabric hung off his frame, at least two sizes too big for him, his small shoulders barely filling it out. His youthful features were obscured by dirt and dried blood, making it hard to tell just how young he really was.

A surge of compassion welled up within Krista as she knelt beside him. 'How old are you?'

'Fourteen,' he said, his eyes wide and haunted.

Krista's breath caught in her throat, her heart aching for the boy who was far too young to be caught up in the horrors of battle. She swallowed hard, pushing back her emotions as she looked down at the fresh cuts to his forearm. Someone had cleaned them already and there was a particularly nasty wound waiting to be stitched.

'How did this happen?' she asked.

'A grenade.' His voice betrayed no hint of the fear he must surely have felt. 'Will this take long?'

'Only a few minutes,' said Krista.

'Good. I've got to get back.'

As Krista opened her mouth to argue, an ear-splitting boom shook the ground beneath them. The walls rattled and dust rained down from the ceiling, coating their hair and clothes. Krista quickly covered the boy's wounds with her hands.

He smiled at her. 'Thanks. The nurse who cleaned me up would not have been pleased if that dust had fallen in the cuts.'

Krista returned his smiled, threaded her needle and set to work suturing the boys ragged flesh with precise and steady movements. The boy tensed his jaw and sat perfectly still while she worked.

The girls worked almost non-stop for hours, going from one wounded person to the next and doing their best to patch up injuries with dwindling supplies. The hallway was a hectic blur of bodies constantly moving in and out, as those with minor wounds were quickly treated and hurried on their way to rejoin the uprising. Exhausted, Krista finally found a moment to catch her breath when the corridor of patients quieted down. She stretched her stiff muscles and rubbed her aching hands together for some relief. It wasn't long before the sound of heavy footsteps echoed down the hallway as another group of injured Polish soldiers stumbled in. Krista sprang into action, gathering bandages, suturing kits, and water.

Days passed by as Krista and the other girls tirelessly tended to the wounded, snatching brief moments to eat or sleep a little whenever possible. She couldn't go home; the thought of it brought her mind to Marcin. Not knowing his whereabouts made her feel powerless, but she took comfort in helping others. After all, each person she cared for was loved by someone.

'That's you,' said Krista, having just stitched and dressed a gaping wound in a soldier's leg.

The soldier sprung up from the bed. 'Great. Here we go again.'

She watched as a he strode away, eager to rejoin the fight. A nurse appeared at the end of the corridor.

'Krista Schulz?' the nurse said.

'That's me,' said Krista, raising her hand as though in a classroom.

'Come with me.' The intensity in her dark eyes hinted at the urgency of the situation and Krista hurried towards her.

'We need someone to deliver supplies to an address on the other side of town.' The nurse's uniform was stained with blood and her hair was dishevelled and plastered to her forehead by sweat. 'Can you do it?' she asked.

'Me?' asked Krista. 'I suppose I could, yes. What kind of supplies?'

'Medical supplies. There's a first aid station there and a doctor. It's a critical location and they need to be resupplied. I have everything packed and ready to go. A messenger boy was supposed to carry out the delivery but he's–' The nurse looked down to the floor. 'He's too injured.'

The nurse looked completely beaten, her shoulders slumped and dark circles beneath her eyes. Krista couldn't imagine what traumas the woman had tended to these last few days. 'Don't worry about the supplies. I can help with that.'

The nurse's hand landed on Krista's shoulder. A hint of guilt at what she was asking passed across her face, her lips pressing into a thin line as she hesitated. 'It's dangerous out there,' she said, her voice laced with concern.

Krista met her gaze and nodded. 'I know.'

She followed the nurse to a set of stainless-steel sinks and scrubbed her hands clean under the stream of water. The nurse stood beside her and rattled off the address and brief directions.

'You may need to take a few detours to get there,' the nurse warned. 'I've heard some of the streets in the area have been all but destroyed.'

Krista dried her hands. She turned to the nurse; her eyes steady. 'Don't worry. I'll get there,' she said.

A mixture of relief and apprehension crossed the nurse's tired features and Krista offered a small smile designed to reassure both herself and the nurse that she was up to this task.

'Who suggested me?' Krista asked.

The nurse shrugged. 'I was given your name. That's all I know.'

She led Krista to a room where three bags of supplies waited. Alongside her own bag, Krista strapped two of the other bags across her body, her shoulders taking the weight, and carried the other one in her hand. The nurse gave a nervous smile and wished her luck. Krista's own nerves gnawed at her from the inside as she made her way through the corridors of the hospital and emerged into the darkness outside.

43

DESPITE THE LATE HOUR, THE AIR WAS WARM AS KRISTA walked through the Old Town, her eyes squinting as they adjusted to the dark. The streets were eerily quiet. Buildings loomed high above her, their once-grand facades now battered by years of war and neglect. She crossed Plac Zamkowy. The Royal Castle was no more. She stepped around piles of rubble where she could and trudged across other piles that could not be avoided. The fighting she had heard from inside the hospital walls had been worse than she had imagined. In the dim light she saw shattered windows, overturned carts, and debris littering the cobblestone streets. The scent of burnt wood and gasoline hung heavily in the air. There were no Germans. The people of the Old Town had come together and fought off the Germans. For another day, at least.

As she made her way through the maze of narrow alleys, she occasionally spotted a figure darting through the shadows and kept her mind occupied by making up stories in her head as to who they were: three Polish soldiers planning their next moves, a civilian sneaking out to find food for his family, and two Scouts making covert deliveries.

A door to her right was flung open and her heart beat a little faster. The quiet of the streets was broken by the laughter of people inside the building who had forgotten their struggles for a moment. Two men emerged from the door. She locked eyes with one and was aware of the other scanning the bags she carried.

'Where are you off to?' the man staring at her asked.

'Delivering medical supplies,' Krista answered.

'Hurry along then,' he said, not bothering to ask for further details or inspect her bags.

Krista scarpered away.

It took another twenty minutes for her to reach the street she was looking for. A man waited for her in the open doorway, a rifle aimed up the street as if also waiting for trouble. Despite its surroundings, the three-storey building looked untouched, standing strong, unlike its crumbling neighbour.

'Are these for you?' Krista asked, lifting the bag she carried.

'The doctor is in the back room,' the man said. The man's face was weathered and lined with deep creases. His eyes sharp and alert, constantly scanning the surroundings.

Krista stepped into the building behind him. A grand staircase rose up from the centre of the house, its intricately carved banisters hinting at its former glory. Ornate light fixtures adorned the walls in the hallway, but they were shrouded in layers of dust. She guessed this once beautiful home had been abandoned some time ago.

She found the back room and a man she presumed was the doctor standing over another man in a military-style metal bed.

'Hi, I'm Krista. The hospital sent me.'

'About time.' The man didn't look at her, but she recognised his voice instantly.

Krista gave a sharp intake of breath. 'Doctor Kowalski?' she asked, her voice laced with disbelief. She had a hundred question, but no time to ask them.

'There's a bottle of vodka on the table,' Kowalski said, still not looking up. 'Can you bring it to me?' Kowalski's clothes were soaked in blood, and only then did she notice he was applying pressure to the injured man's bleeding arm.

Krista put the bags down and hurried to the table. She grabbed the bottle, screwed the lid off, and handed it over. The doctor put the bottle to his lips and took a swig, his other hand still pressed against the man's arm. He gestured for Krista to take over. She put both her hands on the blood-soaked rags and pressed hard. Warm blood seeped through her fingers. The man's arm gave way under her weight and bile rose up in her throat. She swallowed it down. She glanced at the ceiling and thanked whoever might be listening that the man was unconscious.

The doctor doused a knife in vodka. He took another swig. 'You might want to leave,' he said, holding the bottle towards her.

Krista nodded and took her hands off the patient's arm. She had seen some horrifying things since the war began and she didn't need to see any more.

She took the vodka and left the room, stopping in the hallway to take a swig from it. The alcohol burned her throat on its way down, but at least it provided some sensation other than the nausea she was so far holding at bay. Her hands were stained with blood, and she heard voices nearby.

'We've held off the Germans and re-captured much of the Old Town,' someone said. 'The uprising is working.'

'Is it?' another voice asked.

'Yes. Most of Warsaw is now in Polish hands.'

'The Germans still have control of the railways, electricity, the water supply. We've had the benefit of surprise. They're ready for us now.'

'We only have to hold out for a few more days.'

'Says who? The Soviets are not coming to help us. We're on our own and it's a fight to the death. We all saw what had happened in the Jewish ghetto. The people were massacred, and the ghetto flattened. There's nothing left. If we even think about surrendering, Warsaw will be wiped off the map. We must win, no matter the cost.'

The man was right. The Nazis had reacted with fury against the Jewish uprising and what had once housed a community, albeit in dire conditions, now ceased to exist. Scorched, charred earth was all that remained. She couldn't bear the thought that the same thing would happen to the rest of Warsaw. She had come to this city with nothing, but it had become her home. It was where she had learned to take care of herself and where she had spent the last few years caring for others. The Allies were coming. The war was almost over. Everyone except the Nazis knew that. But still her heart ached to think that the Nazis might destroy what was left of the city in one final act of evil.

The crunch on rubble behind her alerted her to someone's presence. She turned. It was the man who had been waiting for her at the door. 'Follow me,' he said.

She followed him into a room that had once been someone's kitchen. Piles of crockery decorated with sunflowers were shattered on the floor and rubble lay in every corner.

The two men whose conversation she had overheard were sitting on the floor, their backs leaning against the wall.

'There's no running water in the house, only buckets of water. We've collected it from dripping pipes and water pooled in bomb craters so use it sparingly.' The man plucked a cup from the floor and plunged it into a bucket of water.

He poured the water over Krista's hands, and she rubbed them together vigorously, doing what she could to scrub them clean. 'Thank you,' she said. 'Are there more patients here?'

'Yes, three more in the other room.'

'I'll go and check on them.' She dried her hands as best she could on her clothes, avoiding the dark patches where blood had already soaked into her clothing. She paused at the door, feeling the need to prepare herself for whatever was behind the door. 'How serious are the injuries?' she asked.

'Everyone is conscious,' the man said.

'Right. I'm Krista, by the way.'

'Aleksy.'

The whistling of a bomb hurtling towards the earth rang out. Krista gripped the door handle with clammy hands and braced herself for the impact. It struck the ground somewhere in the distance. A stream of white dust fell from the ceiling, showering Krista. She coughed as the dust tickled the back of her throat. She looked up the ceiling and back at Aleksy.

'They're coming,' said Aleksy as he lit a cigarette and wandered away.

She stared after him, her chest tightening at the thought of what other horrors they would have to face in the days ahead.

Krista distracted herself for the next hour by tending to the three injured men. She changed bandages and restitched a wound that had burst open. The supplies she needed were already in the room. She'd left the bags she'd brought from the hospital with the doctor and was glad she hadn't had to go back for them.

The men were beaten, bloodied, and, in the case of one of them, severely burned. But they were in high spirits and were eager to continue the fight. One of them wore a Gestapo uniform and the only thing preventing him from being shot at by his fellow Poles was a painted red and white stripe on his helmet to match the armband he wore on his sleeve.

'We're waiting for a resupply of our ammunition.'

'Well, you can't go anywhere until the doctor has seen you again,' said Krista. It was a pointless instruction, she knew. As soon as someone arrived with ammunition, the men would be gone. All she could do was patch them up. Whatever they did next was up to them.

When Doctor Kowalski emerged from his makeshift operating theatre, he came to check on the other three men. He had somehow found a change of clothes. His grey shirt was grubby, but there was no evidence of the bloody operation he had just performed. He inspected the fresh bandages on each of the patients.

'How is he?' one of the men asked. His voice was quiet, full of concern, and Krista suspected he knew the other man well.

'He's alive,' said Kowalski, his tone curt.

'And his arm?'

'Gone.'

Krista flinched as the door burst open and two unfamiliar men stumbled in, one carrying a woman who was bleeding profusely from her abdomen. The woman's face was contorted with fear and pain, and she clutched onto the man's arm for support. A small boy wailed in the other man's arms.

'My son!' the woman screamed; her voice raw with desperation.

'He's here,' the man carrying the child replied, his own voice trembling.

Kowalski's gaze was steady as he looked at the scene before him. 'What happened?' he asked, his voice even and controlled, not betraying any emotions he may have been feeling.

'The Germans are using women and children as shields for their tanks.' The man gently lowered the woman onto one of the beds. 'What are we supposed to do? Allow the Germans to recapture our positions or keep fighting and risk killing the people we're trying to free?'

The other man thrust the crying toddler towards Krista. 'Is he injured?' she asked, taking him into her arms.

'I don't think so,' the man replied before turning away.

Krista quickly assessed the little boy in her arms. He was physically unharmed, but given his whimpering and shaking, he was traumatised by whatever had just happened.

'I'll take him,' the other man said to Krista. 'You might be needed here.'

Krista handed over the child and rushed to assist Kowalski who was already tending to the wounded woman. She couldn't shake the queasy feeling in her stomach. The thought of the Nazis using people as shields for their advance filled her with horror and anger. She snatched up a pile of clean cloths and pressed them hard to the woman's abdomen while Kowalski administered pain relief.

44

THE SHARP CRACK OF GUNFIRE ERUPTED, EACH SHOT A reminder of the violence that inched ever closer to the makeshift medical station. Despite the predictions of a short-lived uprising, it had now been nearly a month since the fighting began. Krista had spent all her time patching up endless people and sending them away again, for some, to their certain deaths. It was obvious even to her that the allies were not coming to support them. She'd heard talk of packages being dropped from the skies containing food and weapons, but they were much fewer in number than the Home Army needed. The Old Town was on the brink of collapse.

Aleksy had disappeared that morning as he did every morning. Only this time he hadn't gone to fight. He had gone in search of an escape route. As they anxiously awaited his return, Doctor Kowalski and Krista tended to the latest group of Resistance fighters to show up at their door. Three of the patients had burns and bullet wounds, and one other lay unconscious, barely clinging to life after Kowalski had revived him twice.

The doctor checked the man's vital signs and shook his head. 'I need a hospital.'

The thought of the destroyed hospital brought tears to Krista's eyes – according to Aleksy, it had been attacked by Nazis who had killed everyone who worked there and set the building ablaze, leaving patients trapped inside. She couldn't bear to think about the girls she had worked alongside and what might have happened to them.

Behind Krista, there was a commotion, and she turned to see Aleksy, trailed by a boy. The boy's face was flushed and his eyes bright with youthful energy. She dried her eyes and steeled herself for what was to come. They had no choice but to keep fighting until the end, whenever that may be.

Aleksy carried a mallet in one hand and a handgun in the other. Dark circles were visible under bloodshot eyes, betraying his sleepless nights. His posture was rigid, his muscles stiff and ready for action.

'I'm Pavel,' the boy said. His gaze was steady, showing no signs of fear or hesitation. He passed around cigarettes, which the injured men snatched. They scrambled to light them and inhaled their first drags with appreciative groans.

'We're leaving today,' said Aleksy. 'As soon as we can. Pavel here is going to lead us out through the sewers.'

There was a hardness in Aleksy's voice that left no room for debate, but still, Doctor Kowalski looked the boy up and down with something close to humour. 'How old are you?' the doctor asked.

Pavel stood a little taller, pushed his shoulders back, and lifted his chin slightly. 'Twelve.'

'And do you know your way around the sewers?' the doctor asked.

A small grin crossed Pavel's face. 'I'm a Scout,' he said, as if that told the doctor everything he needed to know.

Kowalski looked unconvinced.

Krista clapped her hands together. 'Right,' she said. 'What do you need from us?'

The doctor gave her the same look he had given Pavel and shook his head. 'There must be another option.'

Aleksy shrugged. 'You can stay here and die.' He tucked the gun in the waistband of his trousers and held the mallet up. 'I'll make the hole.'

'The hole?' asked Krista.

'We can't walk out of the front door,' said Aleksy, putting a protective hand on Pavel's shoulder. 'Pavel and I barely made it inside. There are snipers everywhere, and the downstairs windows in the back are bricked up. We'll have to smash our way through.'

'We'll need a hole big enough for a stretcher to fit through,' said one of the injured men, nodding to his unconscious friend on the bed.

Aleksy and Kowalski exchanged a glance. The doctor nodded his understanding of whatever silent instruction he had been given. Krista looked at the injured fighter who stood now puffing on a cigarette, looming over his friend. He hadn't noticed the look between Aleksy and the doctor. Probably for the best.

The deafening screech of a bomb slicing through the air filled their ears. It was the loudest one yet. And then, the explosion. The ground beneath their feet trembled violently and the walls shuddered. A piece of the ceiling loosened and plunged to the ground, narrowly missing Pavel. It was as if the world was crumbling, and they were powerless against it.

'Best get organised,' said Aleksy, heading out of the door with one of the less injured patients.

Pavel gave Krista and the others an overview of what to expect in the sewers. He spoke confidently and knowledgeably. If the doctor had any doubts about the boy's ability to lead their way underground, they had surely been quashed by Pavel's vivid descriptions of the conditions they were about the enter.

Gunfire rang out. It was close, and a sign that it was time to go. Pavel seemed confident that they could escape through the sewers. But first they had to run the gauntlet of bombs falling from the sky and Germans on the ground firing at anything that moved.

In the time it had taken Krista to bag up as much of the medical supplies and food that she could carry, Aleksy and the others had bludgeoned a hole in the back wall of the building. There wasn't much food, a few cans of fish, a tin of peaches, and a couple of small potatoes. But food was scarce enough. There was no point in leaving it behind to be buried under a pile of rubble when it could keep someone else going for at least a little while.

'We're ready when the doc is,' said Aleksy, covered head to toe in white dust and still holding the heavy mallet.

Doctor Kowalski appeared at Krista's side. 'We're walking wounded only,' he announced.

Aleksy hooked the mallet in his belt. 'Then let's go.'

One of the injured men shook his head. His eyebrows drew together, but whatever he was thinking remained unsaid. The others scrambled through the hole in the wall.

Krista grabbed her bags and passed them through. There was no time to mourn for the man who had lost his life. He was too gravely injured to have survived the journey ahead of them. Regardless of what had happened in that room, the Nazis were responsible for his death. And if they didn't get going, the same fate would belie them all. She dropped to her stomach and awkwardly shuffled her way through the hole. The dust threatened to choke her, and she clamped her lips together and held her breath to avoid inhaling it. The man on the other side put out his hands and she reached for them. He yanked her free and she stepped aside to make space for Doctor Kowalski following behind her.

The air outside was heavy with smoke and the sky lit up with a fiery orange as Warsaw burned. A plane roared above their heads drowning out the whistle of the bomb it dropped. An explosion rang out and the ground beneath their feet shuddered again with the impact. A crash was heard from inside the house as another piece of the building gave way.

Krista strapped her bags across her body and peered through the hole, watching everyone else hurry through.

Aleksy was last out. He looked up towards the smoke billowing into the sky. 'They're burning us out building by building. It's now in a race to stay ahead of the Germans and the flames.'

'Follow me,' said Pavel, taking charge as soon as everyone had cleared the building. Aleksy readied his weapon, a rifle that he had added to the handgun in the waistband of his trousers and moved alongside him. Krista and the others fell into line behind them.

They left the cover of the building and made their way steadily along the narrow street behind, keeping close to the walls.

Pavel made them stop at the corner. 'We need to run here. Stay low. When you get to the other side, get in the ditch.' He looked up and down the street and signalled for them to move.

Aleksy crossed the street first. The three patients sprinted across the street behind him as fast as their weary legs would carry them. Krista followed. Shots rang out and rubble from the ground sprung up around her ankles. She kept her head down and ran as fast as she could. Aleksy returned fire, shooting indiscriminately at some unseen target. One by one, they dropped into a recently dug six feet deep ditch. Krista's heart raced. She hoped the ditch led all the way to the sewers.

They trudged their way along the narrow trench until they had gone as far as they could then they helped each other to scramble back up onto the street. They were a bloodied and muddy mess, exhaustion visible on all of their faces, but they had no choice but to carry on.

They advanced steadily through the rubble and smouldering ruins of the city. Krista jumped each time she heard shots fire. The sounds of war from inside a building were one thing. Hearing them when you were walking in the open air was something different entirely.

Krista covered her nose with her hand. The acrid smell of smoke and death was impossible not to notice. Shadows lurked at every corner, yet Aleksy never flinched. He kept his hands loosely on his rifle, ready to spring into action if needed. Krista supposed that this had become somewhat normal to him. He had spent many hours in these streets when she and the doctor had been holed up in the relative safety of their makeshift hospital.

Suddenly, a burst of gunfire erupted, ricocheting off the ground around them. The sounds seemed to come from all directions.

'Take cover,' yelled Aleksy.

Krista and the others ran, seeking refuge behind a crumbling wall. Her whole body trembled as she huddled behind the wall, stealing glances every so often at the streets surrounding them. In the distance, she could see figures darting back and forth, the clatter of boots against rubble growing louder as if the Nazis were closing in. Every nerve in Krista's body screamed for her to run, to find somewhere safer to hide, but she gritted her teeth and stayed put.

Aleksy inched his way further into the open then crouched down as if trying to blend into the earth. He scanned the landscape in front of him. Another deafening shot fired in their direction and Aleksy fired back, without hesitation.

There was a moment of silence, save for Krista's ragged and panicked breaths, before Aleksy stood up. He turned to Krista and the others. His eyes were ablaze with the certainty that he'd hit his target. 'We must move quickly,' he urged. 'They know where we are now, and they'll send others.'

With a swift hand signal, Aleksy motioned for them to move. Krista and the others obeyed, following closely behind him. Her senses felt heightened as they weaved their way through the maze of broken buildings and twisted metal. She focused on each step, taking what comfort she could from the weapon in Aleksy's hands and his seemingly deadly accuracy.

45

As they continued their way through the streets of Warsaw, Aleksy and the other three men walked closely together, whispering as they went. Krista couldn't shake the sense of vulnerability that came from being out in the open. It seemed impossible that Aleksy had taken out the only sniper in the area. There had to be others, and Krista felt like they were being watched, stalked even, by someone in the surrounding buildings, just waiting for the perfect opportunity to take a shot. She strained to catch snippets of Aleksy's hushed conversations.

'But only when fired upon,' Aleksy said. 'Unless they find us again, we don't want to give our position away.'

Their hands gripped their respective weapons, ready to fire. Krista had stopped thinking of them as her patients. They were Resistance fighters once again, somehow managing to push through their injuries and, she hoped, get them all to safety.

Eventually, Pavel stopped at a hole in the ground. The metal grate marking the entrance to the sewer had already been opened and cast aside on the cobbled road. Pavel paused, looking uncertain. He dug a torch out of his pocket, crouched down, and shone the light into the space beneath their feet.

'We're good,' said Pavel, straightening up and flicking his torch off.

Krista and the others peered into the darkness of the sewer. She gagged at the smell that flooded her nostrils.

'You get used to it,' said Pavel. He climbed down first.

'You go next,' Aleksy said to Krista. He steadied his rifle and turned away from the manhole to watch for anyone sneaking up on them.

Krista gripped the metal ladder and climbed down into the sludgy water beneath the Old Town. The air in the sewers was stifling hot and in sharp contrast to the icy water sloshing up Krista's legs. The tunnel was tight. Even she couldn't stand up straight. She pressed herself against the wall to make space for the others.

Once everyone was safely underground, Pavel unwound a length of rope. 'Everyone grab a section,' the young sewer rat instructed.

'Should we tie it around us?' asked Krista.

'No, don't do that,' said Aleksy. 'If one person goes down, they'll take the rest of us with them.' He flicked on a tiny light and shone it against the wall. A white symbol had been etched onto the brick. 'Stay together. We'll be navigating most of the way in the dark, but, if you get separated, follow these signs if you see them. Stay quiet and keep moving.'

Aleksy waited for a beat. When no one spoke, he switched the light off and plunged them all into darkness. 'Let's go,' he whispered.

Krista gripped the rope tight. She couldn't see the marks

on the wall so she intended to stick as close to Pavel and Aleksy as she could.

The water rushed past them like the Vistula on a stormy day. She had expected still, stagnant water. She reassured herself that tunnels amplified noise, and it sounded worse than it was. The tension on the rope to the front of her and the weight dragging behind her brought a small comfort. Whatever happened, she wasn't alone.

After a time, Krista's steps became heavier as she lost the feeling in her toes. It was almost too much effort to lift her legs. She allowed her feet to glide through the water and along the floor of the sewer. As they ventured deeper into the tunnels, the sound of rushing water faded away as the current became more subdued. The only noises were the quiet rhythm of her heartbeat and the shuffling of her companions sliding through the mulch.

Without warning, the tension on the rope to the front of her slackened and she bumped up against Aleksy in the dark, Doctor Kowalski bumping up against her. The group huddled together.

'There's an open manhole,' Pavel whispered.

'Should we look?' one of the men asked.

'Only if you want to get shot in the head,' said Pavel, his voice flat and emotionless as he uttered words that no child should ever have to say. The threat hung heavy in the already stifling. 'We're going to move slower. If anyone is up there, we don't want them to hear us. The Germans know we're using the sewers. They've been trying to blast and burn us out.'

The rumbled of vehicles echoed above them.

'We should go back,' whispered Aleksy. 'We'll find another way.' His usual confidence was replaced by a rare uncertainty.

'It's too far to go back,' said Pavel. 'And we'll be heading in the wrong direction. This is the only way.' He may have been young, but he spoke with authority. This was his territory, and everyone seemed to respect that.

Krista gripped the rope with both hands and readied herself to move again.

'Stay slow,' whispered Pavel. 'If you hear shots, run.'

The group crept onwards. Krista spotted the outline of the manhole just ahead of her. Pavel must have past it already. Aleksy would be underneath it now and then it would be her turn.

A beam of light shone into the tunnel, and she froze. No one bumped into her this time. They too must have seen the light and stopped. She heard voices. They were German, she was certain of that, but whatever they were saying didn't travel into the dark depths of the underground.

The light flicked off and Krista felt a tug on the rope. She took it as a sign to keep moving. She stepped forward until she was directly under the opening to the sewer. One more step and she cleared it. She dared not look back at the others. All she could do was keep moving and hope that the Nazis didn't stick their heads into the hole for another look.

Doctor Kowalski bumped into her back. 'Speed it up,' he said. 'They're pouring fuel into the tunnel.'

Krista quickened her stride, catching up with Aleksy. She told him what the doctor had said. Everyone upped their pace and moved as quickly as possible through the dense water, no longer caring if anyone heard them. They were now running for their lives.

Pavel led them around a corner to a dead end. 'Get low and cover your faces,' he said.

Krista was shoved against the wall; a hand grabbed her shoulder and pushed her down into the water. Crouched down with her face buried in her knees, she was pinned in from all sides. An explosion rang out and a burst of unbearable heat flooded the air around them.

46

After what felt like hours of navigating the intricate maze beneath the besieged city, they reached another ladder leading upwards. Pavel climbed up first. Once clear of the sewer, he shone a torch down towards the others. Aleksy motioned for Krista to climb. With trembling hands, she grasped the cool metal rungs and pulled herself up.

As Krista neared the top of the ladder, she heard voices in Polish and then laughter. Tears welled up in her eyes as she emerged from the filth of the sewer into a different world.

The fresh air was the first thing Krista noticed. It was the sweetest smell she could ever remember after so long underground. Gunfire still echoed through the air, but it was reassuringly distant. If she covered her ears to muffle the sound, it was like an entirely different country, one not at war. There was little rubble, the sky was clear, and the buildings had glass in their windows instead of it being crunched underfoot. The street too was alive with activity. Girls served food and water, and boys hurried around carrying boxes or delivering armfuls of weapons to soldiers milling around.

Aleksy emerged from of the manhole last, his clothing scorched and revealing patches of burnt flesh on his upper body. Doctor Kowalski picked at a piece of burnt fabric, but Aleksy batted his hand away.

'You did it,' said Aleksy, giving Pavel a firm slap on the back for a job well done. The boy had led them safely beyond the clutch of the enemy.

A familiar girl with dark hair and a bright smile on her face approached Krista. 'Larysa?'

'Yes,' Larysa nodded her head enthusiastically. 'I wondered if you would recognise me. It's been a while.'

'I can't believe you're here.'

'The Guides and Scouts are helping. Come on. I'll show you where to get cleaned up.'

Krista looked down at her sodden clothes. A sickening stench of waste and dampness clung to her. 'Thank you. I really need it.'

Larysa led her to a nearby building. Krista stared again at the glass in the windows, glad to see a part of the city still looked strong. A breeze from behind her brought warm air and the faint aroma of smoke. She had a sinking feeling the neighbourhood wouldn't stay like this for long.

Inside the building, Krista was met with a wave of warmth and the comforting scent of hot food cooking somewhere. Larysa handed Krista a change of clothes and a small piece of broken soap. 'You can get changed in there.' She pointed to a door off the hallway. 'The water still works. We don't know how long that will last so use it while you can.'

'Have you heard from Nelka?' Krista asked.

Larysa shook her head. 'Not since the uprising began.'

'I'm sure she's fine,' said Krista, more to reassure herself.

She headed into the bathroom, wasting no time in shedding her filthy clothes and scrubbing herself clean. She dressed in a set of trousers that had to be rolled up several times at the ankles and a crumpled blue shirt. But the clothes were clean and dry so she couldn't complain. Her shoes, on the other hand, were soaked. She put them in the sink and turned the tap on, watching the water turn murky brown as it flowed over her shoes.

Once the water ran as clear as it was likely to get, Krista put her feet into the sopping shoes and headed back outside where she found Aleksy and Doctor Kowalski. Aleksy had spread out a map on an upturned crate, his brow furrowed in concentration. Doctor Kowalski sat on the grass nearby, sipping from a mug of steaming liquid. They both looked up as Krista approached and she smiled, grateful that they had all survived.

Krista took a seat beside the doctor and Larysa reappeared, handing her a mug. Krista wrapped her icy hands around the drink and took a sip. It was a watery boiled barley soup, but it was hot, and her stomach growled in anticipation.

'I snagged you a piece of this, too,' said Larysa, slipping a small chunk of bread to Krista.

Krista bit into it. Her mouth filled with crusty bread and a sweet fruit filling. Leave it to the Guides to find jam in the middle of a war zone.

Larysa sat down on the grass. 'Have you been home?'

Krista shook her head. 'There didn't seem to be much point at first. We were so busy. So many people needed our help. And then I got scared – afraid to step outside and afraid that there would be nothing left to go back to.' The apartment wasn't her home. It didn't belong to her. It was just a temporary shelter to store her borrowed belongings and rest her head at night. There had been a stockpile of weapons in the wall, and she hadn't even known about it. But despite that, she couldn't go back to the apartment. When the war finally ended, there was no one waiting for her. She had no family left to return to. And the fear of finding the apartment in ruins and losing one more thing was too great.

Larysa's shoulders drooped and her vibrant demeanour dimmed. 'I went home. The building was destroyed. Thankfully no one was inside. Now, there are eight of us cramped into my grandmother's two-bedroom apartment.'

'I'm sorry,' said Krista.

Larysa shrugged. 'It's only a building. That's what my mother says anyway.'

'Your mother is right.'

When Krista had finished eating, she rummaged through her bag to find that much of what she carried was wet. She spread her damp clothes out on the ground to dry in the air, hoping they would be salvageable.

While she sipped her soup, she flipped through the pages of her address book. The edges were slightly damp, but its leather cover and the clothing it had been nestled beside had shielded it. Other than a few wet smudges, the ink was still legible and Ayala's drawing still intact. She squeezed the book against her chest, relieved that it had survived the water.

A man with a wide grin on his face and a bag slung over his shoulder strode towards them. He slapped Aleksy on the back a few times. 'Good to see you alive and well, my friend,' he said.

'You too,' replied Aleksy, but his tone was more serious. 'What do you have there?'

The man opened the bag and began tossing weapons

onto the ground. Guns, ammunition, and even grenades were tossed carelessly, with no fear of accidental discharge or detonation.

'We found a squad of Nazis hiding in the basement of Andrej's apartment building. There were fourteen of them and only two of us, but they dropped their weapons, put their hands up, and came quietly into our custody.' The man's grin widened further. 'Looks like the Germans are finally giving up.'

Larysa stood up. 'I heard that Paris has been liberated. Is that true?'

The man nodded. 'It's true.'

Larysa turned to Krista; her eyes once more sparkling with joy. 'Liberated! It won't be long until we can say the same.'

Krista felt the tension in her body ease. The imminent fall of the Old Town was a significant setback, but this wasn't the end. For the first time in weeks she felt hope, as though the uprising still had a chance. She just wished in that moment that she hadn't turned around to see the doubt etched on Aleksy's face.

47

2 OCTOBER 1944

Krista's hands shook as she pressed down on the man's chest, trying to stop the blood gushing from the bullet wound. He let out a guttural scream and his eyes pleaded with her for help. It was too late. He was dying right in front of her and there was nothing she could do. Doctor Kowalski injected something into the man's veins, and he quietened down, eyes glassing over as he slipped away.

'He wouldn't have made it,' said Kowalski.

Krista nodded, but a wave of guilt washed over her, as if she were responsible for pulling the trigger that had torn through the man's flesh. He had been their last patient, and they hadn't been able to save him. Her hands dropped to her sides and she looked down at her clothes, drenched in the man's blood.

Kowalski picked up a scrap of metal from the floor and scratched a line next to the others on the wall. The uprising, which should have lasted a few days, had reached day sixty-three and it would go no further. The Polish army had surrendered and agreed to march into German custody. There had been no other choice. The army had no ammunition, no food, no water. The Germans had retaken the power plant, so these last few weeks had been fought without light or electricity.

Aleksy appeared in the doorway. He carried the weight of the failed uprising heavily on his shoulders, evident in every crease and line etched into his face. 'It's time,' he said. He handed Krista and Kowalski a bundle of clothing each. 'Put these on. The Nazis are indiscriminately executing people. This is the one time it might be useful to be caught in uniform. Maybe we'll have a chance if we all stick together.'

Thousands of civilians had been forced out of the city, after being assured by the Nazis that they would be treated humanely. Despite doubts about the sincerity of this promise, the Nazis had followed through. There was still uncertainty about what exactly would happen to those who were expelled, but it had not been the violent massacre that many had feared. Now was different though. The Nazis seemed to consider everyone who remained in the city Resistance fighters. There was a supposed agreement for fair treatment of the Home Army, but the Wehrmacht appeared selective about applying it.

The doctor and Aleksy left the room and Krista changed out of her blood-soaked clothes, wiping the blood from her hands as best she could. The stench of death clung to the scratchy fabric of the uniform. Now wasn't the time to wonder who had last worn it. She tucked her address book in the waistband of her trousers, determined to hang on to it for as long as she could, and grabbed her bag. Turning back to the man on the bed behind her, she whispered, 'I'm sorry.'

She joined the others in the street, her heart thundering in her chest as she stepped outside, mouth agape as she took in their surroundings. The city had crumbled. Entire streets had been ravaged by fire. Somehow the row of townhouses that sheltered their latest medical station still stood, albeit barely. The walls had rattled every time an explosion rang out.

Kowalski and Aleksy had been joined by a larger group of Resistance fighters. The weight of their impending surrender bore down on them all as they walked, their footsteps echoing off the cobblestone streets and bringing them closer to their fate.

The bleak procession marched by a gated garden, filled with perfectly lined rows of wooden crosses marking recent burials. Each one represented a life cut short, a story left unfinished. But those were the fortunate ones, laid to rest with dignity and honour. Elsewhere, bodies lay piled on top of each other, a grim reminder of the widespread devastation that had consumed every corner of the city. It was a scene of unimaginable tragedy.

As the group neared the pre-agreed checkpoint their hushed whispers became a sombre silence. They raised their hands in surrender and fell into line. Krista stole a glance at Aleksy, his expression unreadable behind the facade of stoicism he wore like armour. Beside him, Doctor Kowalski cast furtive glances over his shoulder, his eyes betraying the same fear that Krista felt pulsing through her veins.

The waiting Nazis eyed them warily, rifles at the ready. Any weapons still in Polish hands were tossed to the ground and they were herded forward towards waiting trucks.

Krista climbed aboard the truck. The atmosphere was thick with tension, the air charged with anticipation of what was to come next.

Suddenly, a commotion erupted behind her. She spun around just in time to see a Wehrmacht soldier pointing his rifle at another man dressed in civilian clothes. Before anyone could react, the deafening sound of gunfire pierced the air, causing screams and chaos to erupt among the others waiting in line. The man fell to the ground, crimson blossoming on his chest as he gasped for air. A group of men surged forward and surrounded the injured man.

The soldiers began shouting orders, pushing and corralling the group onto the trucks. Furious arguing ensued until another shot rang out and silenced everyone. The men had little choice but to step around their fallen friend lying lifeless on the ground. Their own lives hung by a thread, at the mercy of men who saw them not as people, but as threats to be eliminated.

Krista found a space on one of the truck's hard wooden benches and sat down. The truck rumbled to life, jolting forward as it joined a convoy of other vehicles, its metal frame creaking and groaning with each turn. As the landscape blurred past her, Krista's thoughts drifted to Marcin. Had he too surrendered? Or was he somewhere else continuing the fight? The uncertainty gnawed at her insides, a knot of fear tightening in her stomach. She exchanged a glance with Doctor Kowalski and Aleksy. As they were driven away into the unknown, she found solace in the fact that they had faced their fate together, and dared to hope that maybe, just maybe, they would all make it out alive.

48

KRISTA STRUGGLED TO FIND ANY SENSE OF TIME WITHOUT A glimpse of sunlight or stars, but she guessed she had been crammed into a cattle car for three, maybe four, days. The heat from the crowded bodies seemed to cling to Krista's skin, squished between strangers whose sweat mixed with her own. Her breath came in shallow gasps, unable to expand fully in the tight space. She felt every movement of the other passengers, like a constant pulse around her. It was suffocating and claustrophobic, and yet she knew this was still better than what awaited them at their destination.

'Albin Dabrowski,' someone called into the darkness. 'Are you here?'

No response.

'Does anyone know Szymon Chmeil?' another voice asked.

Krista's heart ached to call out for Marcin, to hear his name on her lips and feel his presence once again. But the thought of the deafening silence that would follow was almost too much to bear.

Names continued to be called out, but no one had yet been reunited with their missing companion. As each name went unanswered, the anticipation and longing in their voices slowly dissipated, leaving behind a palpable sense of sorrow.

The stench in the carriage was putrid and overwhelming. It made Krista's nose burn and her eyes water. The strong odour of urine and vomit was eventually overtaken by the lingering scent of death and decay. Krista clung to her spot near the doors as people pushed their way towards the edges, desperate for a hint of fresh air creeping in through the slatted wood. The constant chugging of the train had become background noise after travelling for so long, but a new sound caught Krista's attention. It was the hum of aeroplanes.

'Does anyone else hear that?' she asked. Her ears strained to catch the faint sound.

'I do,' someone said. 'What is it?'

'Planes,' another voice answered, the word carrying a heavy weight of dread.

The person next to Krista bumped into her shoulder, their elbow jabbing into her side as they struggled to stand up.

'I can't see anything,' they muttered.

Krista imagined her neighbour's eyes squinting against the dim light, trying to peer through the gaps in their carriage and glimpse the outside world.

'We're stopping,' another voice chimed in, cutting through the growing tension.

Krista felt it too; the train's pace had changed, the grinding of the train's wheels slowing with an ominous groan. She reached out and placed her hand on the floor in the gap created by her standing neighbour, steadying herself as the train screeched to a halt.

The noise of the aircraft was now deafening, a roar that rattled her bones. Instinctively, she ducked, her pulse racing. Seconds later, a thunderous boom rang out, the force of it slamming into the carriage. The entire structure shuddered violently, as if it, too, trembled with fear.

Someone on the outside yelled in German, the command sharp and panicked, telling everyone to take cover. Krista's stomach twisted as she understood that by "everyone", he meant his fellow Nazis, those who were not caged inside, like her.

The doors of the carriages remained shut, amplifying the sense of being trapped, sealed off from any chance of shelter or escape.

Another explosion sounded, followed closely by a third.

'There's a hole,' someone yelled. 'The Germans have fled to take shelter.' The words burst out in a rush, providing a glimmer of hope that had been hidden in the darkness, now shining with clarity and urgency.

The sound of gunshots outside was met with frantic kicks against the carriage doors, a cacophony of desperate thuds as those nearest the doors tried to break free. Eventually, the doors gave way and a stream of fresh air rushed in. Chaos erupted as passengers scrambled over each other in a frenzy to escape. Krista froze, her body rooted to the floor in fear.

A man already outside of the train fixed his gaze on her. His striking green eyes shone like guiding lights, beckoning her forward towards him. She shuffled closer to the edge and leapt from the carriage, unable to see where the train began or ended in the pitch-black of night.

A slight breeze on the backs of her legs brought a few

seconds of cool air after the stifling carriage. The guards appeared from their hiding places and a torrent of gunfire raged towards anyone attempting to flee. As the crackle of gunfire echoed around her, Krista dropped to the ground feeling closer to death than she ever had before. There was only one way to go. She lay on her stomach and crawled under the train. Every muscle in her body protested after days without use. Another thundery roar rang out in the sky above her and, for once, she hoped the air raid would continue. It had to last long enough for her to crawl out of the other side of the train before the Germans fully emerged from their hideouts and the train started moving again.

As she crawled out from under the train, something metal scraped against her shoulder and ripped into her skin. The sounds in the sky faded away and an eerie silence took over. Suddenly, a single gunshot shattered the stillness, followed by dogs barking and shouts in German; warnings to those who had escaped the train. Another shot rang out, then another. Her heart drummed in her chest, drowning out all other sounds and filling her with a deep, primal fear. Krista scrambled to her feet and fled into the darkness as fast as she could.

Krista ran across the fields surrounding the railway track, her breath coming in short raspy gasps, and the wound on her shoulder throbbing with each step. She reached the woodland and slipped between the trees, guided by the pale moonlight filtering through the canopy above. The only sounds were her ragged breaths and the distant echo of barking dogs.

She pushed past branches and bushes that clawed at her

clothes. Her feet stumbled on gnarled roots and rocks hidden in the undergrowth, but she didn't dare slow down. Adrenaline coursed through her veins, driving her forward.

She trudged on for what seemed like hours, her legs heavy with exhaustion. Eventually, she stumbled onto a dirt path cutting through the woods. She turned on to it, hoping it would lead her somewhere away from danger. Just when she thought she could go on no longer, she spotted the silhouette of a small farmhouse nestled amongst the trees.

She approached the front door and knocked, her knuckles rapping against the wood in a desperate plea for help.

Minutes passed before the door creaked open, revealing a woman standing in the threshold. Her long, silver hair hung loosely by her shoulders and a jagged scar ran down her cheek.

'Please help me,' Krista pleaded, her voice hoarse and tears streaming down her grimy cheeks.

The woman hesitated, a flash of fear in her eyes as she took in Krista's scruffy and exhausted appearance. Krista felt a sudden panic that her Polish words had not been understood and the train had crossed into Germany without her even realising it. The woman's gaze darted between Krista and the darkness beyond. After a moment of indecision, she stepped aside and gestured for Krista to come in.

Krista stepped into the dimly lit farmhouse. The woman shut the door behind her, sealing them inside. A stack of books rested on a side table near the door and a wave of relief washed over Krista as she took in their Polish titles. She removed the bag strapped across her body and placed it on the floor, stretching out her stiff shoulders and taking a moment to catch her breath.

The woman hovered nervously near the door, wringing her hands as if unsure of what to do next.

'I... I escaped from a train,' Krista began, her voice barely above a whisper. 'The Nazis... they were everywhere. I had to run.'

The woman's eyes widened in fear at the mention of the Nazis. She pulled back her curtains and glanced out the window, as if expecting to see them approaching at any moment.

'You can't stay here,' the woman finally whispered, her quiet voice trembling. 'I'm sorry.'

A fresh wave of tears welled up in Krista's eyes and trickled down her cheeks. She had hoped that this farmhouse would offer her a temporary sanctuary, but she understood. Harbouring someone on the run from the Nazis was enough to get the woman killed.

Krista nodded and wiped away the tears from her face. She picked up her bag and walked towards the door.

'Wait.' The woman opened her front door, its creak echoing through the quiet night air. She stepped outside. Krista followed, scanning the surrounding trees and listening for any unnatural noises. She heard only the gentle rustle of autumn leaves, a delicate sound that would have been soothing in any other context.

The woman ushered her back inside the house and quietly closed the door. 'The bathroom is at the end of the hall. You can clean yourself up before you leave.'

Krista smiled. She wanted to reach out and hug the woman. It wasn't an invitation to stay, but it was a gesture of kindness that Krista desperately needed after what felt like unending horror. Instead, she simply said, 'Thank you.'

She made her way down the dimly lit hallway, her footsteps muffled by the threadbare rug beneath her feet. The bathroom had floral wallpaper peeling at the edges and a cracked porcelain sink.

Krista turned on the tap, relishing the feel of warm water running over her dirt-caked skin. She scrubbed away the grime and blood, watching as they spiralled down the drain, carrying away the horrors of the night. She dried off with a faded towel hanging on a hook then bent down and pressed her lips against the cool metal tap. The clear liquid flowed out in a steady stream. She closed her eyes and gulped down the water, quenching her parched throat.

After cleaning up as best she could, Krista took a deep breath and opened the bathroom door. The woman was waiting for her just outside. In her arms, she cradled a bundle of clean clothes – a simple blouse and dark trousers, neatly folded.

'Here,' the woman said softly, handing Krista the clothes. 'These should fit you.'

Gratitude swelled in Krista's heart, her eyes stinging with the emotion she fought to keep in check. She accepted the offering with a nod and retreated back into the bathroom. She quickly changed into the fresh clothes, savouring the feel of the clean fabric against her skin. As she tucked her address book securely into her new waistband, she glanced at her reflection in the mirror – a stranger once again in someone else's clothes, but with a renewed sense of purpose.

When she emerged from the bathroom, she found the woman waiting for her in the living room. She held a small parcel in her hands, wrapped in cloth.

'Thank you for the clothes,' said Krista.

The woman nodded, her lips curving into a sad smile. 'I'm truly sorry I can't help more,' she said, her voice tinged with regret.

'I understand,' Krista replied, knowing they were doing what they could.

The woman stepped forward; her hands slightly trembling as she handed Krista the parcel. 'It's some food and water for the journey. It's not much.'

Krista cradled the parcel in her hands, the weight of it somehow heavier than it seemed. 'It's more than I have,' she said, her voice soft and filled with gratitude. She tucked the parcel in her bag. 'Can you please tell me where we are?'

The woman disappeared from the room and returned with a folded map in hand. She spread it out on the sideboard and pointed to a square of Polish countryside. Krista glided her finger along the route she intended to take, making sure to avoid larger towns and potential checkpoint locations. It would be a journey of several days, maybe even longer.

The woman folded the map back up and held it towards Krista. 'Take it with you.'

Krista tucked the map in her bag and followed the woman out of the house.

'Good luck,' the woman said in a hushed tone, glancing over her shoulder as if afraid of being overheard.

With a final nod, Krista set off back into the woods, still heading away from the railway tracks. She glanced back at the farmhouse. The woman was outside with a heavy broom, sweeping the dirt on the ground to remove any trace that someone had been there.

Krista's thoughts turned to the aerial attack. The planes had been attacking the Nazis not the train itself. That had to be good, a sign that the allies were close to ending this nightmare. If she could just hold on a little longer then she might survive this war. As she walked, she carried with her the memories of her grandparents and the sacrifices they had made for her. And Marcin. She had to hang on to the belief that he had survived the uprising and that she still had something worth fighting for.

Krista hiked through the night, emerging from the woods as dawn was breaking, painting the sky with hues of pink and gold as if nature itself was offering her a glimmer of hope.

49

FOR FIVE GRUELLING DAYS, KRISTA TRUDGED ON TOWARDS THE farm belonging to Irena's cousin Maja, sometimes hitching a ride on the back of farm vehicles for part of the way. She had stretched the parcel of food out for three days, allowing herself a meagre ration each morning. Now, her stomach was empty except for the cloudy river water she sipped when her dehydration became unbearable. Each passing day was a blur of pain and exhaustion, her feet were bleeding and her body trembling with weakness. But still she persisted, driven by the thought of finally reaching her destination.

The farmhouse appeared before her, beckoning her towards it like a symbol of liberation amidst the endless expanse of fields and hills. Its walls were weathered from years of exposure to the elements and its roof sagged in some places, but to Krista it was a haven after days of relentless travel.

The air was filled with the scent of fresh hay and wildflowers. Birds chirped nearby, a peaceful melody to welcome her as Krista limped across a field. The sun was sinking in

the sky, casting a warm glow over the farm. She heard a
child's laughter in the distance, a sound so pure and joyful
that it momentarily eased her weary soul. Looking up, she
saw a little girl with shining black hair skipping around the
garden, giggles ringing out like tinkling bells. But what truly
caught Krista's attention was the woman with her. Her red
hair cascaded down her back like a fiery waterfall, shim-
mering in the sunshine. She walked with her arms stretched
out in front of her, her eyes covered by a green silk scarf that
had once been used to disguise her distinctive hair.

The girl suddenly spotted Krista and called out, 'Krista!
Krista!'

The woman halted in her tracks and pulled the scarf off
her face. Her eyes met Krista's gaze, the initial shock fading
quickly to recognition and relief.

Krista crumpled to her knees, her legs giving out under
the weight of her exhaustion and the storm of emotions
crashing over her. Every breath felt like it was being ripped
from her lungs, her body trembling as a raw, guttural sob
tore through her chest. The sound echoed across the empty
landscape, a cry of anguish and release that reverberated in
the still air.

With tears streaming down their faces, Emilia and Ayala
raced towards her, their squeals growing louder as they
closed the distance. They threw themselves at Krista, their
arms wrapping around her like a protective shield. As their
warm bodies pressed against hers, Krista felt a deep, overwhelming sense of relief. She clung to them desperately, her
fingers digging into their clothes as if they were the only
thing stopping her from plunging back into the abyss from
which she had barely escaped.

Irena and Maja appeared in the doorway of the farmhouse, drawn by the commotion. Irena's eyes widened in

disbelief before softening into a look of pure, unfiltered joy. She rushed towards the trio, her steps quick but deliberate, as if afraid the moment might slip away.

When she reached Krista, she knelt beside her, her breath catching in her throat as she placed her warm palms on either side of Krista's tear-streaked face. Irena's fingers trembled as she cradled Krista's cheeks, wiping away the tears that continued to fall. The lines of worry across Irena's forehead melted away, replaced by a tender smile.

'Krista,' Irena said softly, her voice thick with emotion, barely holding back her own tears. 'You made it.'

More tears welled up in Krista's eyes, her vision blurring. She nodded, knowing that Irena's words held much more meaning that just her physical arrival at the farm.

'I made it,' said Krista. Her voice is strained and weak, but her tone holds a quiet triumph that radiates through her body. 'I made it,' she says again.

With Irena's arm wrapped around her waist for support, they rose together. Emilia and Ayala led the way. Maja stood waiting in the garden, her smile warm and welcoming. As they walked towards the farmhouse, arm in arm, Krista felt a sense of peace she hadn't known for so long. She was safe, surrounded by people she had grown to love, and for the first time in a long time, she believed that everything might just be alright.

EPILOGUE

Krista sat up straighter in her seat and stretched out her legs, checking the time. Ten minutes and the train would arrive in Berlin. She had spent almost a year hiding out on the farm, sheltering from both the retreating Germans and advancing Soviets. They learned about Poland's liberation on Maja's forbidden radio, but it didn't feel real until Armin showed up one day looking for Irena.

When she returned to Warsaw, the extent of the destruction had been worse than she ever could have imagined. Entire neighbourhoods were just gone, reduced to nothing but a pile of rubble. The people's resilience remained strong though. Everyone pitched in to rebuild their beautiful country. Soldiers had cleared rubble, assisted by Scouts, while churches provided meals to those in need. And the Guides had been out in force supporting soup kitchens and first aid stations for those working among the ruins, and collecting food, clothing, and household supplies to help friends and neighbours rebuild their lives. But as time went on, it became apparent that the oppressive forces of the Wehrmacht and the Gestapo had been replaced by the Red Army and the Soviet secret police. With the Soviet-backed government suppressing any opposition, liberation became another hardship for the Polish people to endure.

Krista watched the countryside speed past the train's windows, hoping to recognise something that would stir her childhood memories, but no. She wasn't sure she remembered anything from her life in Germany, except for her parents. Even then, some of the images that came to mind were hazy and uncertain.

Her thoughts drifted to her grandparents and how happy they would be that she had survived the war. After the Nazis fled Zawica, Olesia and her mother returned to the village to wait for Olesia's father to return. They were still waiting. Anna had gone to Krista's old farmhouse in search of anything belonging to Krista, but she found nothing – not even a photograph. The house was still standing but all traces of Krista's family had been erased. Krista had wondered if her Girl Guide uniform was still hidden under the floorboards of her bedroom, but she'd decided not to ask her friend to look. She liked to think that a girl, many years from now, would stumble upon it and discover how the Nazis had been so afraid of girls that they had forbidden them from gathering.

Along with the disappointment of finding nothing belonging to her grandparents at the farm, Anna brought the wonderful news that she had been reunited with her cousin Nelka after months of no communication. Nelka had surrendered in Warsaw after the uprising and had spent the final months of the war in an internment camp before its liberation. Every person who made it home felt like another small victory and filled Krista with hope for the future.

As the train slowed down, Krista's pulse quickened. Ahead lay Berlin, a city that held both the promise of new beginnings and the weight of a traumatic past.

'Are you ready?' asked Emilia from the seat beside her.

'Are you?' Krista asked.

Emilia laughed. 'No, but we're doing it anyway.'

Despite all that Emilia had done during the war, her life in Poland was over. Her own community branded her a collaborator while the communist government saw her as an enemy of the state due to her involvement in the Resistance. The government had launched a propaganda campaign vilifying anyone associated with the Resistance. Arrests were becoming more frequent.

Emilia took out a small fabric love heart from her pocket and breathed in its scent. 'It's dried lavender. Ayala made it for me.'

Krista smiled, thinking of little Ayala who had been the reason Krista and Emilia had reunited and formed a strong friendship. Krista had given Ayala her trefoil pin when they last saw each other. No one had come looking for Ayala yet, so she was living with Irena and Armin in a small town close to Warsaw. They had all agreed that the farm was too isolated for a young girl; Ayala needed education and friends. Despite the challenges of living under Soviet rule, schools were slowly reopening.

The train came to a halt at the station and Krista and Emilia gathered their belongings.

Emilia turned to Krista. 'I'll see you on Saturday then?'

Krista nodded, her hands fidgeting with the straps of her bag.

'Have you made a decision about seeing Klein?' Emilia prodded gently.

Krista bit her lip, her brows furrowed. 'I think I have to. There's so much I didn't know about my family and may have some answers.'

Emilia pulled Krista into a tight hug. 'Good luck,' she whispered before they left the train and went their separate ways.

Krista strolled through the streets alone. She'd tracked down an address for Konrad Klein, but hadn't been certain she wanted to see him again. His revelation that her grandfather had been a member of the Nazi party was something she still struggled with, and she wasn't sure she was ready to hear more. But she would have to face it one day.

The streets were bustling, full of people from all walks of life. Shoeless children played in a pile of rubble while women in pretty dresses and men in fancy suits dined in a nearby restaurant that had survived the bombing.

'A beautiful bouquet of flowers for your windowsill, Fraulein?' a street vendor called out, her hand sweeping across her vibrant display of blooms. From deep reds to bright yellows and everything in between, the cart was a kaleidoscope of life releasing a subtle fragrance into the air.

'Maybe later,' Krista replied, but her words were drowned out by drilling from a construction site nearby.

Berlin was being rebuilt. It was a city in transition, just like Krista herself. The sign ahead announced in bold black letters that Krista was now entering the British sector and that the carrying of weapons was forbidden. Krista shivered, despite the spring sunshine. If the sign was meant to be reassuring, it had the opposite effect. She continued down the street, scanning numbers on the buildings until she found the one she was looking for. She reached up and knocked on the door, her stomach knotting with nerves.

The door creaked open, revealing a bright hallway with peeling yellow wallpaper. A woman peered around the edge of the door, her features weathered and tired. She stepped out from behind the door's shadow. 'Krista Schulz?' the woman asked.

Krista nodded. 'Yes.'

The woman's face brightened and the deep wrinkles in her skin seemed to relax, giving her a newfound radiance. 'I so hoped you would come. Please, come in.'

Krista stepped inside. The air was heavy with the smell of damp and neglect. The woman led Krista into a small sitting room and gestured for her to sit in one of the two well-used armchairs.

'I'm sorry, dear, I forgot to introduce myself. I'm Edith Klein. Konrad's wife.'

Krista felt a rush of confusing emotions at the mention of Konrad's name. She had spent countless moments wondering about him, about their shared past that seemed to be shrouded in secrets and unanswered questions. And now, here she was, sitting in his home.

The room was brimming with nostalgia, trinkets covering almost every available surface, and the walls adorned with photographs capturing moments frozen in time – Konrad and Edith smiling in a garden, a young couple holding hands by the sea, and a family portrait with children giggling in front of the more serious adults. Krista's eyes lingered on the images, trying to glean some insight into the man who apparently knew so much about her family.

Edith settled into the chair opposite Krista. 'I know you must have many questions, Krista. Konrad spoke of you often. He had hoped to see you again one day.'

Krista swallowed hard, a lump forming in her throat. 'Is he... is he here?'

Edith shook her head. 'No, my dear. After the war ended, the police came for him. They... He's gone.'

Krista felt a pang of loss in her chest. Edith's sorrow seemed to seep into the very walls of the room and Krista reached out to touch the woman's frail hands.

'He left something for you,' said Edith. She stood up and shuffled to a sideboard, her steps slow and deliberate. Opening the cupboard, she pulled out a photo album.

Krista's hands trembled as she took the album from Edith. She flipped through the delicate pages with a smile on her face and tears welling up in her eyes as images of her grandparents in their younger days smiled back at her from sepia-toned photographs.

'You have so many photographs,' said Krista.

Edith gave a gentle smile. 'Konrad loved photography and he and your grandfather were great friends. Our families spent a lot of time together.'

Krista turned to a photograph taken in a garden. The flowers were in full bloom and Krista felt she could almost see the vivid colours they would have been. Her grandparents were sitting on a blanket with a little boy nestled between them. Krista gently touched her finger to the image.

'That's your father,' said Edith. 'There's also one of your parents together.'

Krista flicked through the pages of the album until she saw it. She paused on the image of her parents on their wedding day, basking in each other's love and radiating so much joy that it warmed Krista's entire body all of these years later. The final page held two photographs – one showed a young Krista beaming from her mother's lap, while her mother rested her smiling face on Krista's shoulder; the other photograph captured Krista on a swing, pushed by her father.

She closed the album and clutched it to her chest. She glanced up at a photograph of Konrad on the wall. 'Thank you,' she whispered. Her family was tragically gone too soon, but this precious gift would help to keep their memories alive and reminded Krista of the happy years they'd shared together.

Edith followed Krista's gaze. 'Konrad took many of those photographs,' she said. Her eyes glassed over with tears. 'I miss him. He made some mistakes, goodness knows we all did, but he wasn't the monster that they said he was.'

Krista leaned over and squeezed Edith's hands again. 'I survived because many people helped me. Konrad was one of those people.'

A tear rolled down Edith's cheek and she dabbed it with her palm.

Krista's words were not to excuse the many terrible things that Klein must have done, but rather to acknowledge that the man Edith had married, and the man that Kristian Schulz had once called a friend, had still been in there somewhere.

Krista opened her bag and tucked the photo album safely beside her other most precious gift, her address book that included the names of the women who had helped her survive.

'I should go,' said Krista. 'But would it be alright if I came back to see you again some time?'

Edith's cheeks flushed pink, and a wide smile formed on her lips. 'Of course, dear. Are you staying here in Germany?'

'I am,' said Krista. 'I've got a job with a humanitarian aid agency.' She'd worked for the same agency in Poland, helping to reunite families separated by the war. Her role allowed her to check on the welfare of those she had come to know during her time in Warsaw. She hadn't yet located Aleksy and Doctor Kowalski, but their names never appeared on any lists of confirmed deaths. Krista chose to believe they were alive and well and keeping a low profile because of their Resistance activities.

'I'm happy to hear that,' said Edith.

Krista moved to the edge of her seat. She had agonised over the move to Germany, feeling as though she were abandoning Poland and betraying those who had helped her to survive. But coming to Berlin was the right decision for her. 'Life is becoming ever more challenging in Poland,' she said.

Edith nodded. 'Communism grips hard. You'll be better off here. Konrad thought he could influence the system from the inside. He was wrong. It sucked him in and turned him inside out. Kristian knew that would happen. He got out. Like you.'

Edith led Krista to the front door. As they walked, Krista felt that they both had an extra bounce in their steps, as if they were lighter for having met each other.

As Krista stepped out of Edith's house, she felt a sense of freedom wash over her, as if Berlin itself had welcomed her with open arms.

She made her way towards Alexanderplatz, stopping when a pop of purple on the ground caught her attention and she crouched down for a closer look. Her fingers stroked the soft petals of a flower growing through the cracks in the pavement. She closed her eyes and tilted her face towards the sun. Despite the destruction surrounding her, the world itself continues to thrive. A flower blooms effortlessly between bits of broken concrete, the sun rises each morning, and white fluffy clouds float above, unaware of the man-made torment below. Echoes of the past still lingered in the rubble around her, but she refused to let them overshadow the possibility of a brighter future.

As she approached the bustling square of Alexanderplatz, Krista's eyes scanned the scene until they landed on a lone figure lounging on a bench reading a newspaper.

Marcin glanced up from his newspaper, a gentle smile spreading across his face as he stood up and walked towards Krista. A rush of warmth flooded her chest at the sight of him. Without a word, he enveloped her in a tight embrace and pressed a tender kiss to her lips.

'Did you get them?' Krista asked when they pulled apart.

Marcin tucked his newspaper under his arm and held out his hand, metal glinting in the sunlight from the keys he held. Keys to their new apartment. Marcin had travelled to Berlin ahead of her to find work and somewhere for them to live. And now, Krista was here too, ready to begin their new life together. Germany had its issues. The country was divided and the economy on its knees, but no one was looking to arrest them.

'I want flowers for the windowsill,' said Krista.

Marcin slipped his hand into Krista's, his eyes holding a tenderness that made her heart flutter. 'Then let's go and find flowers,' he said.

Krista rose up on her tiptoes and planted a kiss on Marcin's cheek. 'I know just the place.'

They strolled hand in hand towards the flower cart and Krista smiled at the cool metal of the keys resting between their palms, a symbol of their future together.

THANK YOU FOR READING

Thank you so much for reading *The Clover Girls' Network*. If you found yourself invested in Krista's story, please consider leaving a rating or review. Hearing from readers is both exciting and nerve-wracking for me, but reviews help other readers to discover new authors.

Your help in spreading the word about my books is gratefully appreciated.

Thank you again for reading.

Claire x

ABOUT THE AUTHOR

Claire Anders was born and raised in a seaside town in Scotland. She now lives in Edinburgh with her husband and daughter. When she's not writing, you can usually find her walking her dog in the nearby woods or with a book in one hand and chocolate in the other.

The Clover Girls' Network is Claire's second historical fiction novel. Claire also writes contemporary feel-good fiction with a touch of romance. All of her books feature strong friendships and supportive communities with a secret or two thrown into the mix.

www.claireanders.com

 facebook.com/claireandersauthor

ALSO BY CLAIRE ANDERS

Historical Fiction

Between Moons

The Clover Girls' Network

∾

Contemporary Fiction

Sunrise in Thistle Bay

New Beginnings - A Thistle Bay Short Story

Snowfall and Second Chances